I0534270

FORBIDDEN ADDICTION

FORBIDDEN #4

R.L. KENDERSON

Forbidden Addiction

Copyright © 2017 by R.L. Kenderson

All Rights Reserved

ISBN: 978-1-950918-29-4

Editor: Jovana Shirley, Unforeseen Editing, www.unforeseenediting.com
Cover Art: R.L. Kenderson at R.L. Cover Designs, www.rlcoverdesigns.com

No part of this book may be reproduced or transmitted in any form or by
any means, electronic or mechanical, including photocopying, recording, or
by any information storage and retrieval system without the written
permission of the authors, except for the use of brief quotations in a book
review.

This book is a work of fiction. Names, characters, places, and incidents either
are products of the authors' imaginations or are used fictitiously. Any
resemblance to actual persons, living or dead, events, or locales is entirely
coincidental.

For Colton Robert
July 26, 2015–August 10, 2015
Son, brother, grandson, nephew, friend, angel.
May you never be forgotten.
#RememberColton

ONE

PHOENIX KAPLAN RAISED her hand to the Guardians' entrance, hesitating for a second before knocking. It was always the same. She shouldn't be here, yet here she stood.

She rubbed her hands over her arms. It was early April, and while it was spring, the nights were still cool, and she was wearing only a light sweater.

The door swung open to reveal Lexine Harlow. "Oh, it's you," she said with an air of disappointment and contempt. "He's in his office," she added, not even waiting for Phoenix to come in as she walked away.

One would think that, after the mating of the Guardians' vampire princess to the Minnesota Pride's alpha's son months ago and the birth of their babies around the corner, Lexine would be more cordial. A relationship had formed between the two species, and all the Guardians had been welcoming of Phoenix and her monthly visits, except for Lexine.

Not that Phoenix cared too much. It was more of an

annoyance than a concern. She really wasn't here to make friends anyway.

She was here for Dante.

Phoenix stepped over the threshold and closed the front door behind her before heading down the hall to Dante's office.

Phoenix had a somewhat complicated past with the vampire.

When Vaughn and Naya mated and someone tried to kidnap them along with Vaughn's sister, Phoenix was sent with Naya and Vaughn to stay at the Guardians' compound for safety. Phoenix didn't want to be there from the start. She wasn't prejudiced against the vampires; she just hated being on protective duty, on defense. She wanted to be out in the field, searching and fighting, on the offensive. She hated sitting around, waiting. And she hated her reaction to Dante.

Phoenix had a painful history when it came to the opposite gender and intimacy. She'd had a not-so-great childhood, and as she'd gotten older, she'd had a couple of sexual encounters that both ended in disasters. She wasn't able to be the kind of woman who men wanted in the bedroom. And, even with those couple of men—boys really because it had been years ago—she'd never felt attraction to them the way she did with Dante.

At first, she didn't know what she felt toward him, not recognizing her desire for what it was because she hadn't experienced it before. Her partners in the past had been good-looking with nice, gentle demeanors, and that was basically what had drawn her to them. But, with Dante, it was pure sexual magnetism. Pun intended because Phoenix's cat was very into him.

Good thing she had complete control over her cat since, no matter how much she was attracted to Dante, it wouldn't end well if she let herself go there. Because, now that she knew Dante better, Phoenix liked him. She would rather get in a fight with five to one odds than see that look of pity in his eyes that she'd seen from her past bedroom efforts. She might be damaged, but she still had her pride.

During her stay at the Guardians' manor, they discovered who was behind the abductions, and they were all planning to go out into the field when Vaughn brought up Dante's need to feed. Due to the male cat-shifter's new mate, he had recognized Dante's need, much to Dante's irritation.

Phoenix would do anything for her friends and fellow sentinels—they had proven their loyalty to her, and they were the only family she had—so she volunteered to be the metaphorical sacrificial lamb. It might not be a big thing to some, but for her to offer up her blood and therefore her body, it was a huge deal. The funny thing was, Dante promptly turned her down—informing her that, when he fed, he fucked—but she persisted, confronting him again a few days later.

He tried to intimidate her, which was easy at first. She caught him in his bedroom after coming out of the shower, so he was only wearing a towel, and he tried to use his near nakedness to get her to leave. She swallowed all her nerves and continued on with her mission to get Dante to feed. But, when she offered to have sex with him, most of the fight had left his body, and she was immediately relieved. It felt a little too close to prostitution, even with her unwanted attraction to Dante. Phoenix then thought he would feed from her wrist to maintain a good distance between them, but Dante fed from her neck instead. She didn't know if a part of him was still punishing her for pushing him into the situation or if he wanted to be close to her. Maybe both, but she didn't ask because she truly didn't know what she wanted the answer to be.

So, Dante pulled her close and held her against his bedroom door as he proceeded to sink his fangs into her neck. It scared her. Not because it hurt or because she was a coward, but because she was turned on. That frightened the shit out of her. And, somehow, Dante knew. Over the years, Phoenix had worked very hard to hide her feelings. Shifters and vampires could sense emotions, and she in no way wanted hers to be used against her again, so she had learned to cover hers. Yet Dante knew she was aroused, and he completely shocked her when he cut his thumb and stuck it in her mouth. She never tasted anything like it. Vampire blood was sweet. Not like sugary candy, but more like chili with loads of brown sugar in it. Rich, hearty, and saccharine.

But that wasn't even the biggest shocker.

What completely blew her mind was that, with the combination of Dante sucking on her neck, rubbing his erection between her legs, and putting his blood in her mouth, Phoenix orgasmed. Pathetically, the first one she'd ever had in her life. Not that she hadn't tried to get herself off before—she was a twenty-first century woman after all—but she just hadn't succeeded. Not only that, but her scent, the scent of her lust, filled the room. So ashamed and a little horrified that Dante had gotten her off and exposed her scent, she fled his bedroom as soon as he released her. It was only later she remembered that Dante had climaxed, too. It didn't ease her humiliation, but it was a relief to know she wasn't the only one affected.

Phoenix avoided Dante after that for a while. To this day, they still hadn't talked about it. And any thoughts of discussing it were pushed aside when she was kidnapped by her alpha's corrupt cousin and then rescued by Dante. She found out later that Dante had located her through the blood he'd consumed from her. She was shaken up from her ordeal, and she asked Dante to take her home with him. He hadn't even hesitated before agreeing. And, when Dante had discovered what Gerald had done to her while under his control, he was kind and gentle as he healed her with the enzymes in his saliva. After that encounter, she slept in his bed next to him for the next three weeks because she couldn't sleep alone with Gerald still on the loose. Something else they hadn't talked about because they went to bed and woke up at different times, and with the exception of Phoenix waking to find Dante sleeping on her hair, they hadn't touched.

Then, Dante was shot in the leg and asked Phoenix to feed him again while he was still in his hospital bed. Refusing him hadn't even crossed her mind. That time, she was the one who offered her neck, she was the one who cut Dante's finger and slipped it in her mouth so that she could suck on his blood, and she was the one who rubbed her groin over his. After they both came again, Dante seemed to have some regret, and she left the room before he could say the words out loud. She went back to the bunkhouse that night and ignored all of Dante's phone calls and texts.

Phoenix ran into him at Naya and Vaughn's New Year's party where she learned that him sleeping next to her and feeding from her had been no big deal to Dante. He wanted to make sure he hadn't hurt her since they were *friends*. While she hadn't slept next to another male and had experienced her most satisfying sexual experiences with him, it was "just sleeping and feeding, a form of nourishment" to him. It was way more than a big deal to her. The embarrassment still stung even if Dante had no idea how she felt. That was why she would not attempt a full-on sexual relationship with him. Anything she felt that night would be tenfold worse when he discovered how defective she was in bed.

She probably would have avoided Dante at all costs after that night, but when he later called three times in less than five minutes, she knew it had to be something important. And it was. Dante found Gerald, and instead of informing her alpha, Vance, he called her. She would forever remember that.

Dante and Phoenix went after Gerald, stupidly without backup. Phoenix was so angry at what he'd done to her that all she wanted was revenge. Dante must have known and didn't even attempt to stop her. And it almost got him killed. In their scuffle with Gerald, Phoenix was shot, and so was Dante, but this time, it hadn't been in the leg. Phoenix killed Gerald when she discovered Dante was hurt, and she finally used her brain and called for help before offering Dante her vein and passing out.

When she woke up in the hospital, she discovered that Dante had refused to leave her side and that she'd given him so much blood that she needed a blood transfusion, which Dante had provided because he wouldn't let anyone else do it. They spent the rest of their time in the hospital side by side—not touching, but reassuring each other with their presence. It was just one more thing the two of them hadn't discussed, and instead, since then, Phoenix would show up every month to feed Dante. Dante got blood, and she got skin-to-skin contact that satisfied her shifter DNA. They didn't talk about her coming—he didn't ask, and she didn't offer—but she always showed up, and he never refused her. One thing was for sure, Dante + Phoenix = Avoidance with a capital A.

Like she'd said, complicated.

She knew they couldn't go on like this forever, and she dreaded ending their time together, but she wasn't about to be the one to bring up the subject because it might end sooner if she said something. Nope, she was going to leave things exactly the way they were. She'd take what little she could get.

Phoenix reached Dante's office, raised her hand, and knocked.

☾

Dante Leonidas raised his head from the map spread out on his desk from where he'd been studying it when he heard the rap at his door.

Phoenix.

Usually, he prepared himself before she arrived, but he'd been so lost in thought that he didn't notice her scent or her presence despite her blood in him. He cursed himself for not paying attention, but it didn't really matter. He'd never be truly equipped to see her.

"Enter," he called out.

The entrance to his office opened, and Phoenix slipped through before closing the door behind her.

Dante held his breath as the aroma of sunshine flooded the room, but it was too late. Her scent teased his nostrils, and suddenly, his pants were too tight as his cock hardened under his fly. He had to reach down and adjust himself under the desk before the painful position caused him to wince. Males always talked about having big dicks, but honestly, it wasn't that great. It could really be a pain in the ass sometimes. No pun intended.

"Hey," the beautiful cat-shifter said as she approached his desk.

She was sans makeup with her long red-and-black hair in a ponytail while she wore her usual outfit of shapeless clothing. Today, it was a sweater and jeans. But, despite her baggy attire, Dante could still make out her curves underneath. It didn't hurt that he'd seen her without her clothes in the past. Picturing her naked didn't help his hard-on.

She glanced down at the Minneapolis/St. Paul area map that he'd been reviewing before she entered. "What are you looking at?"

He pointed to the Xs he'd made in red. "I marked all the incidents on the list in hopes that maybe a pattern or something would jump out at me." Dante threw the pen he had been holding on top of the map as he leaned back in his chair and exhaled his frustration. "So far, it's been a bust."

Over the last few months, crimes had been happening to vampire and shifter residences and places of business. It wasn't like the paranormal community was immune to crime, but the unusual part about it was how they were all coming in pairs. Whatever happened to a vampire-owned place, the same thing would happen to a shifter-owned place. The first incident had been graffiti at a vampire-owned restaurant on the same night a shifter-owned restaurant was hit. It was an obvious message to both vampires and shifters. The latest incidents were fires started at vampire- and shifter-owned homes within an hour of each other. The worst part of the entire situation was that the human police were starting to notice.

Phoenix came around to his side of the desk and leaned over to read the map and his notes. Her baggy pants hung on her hips, but when she bent over, they stretched across her ass, and Dante had to fight not to ogle her. His erection got harder, if that was even possible, and he fought his desire to pull her into his lap, strip off her clothes, and bury himself inside her.

But that would never happen.

Despite the fact that she was there to feed him, they were not in a romantic or sexual relationship. Dante didn't know all the details about what had happened to Phoenix in her past, but he knew she had been traumatized. So, while he usually had sex with the females he fed from, the only thing he'd be sinking inside her were his fangs. His little head didn't get it, but his big head did, and he wasn't going to add to her issues. For now, feeding from her and being her friend was enough. But, damn, this celibacy thing just might kill him.

Maybe, someday, he would tell her how he felt about her, but today wasn't that day. She wasn't ready to hear it.

Turning his thoughts back to the task at hand, he asked her, "Have you guys come up with anything?"

She spun around and sat on the edge of the desk, the emerald green of her eyes filled with vexation. "No. Are you coming to the meeting tomorrow?"

"Yes, we'll all be there."

"That's good." She nodded her approval. "One of the wolf-shifter sentinels is an officer in the Minneapolis Police Department. Damien told Vance that the sentinel would fill us in on what the humans knew."

The wolf-shifter alpha was really proving himself to the cat-shifter alpha. Damien wasn't going to let the newly healed bond between the two subspecies get fractured again, it seemed.

Dante furrowed his brows. "You don't have any cat-shifters in the police force?"

"Yes, we do, but none of them are sentinels. They give us information, but we don't share what we know back with them. It's a good idea, what Damien did, having someone work both angles. I just hope Vance doesn't make one of us sign up for the police academy." She made a face of disgust. "At least, I hope it isn't me."

Dante chuckled. "Humans aren't that bad."

She looked at him like he was crazy. "Humans aren't that bad? The same species that traditionally comes at your species with a stake through the heart?"

"Pretty sure none of the members of the St. Paul Police Department are carrying stakes."

"No, just guns."

He laughed again. "I suppose you have a point."

"So, does that mean you have vampires on the force? How does that work with the sun thing?"

"Of course we do. They enter the academy before their conversion, and after, they work the night shift." Dante frowned. "Although I never thought to have one of the Guardians work for us and the police at the same time. It is smart."

The conversation stalled, and silence fell over the room. Their eyes met, but neither moved.

The knock at the door broke the quietness, and Dante looked at the bare skin on Phoenix's neck. "Come back later. I'm busy."

He swiveled his chair to face her and opened his legs. "Come here, Red."

TWO

HUNTER ESMUND WAITED to speak to Dante, keeping an eye out for the office door to open. There had been another incident, and this time, someone had been hurt. It wasn't just property damage anymore.

After what seemed like forever, he watched as Phoenix exited Dante's office, closing the door behind her. As she walked past, Hunter saw the bite marks from Dante on her neck. They starkly stood out against her creamy skin. Dante hadn't healed her all the way, and Hunter had to wonder if it had been deliberate.

Phoenix neared and looked up to meet his eyes. He tipped his chin in greeting, and she nodded back. Not shy in the least about what she'd been doing in his boss's office— or, more accurately, what his boss had been doing to her— she strolled past with her shoulders back and her head high, as if her being there was an everyday, normal thing. Although sexual arousal clung to her, she didn't smell of the actual act.

The whole thing was odd. Everyone in the house knew

that Dante had a voracious appetite when it came to fucking, but since the female cat-shifter had come into his life, he'd refrained. Usually, sex and feeding were a package deal with the Guardian leader, but while something happened as he fed from Phoenix, they never had actual sex. Not only did neither of them ever smell like it, but Dante had also been increasingly testy lately. And, while Dante had regulars, he never fed from the same female twice in a row. Until now. Yet the two of them had made no claims on one another. Like Hunter had said, odd.

Not that Hunter really understood the whole fucking-and-feeding thing. Or, more truthfully, he didn't understand the whole fucking thing. He'd had a handful of lovers over the years, yet he could take or leave all of them. Sure, it felt good, but so did his hand, and it was a lot less complicated. No awkward conversations after. He didn't know what it was, but there always seemed to be something missing when he had sex, and he never felt the rush of desire from feeding either. So, now, he just skipped the screwing part. He fed from a few females who understood that he didn't want anything more from them. It was easier for everyone that way.

He'd once tried to broach the subject with friends, asking them something like why they thought sex was so great and what was so special about female blood. But, after the looks his pals had given him, Hunter had laughed, like he'd been joking, and never talked to anyone about it since.

Maybe he just needed to meet the right female. Then, things would be different, and he might finally understand what all the hype was about.

Dante opened the office door, and Hunter snapped out of his self-pitying thoughts.

"Lexine," Hunter called down the hall to let her know Dante was ready to talk.

He'd warned her earlier that something had gone down, but when she'd seen that Phoenix was still in Dante's office, Lexine had told Hunter to just let her know when they were ready. No one talked about it, but everyone knew she had a thing for Dante. Everyone but Dante, which was probably good because he didn't see Lexine as anything more than a fellow Guardian.

Hunter entered the office, and Lexine walked in moments later. She left the door open since they were the only ones there now that the cat-shifter had left, and everyone else was out in the field.

Dante ran his fingers through his dark hair while Lexine stared at the floor, her white-blonde hair hanging around her face like a curtain.

"What's going on?" Dante asked.

"There was another attack tonight."

Dante cursed, and his deep brown eyes filled with anger. None of them wanted to see their elders in danger.

Lexine didn't seem to have a reaction. Hunter would have wondered if the female hadn't heard him, except she had vampire hearing and stood directly next to him.

"This time, someone got hurt," he added.

Lexine's head whipped up, looking at him for confirmation, her hazel-green eyes round. *"What?"*

So, now, she cares.

"Who?" Dante asked, the ire in his voice apparent.

"Mrs. Howard."

"Shit," Dante said as he collapsed down in his chair.

"Oh no," Lexine said, worry in her tone. She bit her lip, as if she wanted to say more but stopped herself.

Mrs. Howard was about eighty years old, but she was a tough old bird.

"She's fine," Hunter reassured them both. "She wasn't supposed to be home this evening, but she wasn't feeling well, so she stayed home from her regular bingo night. She was sleeping when she heard someone outside. She called her son and then proceeded to go out on her own to confront whoever was messing with her property." Hunter shook his head at the woman's bravery and stupidity. "She slipped and fell on her porch steps, and the noise scared off whoever was out there. Her son pulled up as the trespasser drove off, so he took her to the clinic. She's got a bruised hip, but she's lucky. It could have been a lot worse."

"Has anyone interviewed her yet?" Dante asked.

"Sterling and Ram had just finished up when they called. They should be here any minute to give us an update."

"So, we don't know who did this?" Lexine questioned him. She sounded strangely relieved.

The front door slammed.

"I guess we'll find out now," Hunter said.

☾

The pounding of large boots coming down the hallway sounded louder than normal. The room felt like it was getting smaller, and the oxygen was being sucked out. Lexine had to get out of there.

Dante and Hunter looked at her with concern.

"Lexine, are you okay?" Dante asked her.

He sounded like he was concerned, and she couldn't handle it. Not after seeing Phoenix, the bitch of a cat-shifter, come here tonight to feed Dante. Again. Not after knowing deep in her heart that she should be feeding him. Not after hearing how the nice elderly Mrs. Howard had gotten hurt. Not after knowing it could have been worse. A lot worse. Not after—

"Lexine," Dante barked.

She slowly looked at his face. "I…have to go." She gradually stepped backward, one small step at a time.

"We're not done here."

She never defied an order from Dante before, and while it pained her to do so now, she turned and fled.

Dante and Hunter called after her, causing her to look over her shoulder as she ran down the hallway until she hit a hard wall.

"*Oof.*"

"Lexine, are you okay?"

She looked up into gray eyes filled with tenderness and worry. *Sterling.* Somehow seeing that it was him made her want to burst into tears, and she had no idea why.

He looked over her head at Ram and jerked his chin toward the end of the hall. "I'll meet you in there in a second."

Lexine glanced quickly at Ram, whose hard yellow eyes suspiciously stared at her. He was six-four, and sometimes, it seemed like he was as wide as he was tall. Even though she knew him and worked with him, he was still an imposing figure. Her vision filled with black spots for a second, and as she heard Ram's retreat, she felt Sterling put his hands on her biceps to steady her.

Sterling's grip was warm against her skin, even with the layer of clothing between them, and it sent tingles down to her fingers and up to her face.

She didn't know what to make of this new sensation, and she was already overwhelmed with everything else, so she jerked her arms out of his grasp. "Don't touch me." She couldn't handle his touch. She didn't deserve his concern.

Sterling stiffened before he straightened, his arms falling to his sides, and his eyes lost their warmth. They went from molten silver to hard, cold stone. "I apologize for worrying about you." His words spoke of forgiveness, but his tone did not. His thick lips stiffened into a straight line, and suddenly, his icy demeanor was more than she could take.

Since when had she cared so much about what Sterling thought?

"No," she started, trying to salvage…something. "It's not you." *It's what? Me?* She couldn't really try to feed the most famous breakup line to Sterling. To this male who she wasn't even dating. "Look, I'm just…stressed out."

His eyes softened as he exhaled. "You can talk to me, you know."

She bit her lip and shook her head. *No way.*

The urge to pour her heart out to him was strong, and for that reason alone, she needed to get out of there.

She moved to step around Sterling, but he put a hand out to stop her, placing it low on her abdomen. The warmth from his body seeped into hers and made her realize how cold she was, all the way down to her bones.

"If you won't talk to me, at least talk to Dante or Lennox."

Lexine almost snorted out loud. She wasn't telling Dante *anything*. And her brother? Well, he would never understand or sympathize whether she was his sister or not.

"Yeah, maybe I'll do that," she lied.

Sterling dropped his hand, and his eyes filled with disappointment.

It seemed like he knew what she was thinking, but she didn't understand how. They were friends and coworkers, but they weren't close.

Still, she couldn't handle letting him down. "I've gotta go."

And, this time, he let her.

She grabbed her jacket, put on her shoes, and picked up her car keys. Then, she slipped quietly out the door.

☾

Sterling Wardell watched Lexine leave the compound. He waited sixty seconds before he followed her.

He pulled his phone out of his pocket and dialed Dante as he got behind the wheel of his SUV. When Dante picked up, Sterling didn't wait for him to say hello. "I'll be back later. I'm gonna follow Lexine."

THREE

THE FOLLOWING NIGHT, the doorbell rang throughout the bunkhouse, which was rare. The usual occupants either lived there or in the main house, and they never knocked.

This meant, visitors.

Phoenix opened the door to see Saxon's parents on the other side.

"Phoenix," Saxon's mom, Susana, said in her light and beautiful accent as she stepped through the doorway. She immediately engulfed Phoenix in a hug. "How are you, dear?"

Phoenix hugged her back. "Can't complain." *Too much.* "How are you two?"

"We just got back from Florida," Carl, Saxon's dad, said as he came in the house, closing the door behind himself.

Every winter, Saxon's parents would go to Florida to get away from the cold now that they were both retired.

Susana released Phoenix and stepped back to stand next to her husband. "We came to let our alpha know that we were back in town, and what a surprise it was to find out that our son had been shot." Susana looked at Carl. "What did Vance say again?"

She had a sweet smile on her face, but Phoenix could tell Saxon's mom was not happy.

When Susana heard Saxon enter the room behind her, she looked at her son, and using her mom voice, she said, her accent getting thicker, "*Almost four months ago.*"

Phoenix couldn't help but smirk. Saxon, an alpha male, was being reprimanded by his mommy.

Saxon held up his hands in surrender as he came over to them. "Mamá, I was going to tell you. I didn't want you guys to worry and cut your trip short. It wasn't that bad, and I'm all healed now."

Susana hugged her son tight and stepped back to look him in the eyes. She ran her hands all over him, as if to make sure he really wasn't hurt. "*Mijo*, you don't keep something like that from your mamá and papá. *¿Me entiendes?*"

"Okay, Mamá, I understand," Saxon said.

Phoenix doubted he would tell them if something like that happened again. He loved and cherished his mother too much to worry her if he felt it was unnecessary.

"Humpf," Susana said, as if she didn't believe him.

Carl drew her away. "Stop babying the boy, Sus," he teased his wife.

"Thanks, Dad." Saxon smiled. "So, did you both come here just to yell at me?"

"No," his father said at the same time his mother said, "Yes."

Saxon laughed, and he drew both parents in for a hug. "I'm glad you're home."

Carl's crystal-green eyes, so much like Saxon's, danced

with amusement while Susana's deep brown eyes filled with happy tears. Saxon's black-and-blond striped hair matched his father's blond and his mother's black, and he had also inherited his mother's stunning golden skin. He was the perfect combination of his parents, and looking at them, there was no doubt they were a family.

The sight of them made Phoenix ache with want—to have parents like that, parents who loved their child so much. And Susana and Carl were lucky to have each other and a son like Saxon.

Susana had come to the US when her entire family and most of her pride were killed in the Veracruz earthquake in 1973. Back then, Vince Llewelyn—Vance's father and Vaughn's grandfather—had been the Minnesota Pride's alpha. He had reached out to what was left of the Puebla Pride in Mexico and sponsored them to come to America.

Carl always said he had taken one look at Susana, and he knew he had found his mate. About ten years later, they'd had Saxon and said their family was complete. Though Saxon had told Phoenix that they had tried for more children.

Phoenix mourned for that kind of relationship because her parents never loved her that much, never loved her enough to believe their own child, and it hurt because she would never have what Susana and Carl had. A beautiful relationship filled with love, devotion, and trust, and she would never get to hold a child of her own in her arms.

For one moment, just a fleeting one, Phoenix thought of Dante, and that only depressed her more. It shouldn't, but it did.

Susana must have seen the emotions on Phoenix's face

because she pulled away from her son and husband. "Oh, *mija*, don't cry."

Susana held out her arms, and Phoenix gladly welcomed her warm motherly embrace as Carl squeezed her hand. Phoenix and Saxon weren't related at all, but Susana still called her *my daughter*, and Phoenix secretly loved it.

How Saxon, commitment-phobe extraordinaire, had come from these two wonderful, loving people, Phoenix would never understand. And, even though she was surrounded by their affection, she still couldn't help feeling alone.

Phoenix pulled away from their embrace and looked at the clock. "We'd better get ready," she told Saxon.

They had to leave for the shifter-vampire meeting in under an hour.

Saxon and Phoenix said good-bye to his parents with Phoenix promising Susana that she would call them herself if something happened to Saxon. He rolled his eyes but wisely kept his mouth shut, knowing that, if he protested, then his parents would never leave.

Tegan was just getting home from a date as they walked out the door. She quickly said hello and bye to Saxon's parents. Then, she told Saxon and Phoenix, "Give me a minute to change, and then I'll head over there with you."

The *over there* Tegan was referring to was the main house where they were meeting their alpha along with Vaughn and Sawyer. The two sentinels would be dropping off their mates, Naya and Kenzie, to hang out with their alphena while the rest of them went to the meeting at L & L Construction. Because there were so many of them now— cat-shifters, wolf-shifters, and vampires—there wasn't enough room at anyone's residence. And, since L & L had a big conference room and it was after-hours, it was the perfect place.

Tegan exited the bedroom that she shared with Phoenix, and the three of them trucked over to the main house.

They were the first to arrive, and Lilith offered them cookies while they waited. She loved cooking and baking, and she always seemed to have some treats around the house. Their alpha and alphena had gone upstairs, and about five minutes later, Vaughn walked in. He could only be described as frazzled with his messy black hair and circles under his blue eyes.

"Whatever you do," he warned them in a hushed tone as he set down his mate's purse, "do not ask Naya about being pregnant, giving birth, or babies." He looked at Zane. "I'm serious."

"Hey," Zane protested, actually looking insulted.

Vaughn clenched his teeth and pointed a finger at Zane.

Zane rolled his eyes. "Fine, I won't say anything."

As Vaughn turned to go back outside, Zane added, "I'm only doing this for you, dude, so you owe me one."

Vaughn looked back at Zane and laughed, but the laugh was more strained than full of humor. "Oh no, *dude*, you're doing it for yourself. Trust me, you do not want to get on her bad side."

"Vaughn!" Naya yelled from outside.

It looked as if Vaughn might have winced.

"Coming!" he shouted back. He wiped his hand down his face and then plastered on the biggest fake smile before heading outside.

They all looked around at each other, and Zane said, "Yikes."

Phoenix hadn't seen Naya for about a month, so she wasn't sure what to expect, but what she saw wasn't it.

Naya usually looked so put together, even throughout her pregnancy, but today, she looked nothing like her normal self. Her dark brown hair was pulled back into a messy bun—and not one of those stylish messy buns. This one was of pure convenience. Her skin was free of all makeup, and if Phoenix had thought Vaughn had bags under his eyes, then Naya had suitcases. The normal violet hue was dull. And, while typically happy, tonight, she wore a scowl on her beautiful face. She looked miserable. And very, very pregnant. Phoenix didn't even know how the poor woman walked.

Vaughn helped his mate into the nearest recliner while everyone greeted her. They all made sure to say nothing of her huge belly, even Zane.

"Where are Mom and Dad?" Vaughn asked as he straightened up from helping Naya sit.

"Upstairs," Saxon answered.

The door opened, and Sawyer and his mate, Kenzie, walked in.

Upon seeing her best friend, the human said, "Oh, Naya." Kenzie bent over to give the vampire a hug, and she just had to add, "You look like you're about to explode."

Vaughn visibly cringed this time and muttered, "Shit," under his breath.

"Yeah, well, you smell weird," Naya told Kenzie.

Kenzie stood, her back stiff, and she looked at her mate. Sawyer grabbed her hand.

"Naya, baby, Kenzie wasn't trying to insult you. Remember how we talked about being nice?" Vaughn said.

Naya adjusted herself in her seat and shot a death glare at him. "Fuck you. Don't treat me like I'm a child."

"Naya!" Kenzie exclaimed.

Naya threw her head back against the recliner and groaned. "God, not you, too. Listen, when you have this male's"—she jerked her thumb at Vaughn—"evil spawn inside of you, sucking the life out of you, then you can reprimand me all you want. Until then, shut up, please."

Everyone was silent.

Then, someone said, "Holy shit, Vaughn. I think you broke Naya." It might have been Zane.

Naya grumbled as she put the foot of the recliner up. "Yeah, well, when you're forty-one weeks pregnant with twins, then you can talk to me about how I should behave."

Suddenly, all the anger left Naya, and her eyes filled with tears. She looked up at Vaughn and pleaded, "Why won't they come out? Why?"

Vaughn knelt next to her and rubbed his hand over her hair and down the back of her neck. "I don't know, baby, and I'm sorry you're so miserable. But, remember, Dr. Montgomery said it should only be a few more days."

Vaughn had told them before that human drugs used to induce labor wouldn't work with vampires. Plus, most vampire doctors believed that, if a female was still pregnant, it was because she was supposed to be, and they didn't like forcing the child to come any earlier than they were ready to.

Naya sniffled. "I know." She smiled a smile she reserved only for her mate. "I'm sorry."

"It's ok——"

Naya gasped.

"What's wrong? The babies?" Vaughn asked, alarmed.

Naya shook her head and looked at Kenzie, her face full of surprise. "You're pregnant."

Kenzie's eyes got huge, and guilt flooded her face.

"That's why you smell weir—different."

Kenzie looked at Sawyer, and he nodded.

"Yes," she told her friend. "We wanted to wait until I was a little further along before we told anyone. I'm only about six weeks." She looked around the room. "Please don't say anything. I know you all have stronger noses, so some of you might smell it on me, and if someone asks, you can confirm it, but please don't go around telling everyone."

"Congratulations," Vaughn said. He stood up, shook Sawyer's hand, and pulled him into a man hug.

Naya held out her arms, and Kenzie leaned over to hug her again.

Saxon and Tegan offered their congratulations to the couple.

Phoenix tried to say something, but she was afraid that, if she opened her mouth, embarrassing words would come out. The ache in her chest from earlier had now widened until she was filled with anguish and grief. Even though she had poured out her secret to Sawyer, she didn't think he had told anyone about her deepest wish to be a mother. Kenzie didn't know what her pregnancy announcement along with Naya's pending birth did to Phoenix, but right now, their happiness hurt. Even Naya's misery hurt because the reason Naya was unhappy was because she was going to give birth. Phoenix couldn't help but feel a little resentful of both of them. She knew it wasn't true, but it seemed like everyone was pregnant but her. Or maybe it was because everyone could get pregnant but her.

Most days, Phoenix had come to terms with her past, but abruptly, the bitterness from her past would come out of nowhere. It wasn't fair. Why did she have to have issues? Why couldn't she just be normal? She was only twenty-nine, for fuck's sake. She had plenty of time to have a baby. If only she could make it through the baby-making process. God, she hated being broken. Phoenix worked hard to be strong, but this weakness of hers ate at her sometimes.

Afraid that she would have to leave the room before anyone saw her misery, she was saved by the front door opening. Payton and Damien walked in as the alpha couple came downstairs.

Thankfully, the arrival of the two separate parties in the entryway saved everyone in the living room from having to explain what they had been talking about.

"Are you all ready to go?" Vance asked his sentinels.

Sawyer answered, "Yep," rather fast, but Vaughn looked down at Naya with worry.

"Honey," Lilith said, "don't worry about Naya. Payton, Kenzie, and I will take good care of her. We'll call you if anything is wrong."

"Yes, go." Naya waved him away.

"Okay," Vaughn said reluctantly. He leaned over and kissed Naya. "Be nice," he murmured against her lips, smiling. "My mom's not tough like me," he said a little louder.

Naya grinned back at him and pushed him away. "I know. She's tougher," she teased.

They all laughed as most of them headed for the door.

Sawyer pulled Kenzie close and cradled the back of her head as he kissed her like he was leaving for a month while Payton pulled Damien down to kiss him, as if he were going off to war. Normally, all this PDA didn't bother Phoenix, but it did tonight. At least Payton wasn't pregnant. That was something.

Phoenix made her way around the group and was the first one outside. She took a deep breath of fresh night air, trying to rid herself of the love and pregnancy hormones swirling inside the house. She had a feeling it was going to be a long night.

FOUR

"THIS IS the first time someone has been hurt in these acts of vandalism, and even though it appears to be an accident, it doesn't sit well with us," Vance told Dante and the room.

"I agree," Damien Lowell said. "Something needs to be done."

Dante stood at the head of the conference table along with the cat-shifter and wolf-shifter alphas. This was the first time he'd been to L & L Construction, and he had to admire the business the shifters had built from scratch. The vampires, at least the king and queen and the members of the Vampire Council, came from old money.

Nobody even knew where the king and queen's fortune had started. They had inherited it from the king and queen before them and were able to live off the money and subsequent investments. The king and queen had enough money without either of them working to pay for his and the other Guardians' salaries and for them to live in their large mansion. Many of the council members held vast empires, like the Vanderbilts who owned a chain of five-star hotels around the world, and that was how they made their money.

But the shifters had worked hard for what they had. The L & L Construction company easily brought in millions of dollars a year, but the fact was that they were what some vampires considered new money, and that was one of the reasons the shifters were looked down upon.

Man, vampires were such snobs.

It wasn't as if Dante wasn't proud to be a vampire because he was. It was just that many of them could use some humility and humbleness. It was no wonder Naya had mated outside her species.

Dante's gaze shifted to Phoenix, who was sitting between Saxon and Tegan. Something was off with her tonight, and he didn't know what. Usually, she had plenty of input and thoughts on things, but tonight, she'd been quiet the whole time. She was a hotbed of emotions, judging from the blood he'd drunk from her last night. She seemed irritated yet sad and angry, all at the same time. He wasn't even sure if she was paying attention to what was going on around her.

Not wanting to be accused of the same thing, Dante turned back to the matter at hand. He had just finished telling everyone in the meeting about poor Mrs. Howard's near miss with the trespasser on her property.

The shifters hadn't been as unlucky—or lucky, depending on how you looked at it. No one was hurt because no one had been home at the wolf-shifter residence when they were attacked, but their brand-new home had been burned to a crisp. It was a nice elderly couple who had just moved back to the Twin Cities area after the wolf-shifter exile had been lifted, and they had sunk all their retirement money into their dream home.

Last night's simultaneous attacks had seemed to specifically target the senior generation. That didn't sit well with anyone. One thing vampires and shifters agreed on was that they both respected and cherished their elders.

This time, Dante looked at Lexine. She'd been particularly upset last night when she found out about Mrs. Howard—to the point that she had fled the compound. Something had been going on with her the past couple of months, but no one had any specifics—not even Lennox, her twin brother. Sterling had followed her after she left the night before, but he had reported that she'd only driven around for a little while before going to a bar near the vampire clinic. She'd sat alone for a half hour, nursing a beer before leaving and heading home. Dante hadn't talked to her about her leaving in the middle of their conversation yet, and he wasn't sure he was going to. Something was definitely off with Lexine, and Dante thought it might be better to just keep an eye on her.

"So far, we've warned the public to be careful, but I think we need to step up and do more interviews," Dante suggested.

Vance nodded. "I agree. There are times when someone has seen something, and they don't even realize it."

"How are we going to have time to do interviews when we're needed out there, looking for the perpetrators? We should be out there right now instead of having everyone sitting in here," Phoenix said.

Phoenix might be opinionated, but he'd never seen her question authority before. Something was absolutely bothering her. He wanted to pull her aside and ask her what was wrong. But they didn't have a relationship like that. And did he even want one?

Hell, he didn't know.

The cat-shifter alpha wasn't going to let Phoenix's challenge go. "Seeing as how the assaults on our communities so far have been spread out by days, tonight is the best time to meet. And this meeting *is* needed. Not only are shifters and vampires the targets, but they are also being targeted for a reason. And the more we work together, the sooner these criminals will be caught," Vance explained, looking directly at Phoenix, his words clipped. His eyes shifted to everyone else in the room, even the wolf-shifters and vampires sitting around the table. "Does anyone else have questions for the three of us?" he said, letting everyone know the three of them were a team on this.

Phoenix cast her eyes downward, obviously feeling ashamed. "No, sir," she said.

Dante had the sudden urge to comfort her. While he understood why Vance was upset, as Dante wouldn't like having his authority or decisions being questioned like that in front of everyone, he also understood her frustration. It was hard to be here, knowing the offenders were out there, running free and planning their next act of violence.

"As for the interviews," Damien said, "we'll select a few people to do them, and we'll try to have all the interviewees come to you to save time from traveling from place to place. Also, we will send out notice to everyone and set up a tip line. It will only take one or two of us to man the line, so the rest of us can get out there and find these assholes."

Murmurs of agreement went around the room, but

Dante hardly noticed. Saxon had leaned over and was whispering in Phoenix's ear, way too close for Dante's comfort. And, when Phoenix drew her hair over her opposite shoulder as she looked at Saxon and smiled, the first smile she'd shown all night, Dante felt like the room was shrinking.

Dante liked Saxon and would even go so far as to say they were friends. They'd hung out a few times. And he knew Saxon thought of Phoenix like a sister. But seeing her smile like that at the male cat-shifter pissed him off. And then it pissed him off that it'd pissed him off.

The snapping of the pen he'd been holding drew his thoughts away from the green-eyed monster raging inside him.

Thankfully, no one noticed the broken ballpoint because Damien's phone rang. Except Phoenix. Her eyes locked with his before she looked down at the now-worthless writing utensil in his hand. He tried to hide it from her without being too obvious. Whether from embarrassment or from worry that she would see his little act of uncontrolled anger and be afraid, he didn't know.

She wasn't the only one who wasn't being herself tonight.

☾

The wolf-shifter alpha closed his phone. "That was my sentinel, Quentin. He just got off work and is on his way."

Thank fuck, Hunter thought. He was getting impatient and wanted to leave.

Part of the reason the meeting was still going on was

because they were waiting for the wolf sentinel who was on the Minneapolis Police force. Hunter understood their gathering was important, but he wanted to get out of there and take some action.

He didn't think Phoenix had gone about it the right way, but he saw her point when she'd asked why they were all sitting there. He was itching to get out there and do something. Last night had been his night off, and a part of him wondered if things would have gone down differently had he been in the rotation.

Ten minutes later, there was a knock at the door, and the male who had to be Quentin entered the room and headed straight for his alpha. He shook Vance's and Dante's hands before speaking to Damien. Hunter felt like all the air had left the room.

The police officer/sentinel had a head of buzzed black hair and short black stubble. He was probably only six feet, if even that, because he was shorter than all the other males standing in the front of the room. Hunter wouldn't have noticed if he hadn't been standing right next to them because the wolf-shifter was built like a linebacker. His police uniform looked like it barely fit with his biceps ready to bust out of the short sleeves of his shirt.

Until now, the vampires had mostly worked with the cat-shifters. The wolf-shifters had only just started to settle back in the Cities. The Guardians hadn't had much interaction with them besides their hunt for the wolf-shifters back before Damien challenged his father and won. Hunter hadn't been there that night—he'd just heard about it—so tonight was the first time some of the wolf-shifters and vampires had met one another.

Damien and Quentin had been speaking to each other in lowered tones, but then Damien raised his voice to be heard by everyone. "Quentin, you know all the cat-shifters. But have you met all the Guardians?"

Quentin turned toward them since they were all sitting together in a row. His almost-black eyes along with the beautiful natural bronze of his skin spoke to African lineage while his facial features hinted toward European ancestry. His nose was straight and narrow, and his lips were on the thinner side—although not too thin that they wouldn't feel good kissing.

Hunter shifted awkwardly in his seat. *What the hell?* He had never thought of another male's skin as beautiful or lips as kissable before.

Quentin looked at all the vampires, but when he got to Hunter, who sat on the end, his onyx eyes felt like they looked right through Hunter and into his soul. Then, the heavy rumble of Quentin's voice said, "Nope. I've never had the pleasure."

A shiver ran up Hunter's spine as he stared into the deep pools of Quentin's eyes. Hunter would have squirmed in his chair again if he'd been able to, but for some reason, he was unable to move.

The spell between the two males broke when Quentin looked away as Damien made the introductions. Quentin nodded to each of them, and Hunter was both disappointed and relieved that Quentin didn't shake their hands. He didn't know what would have happened if they actually touched, and it scared him.

Nothing like this had ever happened to Hunter before. He'd never felt such a visceral reaction to anyone, female or male, and he didn't know what to do or even think.

Thankfully, he didn't have to because Quentin was all business as he began to explain what the police knew, and Hunter was once again in full Guardian mode. Finally, for the first time since the wolf-shifter had entered the room, Hunter relaxed.

FIVE

AS QUENTIN TALKED, Phoenix listened, trying to ignore her sense of restlessness.

"We had a couple of witnesses—human—who said they saw a dark SUV. But this is Minnesota, so the number of dark SUVs is in the thousands. It's not much to go on, but it's something. So, everyone, keep an eye out," the wolf-shifter explained. "Unfortunately, the number of perps seems to be inconsistent. We've had reports from two to five."

"Our vampires in the St. Paul Police have heard about the SUV," Dante said. "And we always knew it was a group, but it might be hard to catch all of them at once. Hopefully, when we catch one of them, they'll start ratting each other out."

Phoenix's agitation didn't stem just from the fuckers out there, hurting their people. Or from all the commotion back at her alpha's home. A big part of it had to do with the pure maleness of the vampire standing at the front of the room.

"And the elderly woman who was hurt yesterday didn't hear, see, or smell anything?" Quentin asked.

Dante shook his head. "She scared off whoever was out there before she could see anything. And her sense of smell isn't what it used to be. She couldn't tell how many there were or if they were human, shifter, or vampire. And they must have parked a ways away. They took off on foot, and she didn't hear or see a vehicle besides her son's. Although her hearing and eyesight aren't great either."

"Shit," Quentin said.

Damien barked out a humorless laugh. "Shit is right."

Dante nodded his head in agreement as he licked his bottom lip and then sucked on it, slowly pulling it out between his teeth, the white of his fangs prominent against the deep color of his mouth. She knew he did it because he was frustrated, but it made her think of something else entirely.

Phoenix remembered when Dante had rescued her from Gerald.

Gerald was Vance's cousin who'd had big dreams of killing off the alpha and his family. During an attempt to capture Gerald, he'd escaped, shooting Saxon and Zane in the process and kidnapping Phoenix as he fled. Gerald had planned to rape her but stopped when he smelled Dante on her. He'd taken his anger out on her breasts by biting her nipples, drawing blood. Most females would have been happy that this was all that had happened to them. And Phoenix was grateful that he hadn't raped her, but her past issues made Gerald's punishment seem almost as bad as if he had.

Phoenix shuddered at the memories. The memory of Gerald and the memories of others who'd come before him.

But, after Dante had rescued her and discovered that she'd been injured, he'd healed her. With his mouth. Just thinking about it gave her hot flashes. It was the first time ever that anything had felt good when it came to her breasts. She'd had issues with them for as long as she could remember. She'd developed early, especially for a shifter, and they had brought unwanted attention to her body. But Dante had seemed to sense that she wasn't like other women, that she needed more care, which she was thankful for and embarrassed about at the same time. She sincerely hoped it was something he had just guessed about her rather than something he knew to be true. Because the thought of Dante knowing her past bothered her.

Saxon shifted beside her. Not many knew her past, but he did. Phoenix looked from Saxon to Dante and back to Saxon.

Oh God. She felt panic rise in her chest.

Saxon wouldn't have told Dante what had happened to her, would he? The two of them had managed to become friends, and Saxon knew she had this weird...*thing*...with Dante. Would he have warned Dante about her past and her issues?

She sat forward in her seat. Was that why Dante never tried to have sex with her?

But she didn't want to have sex with Dante. *Right?*

She slumped back down in her seat and stared at her hands. *What the hell is wrong with me? Why am I thinking these things?* She was not normally like this.

It had to be seeing Saxon's happy family along with the

two pregnant females and all the dumb, blissful couples in her life. It was messing with her head. She had decided a long time ago that she would never be able to mate and have a family. She'd thought she had actually made peace with it.

So, why am I acting like a stupid schoolgirl?

She looked up and right into Dante's handsome face, and she pictured the way he had looked at her last night with heat in his eyes.

"Come here, Red."

And she had. She'd walked right over to him and let him pull her down onto his lap. She'd let him sink his beautiful fangs into her neck and take her blood. He didn't even have to touch her anymore for the ache to settle between her legs. He'd just stuck his thumb, which he'd cut with his incisor right before he pulled her down, in her mouth, so she could take his blood, and she'd gone off like a rocket at the first taste.

Phoenix looked away. *How pathetic.* She was pathetic.

It was no wonder that Dante didn't pressure her to have sex. He didn't need a simple creature like her.

He had to know she didn't have much experience. She didn't know why he continued to feed from her because, way back when she'd first met him, he'd told her that he fucked when he fed. And, even though she knew he'd had orgasms in the past when he fed from her, they never came close to having sex. That meant, whatever they had going on between them wouldn't last. Couldn't last. For all she knew, Dante was feeding from someone else. And fucking that someone.

A light bulb went off in her head.

Of course.

Of course, Dante hadn't given up his sex life to, what? Have some weird relationship with her where they didn't even get to first base, much less go all the way.

She felt sick.

So, why did he continue to let her come to his home and feed from her?

She looked up into his eyes again as she felt the room closing in on her.

Of course.

He felt sorry for her.

That was why he let her feed him and why he fed her his blood, knowing she'd climax.

Poor little damaged she-cat. She was lonely and fixated on the big, strong alpha vampire. The big, bad alpha vampire who was also kind and didn't have the heart to tell her to get lost.

Loser. The word taunted her. That was the word her second boyfriend had called her.

"I'm having sex with Sheena because you're a loser who can't even pretend to like sex."

Make that *pathetic* loser because, when she'd been with her ex, she'd known she wasn't doing anything for him in bed.

But, with Dante, she'd thought he was actually getting something out of their feeding sessions.

Phoenix stood so fast that the chair rolled out from under her and hit the wall behind her.

"Phoenix?" Vance said, concern in his eyes. Concern she didn't deserve.

Vance had been disappointed that she had gone after Gerald without the rest of her pride, injuring both herself and Dante in the process. Something that could have been avoided had she asked for help. Vance hadn't said it, but Phoenix knew she had to earn back his trust because the pride and the sentinels were a team, and she had temporarily gone rogue.

"I have to use the restroom," she told her alpha.

It was a lame excuse, and she was pretty sure everyone could tell she was making it up. But it was better than staying there. And, even though they couldn't hear what she was thinking, the thought of them all knowing her humiliation made her scramble out of there even faster.

She practically slammed the door of the conference room open as she hurried out to rush down the hall, bypassing the first set of restrooms that stood right outside. She didn't know how long she was going to be in there, and she didn't need to run into anyone when she came back out.

She'd been to L & L Construction many times and even picked up odd jobs now and then, so she knew her way around the building. The conference room was on the main floor since that was where they would bring clients to show them presentations and have meetings. Phoenix skipped the elevators and headed toward the back to enter the stairwell, taking the steps two at a time until she made it to the second floor.

Several offices and cubicles were up there along with more than one set of restrooms. Thankfully, at that time of night, they were all empty, and everything was mostly dark, except for a few desk lamps that had been left on and the streetlights shining through the windows.

Phoenix walked past an empty office that was used for excess storage and almost went in there, but she needed to go to the ladies' room. She needed to look at herself in the mirror. She needed to face herself.

Phoenix entered the dark restroom and leaned against the door for a minute. The silent darkness seemed creepy but didn't scare her. She almost wished there were someone in there for her to fight because she was in the mood to kick some ass. It would be an easy way for her to vent her frustration and shame. But she was alone.

She reached out and felt along the side of the wall until she flipped the light switch. The bright fluorescent bulbs flickered on, hurting her eyes. She let her pupils adjust and then walked further into the big room and over to the sinks, taking in her appearance in the mirror.

Her face was pale, and her green eyes looked huge. Her hair had come loose from her ponytail, and her baggy clothes were twisted. She fixed her hair and straightened her clothes. She pinched her cheeks to give herself some color and blinked a few times to take away the deer-in-the-headlights look.

She narrowed her eyes and told herself with conviction, "You are not that little girl anymore. You are a grown woman. You are a sentinel. You have trained to fight and to not let anyone take advantage of you again. You're strong. You don't need a man. And you certainly don't need sex. You have yourself. You have your friends. You have the other sentinels, and you have your pride."

She paused and took in a deep breath, but this time, when she spoke, her voice lost the force behind it. "You don't need him," she practically whispered. "He's just another guy. He's nothing special. You. Don't. Need. Him."

She wasn't sure she believed her words, but she felt a

little better. She had needed that reminder of how far she'd come. She'd needed to tell herself that it was okay to be alone.

She made herself look into her eyes for a few more seconds. Then, she stuck up her chin and forced out a wobbly smile. It wasn't the most confident, but it would do for now. She nodded in agreement and turned around to leave the restroom.

She stopped when she saw someone by the door. She hadn't even heard it open.

"I'm nothing special, huh?" Dante asked.

SIX

PHOENIX STUCK her nose in the air and crossed her arms. "What are you doing in here?"

Just like this female to go on the offensive and avoid his question.

Dante stood from where he was leaning in the doorway and walked toward her. "I came to see if you were okay. You left the conference room in a hurry."

She dropped her arms and tried to look relaxed. "I'm fine."

Right. And I'm the Queen of England.

She must have read the skepticism on his face because she added, "Well, I will be anyway. Nothing that hasn't happened before."

Dante had already sensed her…sadness? No, that wasn't right. It seemed almost like despair. He could sense it through her blood, and to hear her depressing words on top of it concerned him. It was no way to live, and his heart ached for Phoenix. For the prison she and the villains of her past had put her in.

Dante glided closer to her until they were a foot apart. He knew he shouldn't mess with her dignity, but he had to know. "Who were you talking about right before you turned around?"

It was a horrible idea, asking whom she'd been referring to, and one that would likely not end with anything good, but Dante so very much wanted it to be him. He'd only been guessing when he called her out on it earlier.

His blood link to her filled with panic. Not a scared panic but a nervous panic—to the point that he would swear that she'd let her guard slip. He smelled it in the air, too.

He doubted she would have been nervous had she been speaking about someone other than him. And, when she didn't answer his question, it basically confirmed his assumption.

He was so pleased to know that he affected her, and it wasn't just one-sided, so he let his own guard down. Phoenix's eyes widened with confusion as, for a split second, he let his own feelings pass back through the blood she'd consumed from him.

He shouldn't have been too shocked at this turn of events. She had been letting him consume her blood once a month, and she'd let him make her come. But it always seemed like, before and after, she was a cold, reserved being. She would momentarily come alive in his arms, but once it was over, she always went back to being the same female he'd met months ago. If he wasn't in the same room with her when she orgasmed, he would never believe it actually happened. All this time, part of him had assumed that she let him drink her blood because she owed him for rescuing her from Gerald and for telling her about Gerald's whereabouts.

To know that she continued to feed him because she wanted to changed the whole ballgame.

But, at the same time, could anything come from it? Phoenix had some deep issues that Dante feared would never let her open up to anyone completely.

Phoenix always seemed so strong and indifferent to many things around her. She was very loyal to her pride and obviously cared about them, but it seemed that her devotion was reserved to only them. Could Dante have penetrated the wall she'd built around herself?

Dante studied Phoenix and tentatively lifted his hand to touch her. When she didn't shy away, he lightly touched her hair. "You know you can trust me." *With your body. Your heart. Your mind.* But he didn't say any of that aloud because a part of him knew she would balk at his words. "I would never hurt you." More than anything, he wanted her to know that he would die protecting her if he needed to.

Phoenix looked up into his eyes and opened her mouth, but the words didn't come out because both of their phones beeped, breaking whatever spell had been cast around them.

Dante stepped away from her and pulled his mobile out of his pocket.

Before he finished reading the message, Phoenix said, "Naya's in labor."

☾

Hunter and his fellow sentinels had been summoned to the vampire clinic. With the impending birth of Princess Naya and her mate, Vaughn's, babies, their meeting at L & L Construction had been postponed. However, over forty-eight hours later, Naya was still in labor. The vampires' and shifters' fearless leaders knew they still needed to take care of the matter at hand, so they commandeered an empty room for them to finish their meeting.

Basically, they all showed to get their assignments, which was good because they barely all fit in the much smaller space. It was not made to fit the almost twenty people who were currently crammed inside.

Hunter was beginning to feel claustrophobic, but that could be due to the male next to him. Despite someone being behind him, in front of him, and on the other side, Hunter only seemed to be aware of Quentin.

The wolf-shifter was shorter than Hunter but wider, and the male smelled incredible, like evergreens at Christmas, like the outdoors and raw sexuality. And he put off so much heat that Hunter was starting to sweat. The worst part was that Hunter could feel himself getting hard.

What the fuck is going on? he silently asked his dick.

His dick's only response was to become a full-fledged erection, and soon, Hunter had to adjust himself in his pants. Why in the hell was he getting turned on now? This was not the time or the place.

Thankfully, no one, not even Quentin, seemed to notice, as their attention was focused on Dante, Vance, and Damien in the front of the room.

"So, we are going to start placing assignments. We have the city marked off in sections," Vance said. "We're going to have you pair up, and we'll get to that in a minute. First, because of the threats to our communities, we've decided that our mates need protection, especially when some of them are in a delicate position. Vaughn will stay with Naya, of course, since he will already be home with the babies. My mate and my daughter will stay with me, freeing up Damien to go on patrol. That leaves Kenzie, and she will be assigned to Phoenix and Sawyer, of course. The two of you can decide your schedules."

Phoenix was only a few people away from Hunter, so he heard her gasp. He leaned forward to get a look at her face. She looked pissed, but she didn't utter a word. Hunter wondered what Dante thought of her assignment and if he wanted to be with her. On their last job, Hunter had been paired with Dante, and he'd been the one to help Dante rescue Phoenix.

Hunter's mind had wandered so much that he missed the rest of the assignments, but since Phoenix was with Kenzie, he figured he was with Dante again. Due to the overcrowding, Hunter decided to wait for some of them to leave the room before he went and spoke with Dante. He didn't get far though.

"Looks like you and I are together," a deep baritone said beside him.

Hunter's head whipped around to look at Quentin. "Huh?"

"You and I are together."

Others were leaving the room, yet it seemed as if it were getting smaller.

"I'm sorry. I missed that."

Quentin smiled at Hunter like the vampire was a

simpleton and needed an extra explanation. "You"—he pointed to Hunter—"and me"—he pointed to himself —"are assigned to patrol together." He held out his hand. "I'm Quentin. We weren't formally introduced."

Hunter, still in a daze, raised his hand for Quentin to shake. As their skin touched, Hunter felt like a spark had lit inside his body, traveling all around, bouncing off his bones and organs until it settled in his groin. It was then that Hunter realized he was shaking the shifter's hand with the same hand he'd adjusted himself with less than fifteen minutes ago.

Ashamed, Hunter yanked his arm away and out of Quentin's grip, but it was too late.

Hunter was hard again.

Quentin, however, didn't seem to notice. He looked at Hunter and slowly lowered his own arm. He frowned at Hunter with what looked like hurt and disappointment in his eyes. "Maybe you should go and ask your leader for a new partner," the wolf said, his voice clipped.

Hunter was confused. Quentin was obviously mad, but he didn't understand why. Then, Hunter looked down to where he was clutching the hand he'd used to shake Quentin's, as if the shifter had the plague.

Hunter immediately dropped his hands. "No, this is not what it seems."

Quentin raised his brow, as if to say, *Explain it to me then.*

No can do. There was no way Hunter was going to tell this stranger that he'd gotten a boner.

Quentin snickered. "That's what I thought. Either go ask to work with someone else or come find me when you're ready. Either way, get your shit together because we have work to do."

"But—"

Quentin didn't give Hunter a chance to finish. Jaw clenched and fire in his eyes, he pushed past Hunter and exited the room.

SEVEN

THIS MADE the second time that Phoenix had gotten babysitting duty. The first time was when Gerald had kidnapped Payton and tried to kidnap Vaughn and Naya. Technically, it should have been someone else's turn, but she knew she was still proving herself to Vance for going after Gerald without backup.

She was not happy about the assignment, but she wasn't going to dare complain. She was in this situation due to her own zealousness. She had no one to blame but herself. But, minus her and Dante's injuries, she didn't regret it. She'd take the next ten babysitting assignments for the pleasure of killing that asshole Gerald.

Phoenix left the quick meeting in the clinic room to find Sawyer and Kenzie since she needed to figure out how she and Sawyer were going to trade off shifts.

Kenzie was in the waiting room, sleeping in a chair, and Sawyer was nowhere to be found. So much for looking after his own mate. Of course, Kenzie was pretty safe in the clinic, surrounded by everyone waiting for Naya to give birth. Lilith and Payton were several chairs away, also napping, and neither of them would let anything happen to Kenzie.

Phoenix sat down next to Kenzie and waited for Sawyer. She had her fingers crossed that she could go back home and sleep, and she wouldn't have to be here when Naya delivered. Since Sawyer was Vaughn's best friend, Phoenix assumed that Sawyer would want to stay, and she would be able to leave soon. Then, she wouldn't have to pretend that all this excitement didn't bother her.

As she waited, she watched most of the meeting's members file out of the clinic to go home or go on duty. Only a few people remained. As long as it was still dark out, Dante was responsible for bringing the king and queen to see their grandchildren once they were born. Vaughn stayed because he was obviously going into the delivery room. The last few people staying behind were Vance, the soon-to-be grandfather; Damien, who was with his mate, Payton; and Sawyer because he was friends with Vaughn and his mate was friends with Naya.

Kenzie stirred beside her. When she saw Phoenix sitting next to her, she quickly sat up. "Hey. Where's Sawyer?"

Phoenix pointed to Sawyer and Vance, who were still in the hallway, talking. "Over there."

Kenzie relaxed. "Oh, good. I thought maybe something had happened."

"Nothing exciting."

"So, what are you doing here?" Kenzie asked.

Phoenix admired her directness. "You've got yourself a new watchdog."

Kenzie frowned. "What do you mean?"

"Didn't Sawyer tell you that you were going to have twenty-four-hour protection?"

"What the hell? No. That's ridiculous."

As much as Phoenix didn't want the job, it wasn't exactly ridiculous.

"Not when a group is out there, committing crimes against shifters and vampires. And since you're…" Phoenix couldn't bring herself to say pregnant, so she gestured toward Kenzie's abdomen. She was turning into such a wuss.

"Great. I go from being an independent woman who doesn't need a man to someone who needs a babysitter. Be careful what you wish for."

Phoenix chuckled. She liked this human. "Sorry."

"No, I'm sorry. My life is very mundane, and you will probably die from boredom." Kenzie winced. "Does this mean you'll have to follow me around at work?"

Phoenix shrugged. "I don't know. Sawyer and I have to figure out the details."

"Great."

Sawyer and Vance broke apart, and Sawyer walked toward them. Kenzie crossed her legs and arms as she waited for her mate. When Sawyer approached, he must have sensed Kenzie's irritation because he stood in front of her instead of sitting down.

"Have you heard anything?"

"No, I haven't heard *anything*. Is there something you would like to share with me?"

Sawyer nervously rubbed the back of his neck.

A few months ago, Phoenix wouldn't have believed that

she would see this side of Sawyer. Frankly, she hadn't even realized that he had it until recently. It was quite comical.

"Uh...well...Vance and I decided it would be safer to have someone watching over you all the time, just in case."

"Vance and you?" Kenzie asked skeptically.

"Yes."

Kenzie narrowed her eyes.

"Okay, okay, it was mostly me," he said, plopping down into the chair on the other side of her.

"Sawyer, you are making poor Phoenix hang out with me when I can take care of myself."

"Uh, one, Phoenix is not poor, and, two, you cannot take care of yourself. Not when there are people out there who outnumber you," Sawyer said. "And they might be shifters or vampires who are stronger than you. I can't let you get hurt. Or the baby. It would kill me."

Kenzie's expression softened as she turned to her mate. She leaned toward him and tenderly kissed his mouth.

Phoenix felt like a voyeur, watching their intimate exchange, and it made her feel guilty and really, really alone.

She turned away and pulled out her phone to pretend like she wasn't paying attention to the couple and to give them some space. But then she started to hear kissing noises.

Then, Kenzie whispered, trying not to let anyone hear but forgetting that she was in a room with shifters and vampires, "Let's go find someplace to be alone."

Phoenix heard Sawyer hop out of his seat, and she turned in time to see the big grin on his face. He pulled Kenzie up to follow behind him as she giggled and let him drag her off.

"Hey, wait, we haven't talked yet," Phoenix called after them.

But they were too into each other for either one of them to hear Phoenix.

Wonderful. Who knew how long it would take them to do it? *Why does everyone have to have sex all the time?*

Feeling sullen, Phoenix leaned back in her seat to wait. She really should just leave, but she was already on thin ice and didn't need this to be one more thing she messed up.

She propped her head back to rest, but sleep eluded her. She was halfway to dreamland several times, but she kept waking up when she heard a noise or sensed something. But then she smelled the wonderful scent of cinnamon and male, and before she knew it, she was out like a light.

A couple of hours later, Phoenix woke, disoriented until she remembered that she was at the vampire clinic. She was lying on her back with her head on Dante's lap. He was also snoozing with his head back against the wall. He looked so peaceful when he was asleep. Dante carried a lot of weight on his shoulders as the leader of the Guardians, and while he didn't act like it was a stressful job, it clearly affected him.

Phoenix slowly sat up so as not to wake Dante, but he still was slightly roused from his slumber. Half-asleep, he reached out until he touched her leg, and as if he was eased from knowing that she was there, he went back to sleep.

The action startled her, mostly because it didn't bother her. At all. She liked that she brought comfort to Dante instead of the other way around.

Phoenix looked around the room, as if finally remembering they weren't alone. Sawyer and Kenzie were back with Kenzie resting her hand on Sawyer's shoulder while he looked down at his phone. Vance was on the phone and out of earshot. Payton and Lilith were both awake and playing cards, but Lilith glanced over at Phoenix and smiled and winked before turning back to playing her game.

All of a sudden, there was a commotion from the hallway, and Vaughn came out with a big plastic bassinet. Everyone stopped what they were doing and stood to see the new babies.

Everyone but Phoenix.

Dante woke from all the noise but stayed sitting with his hand on her knee. Now, it was she who was taking security from knowing that Dante was beside her.

"Are you going to go see the babies?" she asked Dante.

"Nah, I'm not close to either of them, and I'd feel like I was intruding." He looked at his watch. "As soon as Vaughn gives me the okay, I'm going to pick up Naya's parents." Dante looked at Phoenix. "Don't you want to see the little ones?"

She shrugged. She was dying to see them, but at the same time, she was absolutely terrified. Sawyer glanced over at her. He was the only one besides Saxon who knew that she really wanted to be a mother. She'd told Sawyer in confidence when he was making some bad decisions about being with Kenzie. Thankfully, he hadn't told anyone else her secret.

For many others, it probably didn't seem that hush, hush. Many beings wanted families. It wasn't unusual by any means. But, for Phoenix, it felt like a vulnerability. She knew she came across as tough and even unfeeling sometimes, so she could just imagine everyone laughing at her once they found out she wanted to be a mom. And she didn't want anyone to know because she hated being pitied.

Poor sexually dysfunctional female who wants a family. She could practically hear them whispering behind her back already.

"I'm good right here," she finally told Dante. "I'm splitting guard duty with Sawyer, and we haven't worked out the details yet. Otherwise, I wouldn't even be here."

Dante nodded, as if he understood, but there was still speculation in his eyes.

"How's Naya?" Lilith asked her son as she cuddled a baby.

"Good. It was kind of scary for a while there. The doctor almost had to take her for a C-section because Naya was getting tired and weak, but that's when these two decided to make their entrances. Naya is sleeping now, so I wanted to give her time to rest."

"After more than fifty hours of labor, I can imagine."

"Well, not all of it was active labor, Mom."

"It's still labor, dear, and until you experience it, you don't get a say," Lilith told her son.

"Yes, ma'am."

"That's it. I'm never having kids," Payton said as she held the other baby. "I don't like pain, and fifty hours is just too long."

"You'll change your mind," her mother told her.

"About pain? I don't think so." She looked down at the baby. "Although you are pretty cute."

Damien pulled his mate close and whispered in her ear, and she smiled.

"Okay, I might change my mind for you."

"What are their names?" Kenzie asked. "Do they finally have some?"

Vaughn laughed. "Yes. The boy is Aidan Vaughn, and the girl is Victoria Anaya."

"Oh, isn't that cute? A.V. and V.A.," Lilith said. "I love it."

Everyone took chairs after that and took turns holding the newborns.

Phoenix thought she had managed to avoid the whole baby-holding situation when Kenzie, who was sitting beside her, put the baby in her arms without asking and jumped up. "I have to use the restroom."

Phoenix looked down to see a little scrunched up face with a pink hat. Little Victoria fussed, and Phoenix instinctively clutched the baby closer to her.

The baby calmed immediately while Phoenix was overcome with emotion. It was easy to ignore wanting a baby when she wasn't ever faced with one. It was easy to pretend that she didn't yearn for the things she wanted in life, that she was okay with how things had turned out.

But holding Victoria in her arms made Phoenix realize just how much she wanted to be a mother. The desire was so strong, she was afraid she wouldn't be able to breathe from the longing. And, without warning, her impending mating heat loomed over her. To know that she would be spending it alone and drugged up in a room by herself was so depressing that Phoenix almost choked on it.

"Phoenix. Phoenix."

She looked up into Dante's deep brown eyes.

"Are you okay?"

No. Not at all.

"Is there anything I can do?" he asked when she didn't answer.

Phoenix thought to a couple of days ago when Dante had told her she could trust him and that he'd never hurt her. There was a moment that night when she could have sworn she'd actually felt what he was feeling, but then the feeling was gone. She believed him one hundred ten percent, and she trusted her feelings. That was why he would be perfect for the job.

"Yes," she told him.

"What can I do?" He looked so sincere in his question that she knew she was making the right choice.

"How about I come with you to pick up the king and queen? I'll tell you all about it."

He looked like he wanted to press, but he nodded his okay.

Suddenly, feeling lighter than she had in days, Phoenix sat back and kissed baby Victoria on the head before snuggling her close.

EIGHT

DANTE OPENED the car door for Phoenix, so she could get in the passenger side. He slid behind the steering wheel and left the clinic before saying anything to Phoenix.

She'd been very distressed at the clinic once Vaughn brought the twins out, and her anxiety had increased when Kenzie put baby Victoria in her arms. But then, out of nowhere, a calmness had settled over Phoenix after he offered to help her. His mind was reeling with the possibilities.

"So, what did you want to talk about?"

Phoenix stared straight ahead, out the windshield. "No judging, please."

"Of course not."

"I have always wanted to be a mother," she said matter-of-factly.

He figured she was keeping all emotion out of her voice in case he said something to make her feel like her dream was less than.

He admitted he was shocked. He would have expected

Phoenix to be the last person to say that, and frankly, he didn't know how to respond. "I can understand that," is what he settled on because it was the truth. "I've always pictured having children myself."

"Good. Then, this should be easier."

What in the world...

"Do you know how babies are conceived?"

"Uh…" *Is this a trick question?*

"I mean, shifter babies."

That question made more sense. "A little but not the specifics. Shifter females have a mating heat that requires constant…stimulation."

"We are only fertile two times a year, about every six months, when we go through our mating heat. It lasts several days, and if we don't conceive, we have to wait again. That is why there are so few of us compared to humans."

"Okay." Where was she going with this?

"You meant what you said to me at L and L, right? That I could trust you, and you would never hurt me?"

"Of course." Now, Dante was completely lost.

Phoenix looked over at him and smiled. "Good. My mating heat is in less than a month, and I want you to get me pregnant."

Dante swerved into the next lane, almost hitting another car. *"What?"*

"I want you to have sex with me during my next mating heat and get me pregnant. The whole process will take a few days, so that is why I wanted to warn you now, so you know you'll be unavailable for a while."

"You misunderstood. I heard you. I just don't understand why."

Phoenix sighed, as if she were talking to an imbecile. "I want to be a mother. I only have two chances every year. I am not getting any younger. Since it looks like I will never be comfortable having sex and therefore finding a mate, I would like you to get me pregnant."

"Did you just hear yourself?" Dante asked. "You will never be comfortable having sex, but you want me to… to…" He couldn't finish.

"Knock me up? Yes."

"No," he told her. *No way.*

"No?" she repeated.

"No."

She threw her hands up. "Why not?"

"Let me get this straight. You don't like sex; in fact, you dislike it. Yet you want me to have sex with you over and over again until you get pregnant."

"Yes," she said.

"And you don't find anything wrong with that?"

"If it gets me what I want, then no."

"I'm sorry, but I can't do that, Phoenix." It was crazy that they were even having this conversation.

"Oh," she said, as if she suddenly realized how ridiculous she sounded. "You can be a part of our child's life if you want. Or you don't have to be. I won't deny or force you to do either."

Holy shit, she just doesn't get it.

"While I appreciate that, I am not going to force myself on you over and over, all the while knowing that you are hating every second of it. Even if you are willing and it was your idea, I don't have that certain kink. I doubt I'd even be able to start, much less...finish."

The thought of Phoenix lying on a bed, simply enduring sex, while he fucked her made him sick to his stomach. His dick and balls were shriveling up, just thinking about it.

"But—"

"I'm sorry, Phoenix. I can't do that to you. Or to me."

She put her back to him and stared out the passenger window. He felt her despair that he'd felt in her earlier at the clinic. It was so strong through their blood link that he almost tasted it.

Had she really felt better after coming up with that crazy, outrageous idea? It seemed so.

He felt awful. He wanted to help her in any way he could, but he just couldn't do it. It felt too much like rape, and he would never do that to a woman. Ever.

They rode the rest of the way in silence. When they pulled up to the king and queen's mansion, Dante got out while Phoenix stayed inside the vehicle. The Kensington's butler, Hans, answered the door and let him in. He had called ahead to tell them that he was coming, but Naya's parents weren't ready.

Left alone with his thoughts, Dante mulled over what Phoenix had said. He wanted to help her but didn't know how.

Just as he heard footsteps on the stairs, the horrible thought of Phoenix asking someone else to help her materialized in his head, and Dante's vision waned. Over his dead body would he give her the opportunity to ask someone else to do that for her. There was no way he was going to let anyone else touch her, have sex with her, put a baby inside her.

He'd—

"Dante?"

He heard his name and looked up at his king and queen.

Dante cleared his throat. "I'm sorry, sir. My thoughts were momentarily preoccupied. Are you and the queen ready to go?"

"Yes. Shall we go?" the king said.

Dante held out his arm to escort the queen down the front steps and into his SUV.

Once the king and queen were settled, Dante introduced Phoenix, "Sir, ma'am, this is Phoenix. She is a sentinel with your son-in-law's pride."

Phoenix turned around and held out her hand. "Hello," she said.

Dante leaned closer to her and whispered, "They don't shake hands."

"Oh," she said as she withdrew her hand. "It's nice to meet you," she told Naya's parents.

"Likewise, I'm sure," the queen spoke, her voice frosty.

The queen might have accepted her daughter's mating but only barely. She wasn't happy about the situation. At least she was going to visit her grandchildren. Part of Dante was still surprised, but maybe even she wasn't that heartless.

"Can you tell us how our daughter is doing, Dante?"

Dante relayed the information that Vaughn had given him while Phoenix sat in silence and listened. After the update, there didn't seem to be any more for anyone to say, and Dante's thoughts returned to Phoenix's request.

He couldn't stop picturing her with someone else.

Someone like Saxon. And, while Phoenix had said she found sex uncomfortable, Dante continued to picture Saxon making Phoenix come with a look of pleasure on her face. It was starting to drive him insane.

He was so lost in his thoughts, he didn't realize that he'd driven all the way to the clinic on autopilot. As he pulled up to the door, he knew what he had to do.

Phoenix reached for the door handle, and Dante lightly touched her arm to stop her.

"Will you stay in here until I park? I need to say something to you."

She studied his face before dropping her hand. "Fine," she bit out.

"Give me one moment," he told her.

Dante exited the SUV, opened the back doors to let the king and queen out, and walked them to the front door. Once they were safely inside, he went back to his vehicle. He found a spot and put the SUV in park before saying anything to Phoenix.

She was sitting with her arms crossed, her wall firmly in place, and he cursed himself. He'd worked so hard to break some of it down, only to have her put it back up with a single conversation.

"Well?" she prompted. She was still upset with him.

"I will help you," he said.

She dropped her arms, and a look of amazement crossed her face.

Dante put up a finger. "On two conditions."

"Deal."

He frowned. "You don't even know what I'm going to say."

"I don't care. I'm just happy you've agreed."

"Well, I care. My first requirement is that I will get to be this child's father. I am not a sperm donor."

She smiled. "I already said you could."

Whew. He'd been afraid that she would fight him on that.

"My second stipulation is that we have to get to know each other, physically, before your mating heat arrives. I'm not having sex with you during your mating heat while you simply lie there and endure it. We will make time to learn each other's likes and dislikes. I want to make the experience good for you. We're going to start slow and take our time before we have sex."

She lost her smile. "Dante," she sighed. "It's no use. It won't make any difference."

"It will to me. It's the only way I'll agree to do this. It's either that or nothing." *Please don't turn me down and ask someone else*, he prayed. Outside though, he played it cool. He didn't want her to know exactly how much this meant to him.

"Fine. But you're just going to be disappointed. Don't blame me when you end up frustrated."

The pleasure Dante felt that she had agreed swept over him. He opened his door and turned to her. "Oh, Phoenix." *What a silly female.* "Don't you know, you could never disappoint me?"

And, with that, Dante departed his SUV and went toward the clinic, whistling all the way. He was going to find a way to pleasure her if it was the last thing he did. Phoenix deserved it.

NINE

LEXINE DROVE past Michelle's house one more time, knowing it was hopeless, before going home. She only had about an hour and a half before sunrise, and she was on duty with Sterling the following night.

She almost kept driving after reaching her destination but did a double take when she saw that Michelle's car was in her driveway. Even better, Lexine recognized the other two vehicles parked on the street.

Lexine screeched to a stop, parking crookedly across the street, and set a foot outside her door before she even had her vehicle in park. She flew up the walkway and pounded on Michelle's door.

When Michelle answered, she obviously hadn't been expecting Lexine because she looked shocked and then guilty. Then, she smiled like she was happy to see the other vampire.

"Let me in," Lexine said.

Michelle laughed nervously as she opened the door further and stood back. "Of course."

Lexine marched through the house until she found the rest of the group in the kitchen. Everyone was there—Dani, Steve, Analeigh, and Mathis—except Lucas.

"Would you like to explain to me what in the hell happened the other night?"

"What are you talking about?" Dani asked with her eyes wide, feigning innocence.

Lexine saw right through it. She was a Guardian after all. She had been trained to spot bullshit a mile away.

Lexine crossed her arms. "Don't pretend like you guys don't know what I'm talking about. Or is there another reason you've all been MIA for the last few days?" She dropped her arms and pointed to the group. "You promised no one would get hurt."

She heard footsteps behind her and turned around as Michelle was hanging up her phone.

"Lucas will be here in five."

It hadn't taken Lexine long to learn that Lucas was the leader of this band of misfits, which was terribly annoying at times. Yes, Dante was her leader, and the king and queen were technically in charge of all of them, but she and her fellow Guardians could still make decisions on their own and were independent in their own way. These vampires wouldn't take a piss without asking Lucas for permission.

"Of course. You guys can't talk to me without Lucas present."

"Why don't you have a seat? I'll get you something to drink," Analeigh, the quiet one of the group, said.

"Yes, good idea," Steve, her boyfriend, said.

"Fine," Lexine said, pulling out a chair at the table.

Everyone else sat around the table for eight and tried to

make friendly conversation, except for Analeigh, who was at the kitchen counter, making Lexine a drink. She could tell they were all nervous, as they should be. They had royally messed up the other night, and Lexine was a Guardian. By vampire law, she should be locking these people up.

Analeigh brought over Lexine's drink and set it in front of her. It was alcoholic, so she almost refused. But, with vampire metabolism, it would take a lot to get her drunk, and she wasn't on duty until sundown that following night. She might as well enjoy it.

When she'd gotten involved with them months ago, she had been angry and hurt from Dante's lack of interest in her. She was still in love with him and hated to see him with that stupid *crap*-shifter, but she was a little less angry now. She had fully supported her new friends' idea to protest the new vampire-shifter truce. She'd even given them information about how to avoid the Guardians, but the plan had been that no one would be injured.

Her new friends continued talking about some lame-ass movie, trying to get Lexine to join in, but after a few one-worded answers, they stopped trying to engage her. After a few minutes, Lexine started to feel really drowsy. She hadn't slept as much as she should have the last few days because she was worried, but this was bizarre. She felt like she had twenty pounds sitting on each eyelid, and her vision was going blurry.

"Are you okay, Lexine?" one of the females asked.

She couldn't tell who had asked.

"I think it's working," one of the guys said.

Lexine tried to tell them that she wasn't okay, but her words came out muffled and didn't make any sense.

Lexine picked up on footsteps coming from the front of the house.

Then, someone said, "Lucas is here."

That was the last thing Lexine heard before she slumped over onto the floor and hit her head.

☾

Lexine awoke, lying on her back, with a splitting headache. She tried to roll over but was unable to move. She opened her eyes to see that her hands and feet were each chained to the corners of a bed.

She had no idea how long she'd been there. The shutters were all closed in the room, which meant that it was probably daylight. But was it the same day, or had more days passed?

"You're awake," a voice said from the corner, startling Lexine.

She didn't say anything as she watched Lucas rise out of the seat and move closer. Her first instinct was to lash out and demand to be let go, but she knew that would get her nowhere. She had to be calm and try to appeal to him, and she had to gain as much information as she could in the process.

"How-how long have I been here?" Her throat was dry, and the words came out hoarse.

Lucas looked at his watch. "About five hours." He dropped his arm and smiled. "You should have only been out about two hours or so. Analeigh gave you a little more sedative than normally recommended. She was afraid it wouldn't work."

"Is that why my head hurts?"

Lucas laughed. "Oh, no. That's because you hit your head when you fell." He shrugged. "Everyone thought you were faking it to get the upper hand, so no one bothered to catch you."

Assholes.

"What is going on? Why am I tied up?"

Lucas grabbed another chair that was against the wall and pulled it closer to the bed. He sat on it backward and casually said, "Because you're no longer useful to us, and you're starting to become more of a pain in the ass. You seem to think that you're in charge because you're some bitch Guardian." He bared his teeth, and his eyes turned frosty. "You seem to have forgotten that this is my group. I'm the one in charge. We don't need your ugly cunt telling us what to do."

Lexine almost shrank away from him. But she couldn't let him see that he really scared her; although he could probably already smell her fear in the air. She needed to think of something else. Like how she couldn't believe that she'd actually been interested in Lucas at one point. How could she have had sex with this guy and not known that he was so horrible?

Once again, the nice, well-mannered Lucas, the one she'd originally known, returned. "Now, I think the two of us need to get something straight."

"That you're going to kill me?"

Lucas shook with a full-on belly laugh. "God, no. We're not idiots."

"So then, what? You're going to keep me locked up

here? Because I'm on duty at sunset, and they'll know I'm missing if I don't show up."

He waved his hand, as if she were being silly. "You'll be back to do your job. You might be a little late, considering you're stuck here until sundown, but you'll be back."

"I don't understand."

"Thanks for asking, Lexine. Yes, I would love to explain it to you." His eyes and voice lost all humor again. "You work for me now, bitch. I'm the one who calls the shots, and I'm the one who gives orders."

Lexine wasn't just going to sit by and do whatever this crazy nut said. He must have forgotten that she was a Guardian and had the power to lock his ass up.

"Okay," she said sarcastically.

"Michelle!" Lucas shouted so loudly that Lexine jumped.

There was a knock at the door, and then Michelle entered. She wouldn't look Lexine in the eyes.

"Michelle, why don't you tell Lexine what will happen if she turns us in?"

Michelle pulled a tablet from behind her back and hit play. There was a picture of her, her parents, and her brother, Lennox. This appeared to have been taken just the other day when Lennox and she were visiting. They knew where her parents lived.

But that was okay. Once she told Dante and Lennox and the others, they would put her parents in a safe place.

"Uh-uh-uhh." Lucas shook his finger at her, as if he knew what she was thinking. "We're not done yet. Keep watching. And, more importantly, keep listening."

Next, she saw a video of her ranting and raving about how much she hated the shifters. She had said it all when she was very angry, but hearing it now sounded horrible. When she had said that she wanted to hurt them, she hadn't really meant it. She had been venting her hurt feelings.

After that, the screen went black, but there was still sound. There were conversations about what they were going to do to stop the vampire-shifter truce, and it was very damning evidence. Some of it wasn't true, especially when they talked about upping the actions to violence. The tape had been edited to make it sound like it was her idea.

The last thing the video showed was her parents again. This time, they were in a windowless room, pounding on the door and yelling for help.

Lexine was furious, and she tried to fight off her chains, but they were too strong. She fought until she exhausted herself, and she lay there, panting and watching her poor trapped mom and dad.

The recording ended, and Lucas clapped, like he was at the theater or something. It was creepy. "That'll be all, Michelle."

Michelle left the room, and Lucas looked at her.

"So, now, you know that your parents are guests of ours. As long as you cooperate, they will be taken care of. And if you don't…" Lucas ran a finger across his throat. "And, if you don't care about your parents and still go to your precious leader, I have plenty of evidence to damn you to the Guardians. It's your word against ours."

"It's a lie," she bit out.

"Now, now, Lexine. Some of it is, and some of it isn't.

But that doesn't matter because your friends will all believe it." He raised an eyebrow. "Now, will you help us?"

What choice do I have? She couldn't let anything happen to her parents. *Anyway, who would believe me?* She was partly guilty after all.

"Fine," she said through clenched teeth. "But how am I going to explain where I was today?" She bet that he hadn't thought of that.

Lucas laughed again, but it was eerie and sent a chill down her back.

"Steve, Mathis, it's your turn."

When the other guys entered the room, Lucas got out of the chair and shoved it out of the way. The three males stood around Lexine, and she was filled with dread.

"Hold her down," Lucas said.

"No, no, no," Lexine chanted, afraid they were going to rape her.

Steve lay across her lower body and legs, and Mathis held down an arm and turned her head toward him. Lucas grabbed her other arm. She tried to see what he was doing, but he put a hand on her head and held it away from him.

She was completely unprepared for their next action. Lucas struck her neck, taking her blood in large gulps. Lexine tried to fight the guys off, but it was no use. With the chains and three against one, she couldn't defeat them.

What was worse was that she started to cry. Lucas might not be sexually assaulting her in the way that regular humans thought of, but vampires normally did not steal blood from other vampires. They only took what was given freely. Lucas was blood-raping her, and Lexine feared she was going to throw up. Now, he would be able to sense her whether she wanted him to or not.

After Lucas was finished and after he'd taken more blood than he should have, he licked her wounds closed, taking more time than he needed to seal them. When the guys let her go, she looked over at Lucas and shot daggers at him with her eyes. She didn't care if she had tears running down her face.

Lucas was licking his fangs and lips. "God, you taste good. I knew you would." He looked up at Steve and Mathis. "This cunt wouldn't let me drink from her when we were fucking." He looked back down at Lexine. "Looks like I got what I wanted after all."

Lexine spit on him, and Lucas slapped her.

He grabbed her face and squeezed. "Don't you ever try something like that again."

Lexine wasn't stupid enough to repeat the action, but she didn't look away from his eyes. She *would not* submit to him.

Lucas let her go and looked at the other males. "Okay, guys, you know what we have to do now."

Mathis pulled out a pair of scissors, and once again, Lexine was scared.

"Lie still, and you won't get hurt," he said.

"Don't baby her, Mathis," Lucas said. "Just cut off her clothes already."

It took all three of them to hold her down again in order to get her clothes off, leaving her in her underwear and bra.

"Go ahead and fight. The sweatier you are, the more you'll sell it," Lucas said.

Then, he unzipped his pants, and the other guys followed suit.

Lexine closed her eyes, not wanting to watch. She was already so tired from struggling and from blood loss that she didn't know if she could fight much more.

This was just going to be another way to discredit and degrade her.

TEN

PHOENIX STOOD at the front of the Guardians' compound, the same place she'd been a few nights ago, but this time, she was there for another reason.

She was going to have sex with Dante.

The idea seemed crazy. Not that long ago, she had sworn to herself that she would never have sex again with anyone, but now, here she was.

She might have gone back on her proposition to have Dante get her pregnant, excusing her impulsive proposal as a moment of insanity, except she had spent all day with Kenzie and her pregnancy hormones. It was enough to let Phoenix know that she was making the right decision.

Phoenix knocked on the door, and this time, Dante answered. He opened the door and quickly ushered her inside because the sun had not set yet. Vampires didn't go poof or burst into a ball of flames in the sun, but they did get severely sunburned. However, they healed so fast that it was invisible to the naked eye. It was only after modern technology that it had been discovered what the sun did to them and why they required extra blood and hours upon hours of rest when coming into contact with the sun.

Phoenix hurried inside, so Dante could shut the door behind her.

"Can I get you something to drink?" Dante asked.

It seemed weird that he was trying to be polite and sociable. Not that this behavior wasn't one hundred percent Dante. It was just that she usually came to feed him. She got in and out, and that was the extent of their interactions. It was usually more like one colleague helping another rather than a social call.

"No, thanks. I'm good." Quite frankly, she wanted to get this over with. She was starting to get really nervous, and it was not a feeling she was comfortable with. It made her feel vulnerable, and she already felt vulnerable enough, knowing that the two of them were going to be getting naked together.

She scanned him up and down, seeing him differently now than before. She never really looked at him like a woman looked at a man. She never looked at any male like that actually. But, tonight, she studied Dante.

He was tall, a few inches over six feet, with thick dark hair and dark brown eyes. He had a Mediterranean skin tone due to his Greek ancestry. He was, without a doubt, attractive, and he would make beautiful babies. She already hoped that their child would end up looking like him.

"Come on upstairs then," Dante said, holding his arm out toward the stairs.

Phoenix went ahead of him. With each step she climbed, her anxiety grew. When she reached Dante's room, she almost didn't go in. Until she pictured Naya's babies, giving her the renewed strength to step over the threshold and into Dante's domain.

She'd been in Dante's room before, so she shouldn't be that scared of it. It was the first place where he had fed from her. Also, after Gerald had kidnapped her, she hadn't been able to sleep alone in the compound's guest room. She'd slept in Dante's bed the whole time she stayed with the vampires.

Dante stepped around her and went to his dresser where a television sat.

"Is that new?" she asked. "I don't remember you having a TV."

"It is," he said, picking up a remote. "So, what do you like to watch?"

"Excuse me?"

Why was he wasting time with asking her what she liked?

"What do you like to watch? TV? Movies? We have just about everything in this joint."

"Um…I don't really watch television or movies."

Dante looked a little defeated. "Yeah, me either." He perked up. "But I've heard great things about *Game of Thrones*. And, if we're really up for something challenging, Morgan suggested *True Blood*. Apparently, they have their vampire facts all wrong."

"Huh?"

Phoenix had met Morgan before. She was another Guardian and seemed nice enough with her beautiful brown skin and her turquoise eyes, but for some reason, Phoenix didn't like the fact that Morgan and Dante were chummy.

"Yeah, it's that show on HBO about vampires, werewolves, and faeries. Along with humans who are addicted to vampire blood."

"I'm confused."

Dante shrugged. "Well, maybe we just have to start watching it to understand."

Phoenix shook her head. "No, I'm not confused about the show. I mean, I am but not in the way you think. I'm confused about why we are talking about watching television. Shouldn't we be...you know"—she gestured to the two of them and then to his bed—"having sex?"

Dante laughed, walked closer to his bed, and then literally jumped on top of it, landing on his back with his head on the pillows. "Come here, Red."

She would never admit it to anyone—*anyone*—but she loved it when Dante called her Red. No one had ever given her a nickname before, not even when she was a kid, and she loved that he had a special name for her. Until now, he'd only used it when he was feeding from her.

Phoenix cautiously sat next to Dante on the bed, unsure of what to do next. *Take off my clothes, take off his clothes, kiss him?* This was why it was easier not to do this stuff at all. She should just go find someone else to get her pregnant. Someone who would just have sex with her during her heat and skip this whole thing.

She looked back at Dante. But he was the only one she trusted. She faced forward again, leaned over, and removed her shoes.

Before she could do anything else, Dante put an arm around her waist and hauled her backward until she lay beside him with his arm around her and her head on his shoulder.

"What-what are you doing?"

"We're going to lie here and watch TV together."

"But—"

"Phoenix, I told you, we're taking it slow. Tonight, we're going to lie here together and just cuddle. I want you to know that you can trust me."

She got up on one elbow and looked down at him. "But you've already taken my blood. You've given me, you know…orgasms. I've slept in your bed. You've sucked on my nipples, for heaven's sake."

He shook his head. "Not the same. While I enjoy making you come, we both know that you're there to give me your blood. You slept in my bed because you were scared and needed to be close to someone. And the nipple thing was because of what Gerald did." He pushed her back down on his chest. "I don't like thinking about what that asshole did to you, so let's not talk about it." He picked up the remote. "I vote for *Game of Thrones*. I am curious as to what everyone has been talking about. Is that okay with you?"

Phoenix didn't really hear Dante's question. She was thinking about what he'd said before that. He liked making her come. He'd said it matter-of-factly, which was almost better because then he really meant it. He wasn't just saying it.

She'd had no idea that he liked doing that to her, and she couldn't help grinning. Thank heavens she was looking away from him.

"Phoenix?"

"Huh? What?" *What else did he say? Oh, yeah.* "Sure, *Game of Thrones* is fine with me. I admit, I've been wondering what all the excitement over that show is about, too."

It didn't really matter what they watched because she was entirely too aware of Dante's hard body and how they were touching from head to toe, so she doubted she'd even pay attention to the show.

The good news was that she wasn't uncomfortable. While she didn't like others touching her, especially without permission, she didn't mind Dante being this close to her. But, even though he'd said they weren't going to do anything tonight, her nervousness returned. Because they were still going to do something in the future. She had been looking forward to getting it over with, but it looked like she would have to wait. The suspense might kill her.

Dante found his HBO Now app, brought it up, and selected the show.

By the end of the first episode, they were both hooked. Phoenix didn't even notice anymore that half of her was lying on Dante. He was warm and smelled incredible—his scent always brought her comfort—and he was fun to watch the show with. He had rubbed her back and played with her hair while they watched, and she confessed to herself that she liked his touch.

The part about the brother and sister made Phoenix uncomfortable, but it seemed to make Dante uncomfortable, too. He gave her a reassuring squeeze, as if he knew just how much it bothered her.

The next thing Phoenix knew, she was waking up on her side with Dante breathing deeply behind her. He had his arm around her, which she was clutching like it was a teddy bear. Her bottom leg was straight, but her top leg was bent at the knee, and Dante's top leg was bent also. It was right behind hers and lying over her bottom leg. She didn't think she'd ever been so comfortable with being this close to another person before.

She liked it.

She took the opportunity to caress Dante's arm. It was covered with a few dark hairs. Vampires were less hairy than shifters, and she kind of liked that about him. Now that she didn't have to hold herself back from Dante, she felt freer. She hadn't realized how much she restrained herself when it came to him.

She was sure he wouldn't want anything to do with her sexually after she went through her heat. She knew it wouldn't end up being great, but she no longer feared it would end horribly. And, no matter what, she trusted Dante to remain her friend.

If she thought about it too much, she knew it would hurt if he rejected her after they slept together. But it was inevitable, and if she got to be a mother out of it, she wouldn't have any regrets.

Dante stirred behind her and rolled onto his back, taking his limbs and warmth with him. Phoenix rolled onto her side to see him better.

He looked around, as if he'd forgotten where he was, and ran a hand down his face. The television was still on, but somehow, the volume had been turned down. "Wow. I was out."

"Me, too," she said.

Dante surprised her when he rolled back toward her and pulled her close to him. "I don't want to get up. You're so warm and smell so good."

She chuckled and hesitantly ran her hand down his chest. "I was thinking that about you," she confessed.

"Are you on duty tonight?"

"No. I'm on babysitting duty, remember? I was with Kenzie all afternoon. And I have to be back there in the morning."

"That's right."

"You?" she asked.

"Yes. Once I leave this room, I have to go to work, and I don't want to. If we could figure out who was doing this, it wouldn't feel like such a waste of time."

Wasn't that the truth?

Dante rolled away from her and stood up. "Would you like to come with me for a while tonight?"

He knew the way to her heart.

"I would love to. But I don't know if I should."

"You're just going to ride along. Nothing is going to happen anyway. I'll make sure you're back in time to get to Sawyer's."

Phoenix still wasn't sure. "Who are you with tonight?"

He scratched his chin. "Ah…tonight, it's Morgan. Do—"

Phoenix jumped from the bed. "Count me in."

Dante grinned at her. "I knew you couldn't resist getting out there."

Yes, that was exactly why she was going along.

Liar.

ELEVEN

LEXINE BARELY MADE it back to the manor. After the sun had set, Lucas had let her go with a list of demands. And, if she didn't follow them, he would show Dante and everyone else the video that he'd shown her.

Just thinking about how everyone would look at her made her sick. Although that could also be the blood loss she was dealing with. She didn't know how she was going to go out on patrol when she could barely hold herself upright.

Lexine snuck into the compound through one of the back doors and was able to creep up to her room without anyone seeing her—the one thing she had going for her that night.

She would have laughed if it wasn't so sad.

Once she entered her room, she stripped off all her clothes, found an old backpack in the rear of her closet, and stuffed her outfit in there. She'd burn the whole thing later.

Next, she got in the shower and turned the water on as hot as she could take it and scrubbed her skin raw.

Lucas and the others hadn't raped her. After they'd all

unzipped their pants, she'd closed her eyes, weak from fighting and Lucas stealing her blood. Nobody had touched her at first. She'd thought and hoped that maybe they were going to leave her alone. Until she'd felt a hot spurt hit her stomach. And another and another. Then, she'd felt it on her chest, her legs, and her arms. They had jacked themselves off and come on her over and over again, leaving no part of her body untouched.

At first, she hadn't understood why they had done that instead of sexually assaulting her. But then she'd figured out that, this way, there would be no proof of her attack because a rape kit would show nothing. And, to top it all off, she had to come home smelling like she'd had sex with three males. Add in the low blood count, and now, she looked like a whore who gave out her body and her blood.

After they'd finished, they had let her lie there, covered in their semen, for the rest of the day. She'd known that she needed to rest to regain her strength, but every time she'd tried to sleep and escape her situation, someone had come along and woken her up. She hadn't slept for over thirty-six hours.

Lexine sank down into the tub and let the water wash over her. Even though she had not been a willing participant, she was mortified. She had let these people into her life. All because she'd trusted the wrong vampires. She'd thought they were her friends. Some Guardian she was. She hadn't even seen them for who they really were.

The water was beginning to turn cold before she reached up to shut it off, but she was too tired to get out. The hot water on top of everything else had made her incredibly sleepy. She lay back to rest for just a minute to regain some strength before attempting to climb out and get herself up and dressed.

She zoned out, her body trying to sleep while her mind tried to stay awake, and she didn't hear someone knocking on her bedroom door. She didn't even hear that person breaking in or charging into her bathroom.

"Lexine! Oh my God!"

She opened an eye. It was Sterling. He was bending over the tub with a horrified expression on his face.

"Of course it's you," she wearily told him.

"What happened to you? You're as pale as a ghost." He leaned closer and frowned. "And you smell like…"

"I'm not a whore. I'm not." She wasn't supposed to tell anyone the truth, but she couldn't have people believing she would do that. She didn't even care that she was naked as long as he didn't really think she had been out, having an orgy.

Sterling's face softened. "I know." He leaned over, grabbed her big bath towel from her towel rack, and wrapped it around her before he lifted her out of the bathtub and carried her into her room. "You need to feed."

She shook her head. "There's no time. We're on duty tonight. And I can't let my brother see me like this."

As an unwedded female, it was preferred that she only drank from members of the same sex or from family members. She often drank from her brother, but there was no way she would let him see her like this.

"Take my vein," Sterling said.

She swatted his hand away, or she tried to anyway. With her weakness, it was like a feather hitting a rock. "I'm not going to do that."

While she was a stickler for the old rules, especially when it came to being a female, she was a Guardian after all, and there was a time when there used to be no female Guardians. She just wasn't comfortable with feeding from any male. And she always envisioned that Dante would be the first one she fed from.

Sterling looked at her like she was crazy. "Okay then, I'd better go find our leader before he goes out for the night because there is no way you can go out like this. Someone will have to cover for you."

He stood, and she grabbed the first body part she touched—his leg.

"No." There was no way she could let Dante see her and smell her like this. She was already having enough trouble getting him to see that she was meant for him. "I will drink from you."

"Thank God." He sat down on the bed, took off his shirt, and spread his body out beside hers.

"What are you doing?" she asked.

Like all Guardians, Sterling was physically fit, but she never really paid attention to how nice his chest looked until it was right in front of her.

"Feeding you," he said, drawing her eyes up to his and away from his body. "You know, you need to drink a lot and fast. You don't have time to feed from my wrist."

Sterling grabbed her around the waist and laid her halfway on his body so that her mouth was right at his neck. He touched her like it was something he did every day, and she wasn't sure how that made her feel. She knew he was helping her, but they didn't know each other that way.

But then she smelled his skin and his blood. How had

she never noticed that Sterling smelled almost like melted chocolate? He smelled delicious, but she was sure it was because she was so hungry.

She sank her fangs in his neck and took the first pull. There was a possibility that her eyes rolled back into her head at the taste. How had she never known that the opposite gender's blood tasted this good? No one had ever told her. No wonder the Vampire Council discouraged it.

She drank and drank from him, climbing on top of his body until she was straddling him. She would have continued, but he gently cupped the back of her head.

"Lexine. Lexine, honey, you need to stop. I just fed last night, but if you keep going, I'm going to need to feed again."

She barely heard his words, but they did penetrate. She remembered what Lucas had done to her and didn't want to do the same to Sterling. She withdrew her fangs and licked the wound closed. Despite lying still for quite some time, she was breathing as hard as if she'd run a marathon. It took several seconds for her to realize that Sterling was aroused under her. She knew it had to do more with her feeding from him than with him being attracted to her, but she was suddenly aware of her nakedness and slid off him, clutching her towel to her.

"Holy shit," Sterling whispered more to himself than to her. He shook his head, as if to clear it, and looked over at her. "You okay?"

She nodded and licked her lips, making sure she got every drop of his blood. "Yes."

"Good." He stood up and adjusted himself. He probably

didn't think she noticed, but she did. "Are you ready to talk about what happened?"

She shook her head. Even if she wanted to submit herself to that humiliation, she couldn't. Not if she didn't want her parents to be hurt.

Sterling looked disappointed. "I figured."

"I'm sorry," she whispered. It wasn't much, but she felt like she owed him something for all his help.

"Will you be ready to go soon?"

She nodded.

He gave her a single nod in return. "See you in ten." He reached for her door handle.

"Wait," she said as she sat up in a panic.

Sterling looked over at her. "Don't worry, Lexine; I won't tell anyone. But you are going to have to talk to me soon."

He reached for the door, and this time, she let him go.

She flopped back on the bed. She was in so much trouble. And, while it was nice that Sterling wanted to hear what she had to say, she was in this by herself. She needed a plan, and she needed one soon because she wasn't going to let Lucas win. He'd messed with the wrong Guardian.

TWELVE

HUNTER DROVE to the same place where he and Quentin had been meeting each other for the last four nights. It was the same thing every night. One of them would get in the other's vehicle, and then they would drive around, get out, and talk to shifters and vampires, trying to find out any clues as to who had been wreaking havoc around the area.

Hunter parked his car, exited, and walked over to Quentin's to get in the passenger seat. Quentin nodded to Hunter, but that was the extent of his greeting. He was always civil and polite but never friendly, except for the brief introduction several nights ago. Hunter had tried to apologize for his reaction that night, but Quentin had told him it was fine even though it clearly wasn't, which was kind of a relief. How was he supposed to explain his reaction to the shifter?

He was still struggling with it because, every time he was near the wolf, explicit images would enter his mind. Hunter would try to brush them aside because they had a job to do, but he dreamed about Quentin almost every night. Dreams that he never had about any female before. Thank God he had a job to do; otherwise, he'd be driving himself crazy.

"Where are we going tonight?" Hunter asked.

"I thought we'd head to the U and chat up some college students. They always seem to have some way of getting gossip."

"Humans or shifters and vampires?"

"All three. Humans sometimes see things that they don't even realize they're seeing."

"Very true. Since it's the weekend, hopefully, we can find some intoxicated blabbermouths."

Fifteen minutes later, they arrived at the campus and found a place to park some distance away. They got out of Quentin's car and decided to head in one direction. They were hoping to come along some house parties or kids hanging outside since it was finally getting nice out.

They heard some voices and laughing down one street, so they turned the corner. Then, they heard a scream, which didn't sound like someone having fun, and both of them broke into a run.

Hunter and Quentin drew closer to the voices.

"Get off me! Leave me alone."

"Come on, baby. You've been giving me the eye all night. I know you want it."

What was it with college boys thinking they could just have sex with anyone?

"I don't want to have sex with you. Get. Away. From. Me."

They heard a grunt and went to the side of the house that had music playing inside. Thankfully, the volume was low enough for Hunter and Quentin to hear the couple outside.

When they reached the college students, Quentin grabbed the punk by the collar. "Maybe you didn't hear the lady. She asked you to leave her alone."

The female looked relieved and scared at the same time. She shrank back into the side of the house as much as she could. Hunter supposed he and Quentin were pretty intimidating to a young woman. Neither of them was small, and Quentin had a don't-fuck-with-me look written across his face.

The young male reached back and pulled his shirt from Quentin's grip. "Who the fuck are you? Go away. Sara and I were just getting to know each other, weren't we, baby?"

The female, Sara, shook her head.

"Yeah, that's not what we heard," Hunter said. "It sounded like you were getting ready to sexually assault this young lady."

The punk actually had the nerve to look insulted. "What the fuck, dude?"

Quentin grabbed the kid by the front of the shirt and pulled him closer. Quentin had several inches and at least fifty pounds of muscle on the punk. Despite that, the kid fought Quentin.

"Listen here, *dude*. When a woman says no, leave me alone, get off me, et cetera, et cetera, she means what she says. She's not playing hard to get. She doesn't want you fucking touching her."

The kid backed up and yanked on his shirt. The only reason he was able to get it out of Quentin's grip was because the wolf let go.

"Listen, kid," Hunter said, "I know you think you're the shit, and the alcohol I smell on you probably doesn't help, but you are not that irresistible. The next time you try something like this with a female, you might not get away with just a warning."

"Fuck you," the punk said.

Hunter rolled his eyes and sighed. This kid really had no sense of self-preservation.

Quentin was flexing his fist and looked like he really wanted to punch the jerk.

Hunter put his hand on the shifter's arm. "He's not worth it."

"I know, but it would be so satisfying."

Hunter turned back to the punk. "Get out of here, kid, and when you sober up, you need to ask yourself if this is really the kind of asshole you want to be."

The punk sneered. "Whatever. Like I'm going to take some advice from a couple of queers." He flicked them off and walked to the front of the house.

Hunter didn't really get a chance to process the kid's parting words before the female stepped away from the house.

"Thank you. I thought he was a nice guy, but I guess not."

"Where are you off to now? Do you need us to walk you home?" Hunter asked.

"No, I'll go back into the party. I have several friends in there, and I won't leave their side for the rest of the night."

"Okay, as long as you're sure," Quentin said.

She nodded again. "I'm sure. Thank you again." She turned and headed for the front of the house. She turned and gave a single wave before she disappeared around the corner.

"Well, that wasn't what we were looking for, but I'm glad we could help someone," Hunter said, giving the front yard one last look and keeping an ear open just to make sure the punk hadn't waited for Sara.

"Yeah," Quentin agreed, but it sounded like he hadn't really been listening to Hunter.

Hunter turned and looked at the shifter.

Quentin was examining his forearm.

Hunter stepped closer. "What's wrong?"

"The little shit scratched me with something. I think it was his fingernail." Quentin grimaced. "Gross. Who knows the last time he washed his hands?"

Worried for the shifter, Hunter grabbed Quentin's arm and looked at his wound. As far as lacerations went, it was superficial and minor. But it was bleeding, and the shifter was right about germs. Even though shifters and vampires had stronger immune systems than humans, they could still get infections.

Without even thinking, Hunter brought Quentin's arm to his mouth and licked the wound closed. "There. Now, it should heal nicely," he said to the wolf right before the taste of his blood hit Hunter.

Hunter's stance staggered, and he took a step back, so he didn't fall to his knees. "Holy fuck." His cock was as hard as a rock.

Quentin grabbed Hunter under his arms. "Are you okay, man? Is there something wrong with my blood?"

Wrong? Not even close.

His blood was perfect. Hunter had never tasted anything

as good as Quentin's blood.

"I just need to sit down for a minute," Hunter said.

Quentin led him over to the side of the house and helped him to the ground.

Hunter leaned his head back against the wall and took some deep breaths.

"Hey, thanks for healing me," Quentin said.

Hunter looked over to see the shifter examining his arm again.

"That sure is a handy trait to have."

Hunter snickered. "Yeah, except for the fact that we need blood to live. That's kind of a make-it-or-break-it sort of thing. You don't need anyone else to keep you alive."

"Huh. I never thought about it like that."

"Yeah."

"So, who do you usually feed from?"

"I have a couple of females who keep me fed."

"Vampire females, I'm assuming."

"Yes."

"So, I noticed you had a reaction to my blood. Is it because I'm a shifter, or is it because something is wrong? You can tell if someone's sick through their blood, correct?"

"Yes, and no. You're not sick or anything."

Quentin looked relieved. "So, it's because I'm a shifter."

Hunter cleared his throat. "I don't know. I suspect it's because you're male."

Quentin frowned. "Male and females taste different?"

Hunter shrugged. "I don't know. I've only ever fed from females." He looked at Quentin's neck and his artery pulsing there. He wanted to taste the male again. Hunter groaned.

"What is it?"

"I don't know if I should say anything since this is the first real conversation we've had since we were paired up."

Quentin smiled warily. "I noticed. But I doubt I could think any worse of you than I did before."

"Ouch."

Quentin laughed. "Well, you did outright reject me."

Hunter shook his head and frowned. "No, I didn't."

Quentin raised his brow. "What do you call jerking your hand out of mine like I had the plague?"

"I really hate this line. But it wasn't you; it was me."

The shifter looked doubtful.

Hunter leaned his head back against the wall and stared up at the stars. "Look, ever since I met you, things have been happening to me. I have always thought of myself as asexual. Until you came along. I find myself"—he cleared his throat—"aroused when you're around. It's like I've never been…so aware of another being. I don't know what to do about it, and I'm kind of freaking out. Then, there are the dreams and, now, your blood. I have never tasted anything so good." Hunter lifted his head and looked at the wolf. "So, no, there is nothing wrong with you. I think there's something wrong with me."

Quentin laughed, and Hunter would have been insulted after pouring his heart out to this guy, except Quentin put his big hand on Hunter's knee.

"Tomorrow is our night off. I would like you to come somewhere with me."

"Okay," Hunter said warily.

The shifter clapped his hands together. "Great. Now, we'd better get back out there." He stood and put out his hand for Hunter to grab and then helped him up.

Hunter couldn't believe that was all Quentin had to say.

He must have read his expression because he said, "I'm not dismissing everything you told me. I'm just putting the conversation on hold until tomorrow. We have a lot to talk about, and we have to work tonight. Okay?"

Hunter nodded. "Okay."

"All right. Let's go then."

Hunter followed, excited but extremely nervous about what the next night would bring.

THIRTEEN

DANTE HUNG up his cell after taking a call from Hunter. He and the shifter, Quentin, had run into a couple of college kids where the male was trying to take advantage of the female. Hunter had wanted to give Dante a heads-up in case anything came of it, but Dante doubted that would happen. The kid would probably wake up the next morning, hungover and thankful that someone had stopped him. At least, that was what Dante hoped would happen.

"Everything okay?" Phoenix asked.

Dante was lying on his bed with Phoenix, watching the next episode of *Game of Thrones*. To say they were both fans was an understatement. The highlight of his night was watching TV with Phoenix.

"Yeah, at least, now, it is," he told her. He hit play again since he'd paused it to take the phone call.

So far, all they'd done the last few nights was snuggle. When he'd said he was going to take it slow, he meant it.

Phoenix probably didn't even realize how stiff she'd been in his arms the first night. Now, she willingly came to him, sometimes lying down before him and telling him to hurry up and get on the bed. She was learning to trust him more and more, and Dante was very pleased.

He would know she really trusted him when she told him about her past, but they weren't there yet. However, Dante did think it was time to up the stakes. Tonight was perfect because he was off duty, so they had plenty of time. He just needed to figure out how he was going to do it without frightening her.

After the last episode of season one, Phoenix sat up and exclaimed, "That was fucking badass. Daenerys is my new hero. Or, more accurately, my heroine. The things I could do if I could walk through fire with dragons."

Dante sat up and grinned at her. He couldn't remember if he'd ever seen her happy with excitement.

"Can we start season two?" she asked.

"No."

She frowned. "No? But don't you want to find out what happens next?"

"Yes, but I'd rather kiss you first."

Phoenix visibly swallowed, but her eyes also lit up for a second. That was a good sign.

"Is this because you saw Daenerys's boobs?"

Dante laughed. "No, Red, this is because you are absolutely beautiful when you smile. You should do it more often."

Phoenix looked down, and if he wasn't mistaken, her face was now the same color as her hair.

Dante put his finger under her chin and tilted it up. "You know I won't hurt you, right?"

"Yes," she whispered.

"Good. I want you to remember that. Always."

Phoenix was staring at his mouth. "I will," she said, still whispering.

Since they were both sitting awkwardly, Dante moved to the edge of the bed and stood up. He held out his hand. "Come here, Red."

Phoenix scooted closer and took his hand to let him help her off the bed. Dante thought it would be easier for her to have control if they were standing up.

He pulled her closer until they were less than a foot away from one another, and he placed her hands on his chest. "I know you aren't comfortable with being close to others, so anytime you don't like what we're doing, you just push, okay?"

She nodded. "Where are you going to put your hands?"

"That depends. I can put them behind my back. Or I can rest them on your hips. It's up to you."

Phoenix bit her lip, and he saw her protruding incisor. It wasn't as prominent as a vampire's, but it was longer than a human's, thanks to her cat-shifter genetics. For some reason, it really turned him on.

She released her lip. "You can put your hands on me."

She shrugged, like it was no big deal, but he could tell by the rest of her body language that it actually was a big deal. She was stiff again even though she was trying to relax.

He was glad that she'd chosen to have his hands on her hips because Dante was already hard. Maybe Phoenix wouldn't even react to his kiss, but if she did and tried to get closer, he would be able to keep her groin away from his ever-growing erection.

Dante rested his hands on Phoenix's sides and brought

his mouth down to lightly brush his lips over hers. When she didn't move away, he pressed his lips against hers.

For a few minutes, he continued to give her closed-mouthed kisses. He wanted her to be good and used to him.

It was strange to think that he'd drunk her blood and given her orgasms and received them in return, yet they'd never kissed. They were long overdue for this.

When Phoenix dug her nails into his chest a bit and her scent flared ever-so lightly, Dante knew it was time to take the kiss to the next level. He licked the seam of her lips, and she hesitantly opened her mouth.

He slowly licked the inside of her lips and then moved on to the rest of her mouth. She let him do all the work, which he was fine with, but he wanted her to kiss him back.

Dante searched for her tongue, and when he got it where he wanted it, he sucked it into his mouth to let her know what he wanted. Then, he waited.

Phoenix slowly, tentatively pushed her tongue in his mouth, and when she did, he groaned.

She dug her claws in deeper and tried to step closer. He almost let her because he was so lost in what they were doing above the neck. But, at the last minute, he remembered that his hard-on would probably scare her and would ruin all the steps forward they'd taken.

Phoenix released her fingernails and moved her hands up and over his shoulders and then down his arms. When she reached his hands, she trailed back the opposite way. Up his arms, over his shoulders, down his chest, and then to his waist.

Dante almost didn't realize where she was headed until

it was too late, but he quickly grabbed her hands and moved them away from his crotch area.

She broke their kiss and took a step back.

He opened his eyes and looked to see her frowning.

"Why won't you let me touch you? Do you not like it?"

She tried to pull her hands out of his, but he held on, something telling him that it was important to not let go.

"No, that's not it at all. The thing is, I like it...too much."

Her frown turned into a scowl. "Then, why did you stop me? And what do you mean, too much?"

Please don't make me say it, Red.

He squeezed her hands. "I like you touching me a lot." He used his eyes to pointedly glance down toward his groin, making sure she saw the movement. "But I don't want to scare you."

She was already going to be scared enough as it was with having sex; she did not need to know how big he was yet.

She sighed, but at least she stopped glaring at him. "I'm not a virgin, you know."

Dante quickly hid his surprise. He never really thought about whether she was a virgin or not, but now that she'd said it out loud, it was clear he had assumed that.

"No, I didn't know that. You don't really tell me much, Phoenix. I'm going at this blind, you know."

Phoenix sighed again. "You're right. I'm the one who asked you to help me, so I should be a little more forthcoming."

This time, he hid his anticipation. *Play it cool, man. Do not let her know how interested you are.*

"That would be nice," he managed to say with a perfectly straight face.

"Can we sit back down?"

"Of course."

They both sat on the side of his bed.

"I'm not going to tell you everything," she said. "I *can't* tell you everything. It's just too hard."

Dante tried not to feel disappointed. He should be happy that she was opening up about anything. "Okay," he agreed with a nod.

"So, some unfortunate stuff happened to me when I was younger."

Dante doubted *unfortunate* was the word to describe what had happened to Phoenix. Unfortunate was a young girl's first boyfriend moving away. She did not have these issues because of something unfortunate happening.

"Because of that," she continued, "I've never felt comfortable with having people close to me and touching me, but I wanted to have as normal a life as possible. I was young and started dating this guy. He pushed me to have sex with him. He was young, too, and probably had no idea what he was doing, but neither did I. It was over in less than five minutes. There was no leading up to the moment or anything. He just stuck his dick in me and pretty much came. Then, he rolled off me and acted like he'd rocked my world. I hated the whole thing. What a way to lose your virginity, huh? Anyway, I thought it was because it was the first time for both of us, but it was always the same. It was awful."

Dante was getting upset. Anyone could see that Phoenix had issues. He wanted to find the little shit who'd taken

Phoenix's virginity and shake him until he apologized to this woman. He realized that young guys didn't know what they were doing, but Phoenix was the wrong person for that.

"So, after that, I decided that maybe it was the guy, and I needed to find someone older who knew what they were doing. I dated this guy who was five years my senior, and things were"—she rolled her eyes—"okay, I guess. Better than my first boyfriend. But I still never really enjoyed it and only did it to make him happy. He ended up cheating on me because I was too boring in bed. It turned out that I'd put myself through it all those times for nothing because he was getting it better from someone else."

Dante closed his eyes. *Oh, Phoenix.*

No wonder she didn't like sex. With two selfish lovers for someone who needed to be taken care of, of course her experiences had ended up being terrible.

"So, now, you see why I think you're just wasting your time with all this," she told him, squaring her shoulders. "I don't like sex, and I'm not good at it."

"Thank you for trusting me with all that. I know it wasn't easy."

She lifted a shoulder.

"But I have a couple of questions for you."

"Okay."

"I need you to be honest."

She nodded cautiously. "Okay."

"I'm not even going to ask if either of those…guys got you off." There was no way he would refer to those lousy males as men. "But did they ever try?"

"I don't…think so?"

Dante wanted to roll his eyes, but his reaction was

toward the fumbling idiots and not at Phoenix. "Was that a question or a statement?"

"Well, they just had sex with me and expected me to like it. So, I always assumed they knew what they were doing, and there was something wrong with me."

"Did you know that something like eighty percent of women can't have an orgasm from vaginal intercourse alone? The study was done on humans, but obviously, there are shifters and vampires who can't either."

Phoenix furrowed her brows. "I think I saw a headline with that or something in one of Tegan's magazines, but I never really paid it attention."

"So, my next question is, when you have an orgasm while I'm feeding from you, are those the only ones you've ever had?"

Her face flushed. "Yes."

Dante nodded, but he was mentally giving himself a pat on the back. Now was not the time to brag or feel overconfident. "And do you like them?"

He would have thought it was impossible, but her face got redder.

"Yes. It's…" She cleared her throat. "It's part of the reason I like feeding you and why I keep coming back. As weird as it is, it's the most normal sexual relationship I've ever had."

Dante wanted to pump his fist in the air, but he played it cool. "There you have it, Phoenix. There's nothing wrong with you. There was something wrong with those jackasses who thought they knew what they were doing."

She skeptically looked at him. "I don't know, Dante."

Dante touched her hair and breathed in her sunshine

scent. "I do. And, thankfully, I'm confident enough about that for both of us."

She cocked her head and raised her brow. "Does this mean, we're having sex now?"

Dante laughed. *Oh, no.*

Phoenix still had a past, so they were going to take it slow. But knowing that he might be able to fix some of the damage that had been caused made him want to celebrate.

"No, Red, it just means that it's time for us to start season two."

FOURTEEN

THE FOLLOWING DAY, Phoenix was beginning to feel trapped. She couldn't stop thinking about the night before with Dante, but she was stuck with Kenzie in the box of a room that she called an office at the hotel where she worked. Phoenix wanted out of there. What she could really use was a run through the forest in her cat form. Instead, she had to settle for standing up and pacing the human's office.

"You are more than welcome to leave. I am perfectly safe here at work," Kenzie said from her desk where she was typing on the computer. "I can call you when I'm done."

"No, I have to stay here."

She had been given this assignment by her alpha, and she wasn't going to disappoint him. But, if someone hadn't needed to come in to work on a Saturday morning, this all could have been avoided.

Okay, that wasn't fair. It wasn't Kenzie's fault that Phoenix was feeling overwhelmed emotionally. But, still...if the human would just hurry up.

Kenzie looked up from her monitor and smiled sweetly

at Phoenix. "Then, you'd better sit your ass down before I kick you out."

Phoenix narrowed her eyes. "You wouldn't."

Kenzie picked up the phone. "Security? Yes—"

Phoenix plopped her butt down in a chair and scowled.

"Never mind, Wayne. False alarm," Kenzie said before hanging up the phone.

"You know, if I wasn't going to die from boredom in a few minutes, I could see us being friends. You don't put up with shit. I like that."

Kenzie snorted. "Give me fifteen minutes to finish up, and we can get out of here. Or will you already be dead by then?"

Phoenix pretended to look at the clock and think about it. "Nope, I can make it."

"Thank God. If you sit there and stay quiet, I promise you that I will be done soon."

"Got it," Phoenix said. She pulled out her phone to waste some time. She didn't have much to do on it though. She wasn't on Facebook or Instagram or any other social media. She didn't get the appeal.

Just as she was about to open up one of her games, she got a text.

Dante: Are you doing okay today?

Okay was such a relative word. Technically, she was okay. She was alive and in good health. But, emotionally, she was kind of a wreck. She couldn't stop thinking about the conversation she'd had with Dante last night. And that kiss.

Kisses actually.

Phoenix had needed to know if her reaction had been some fluke, so she had kissed Dante again as they lay on his bed. But that was as far as it had gone. There was no touching below the neck, not sexually anyway. The part that Phoenix was really tripping balls over was that she wanted more than just a kiss.

This was a whole new experience for her, and she felt out of her realm.

She hated it.

Phoenix: Doing well. You gave me a lot to think about.

Dante: All good stuff, I hope. You're not going to change your mind, are you?

Never. Just because Dante was putting her mind in over-drive did not mean she wanted to stop going through with their plan.

Phoenix: Nope.

"Dude, do you have something going on with Dante? He's hot. Yum."

Phoenix snapped her phone against her chest and glared at Kenzie. "Excuse me, why don't you mind your own business?"

Kenzie shrugged, as if being rude was no big deal. "What's the fun in that? Besides, I called your name like fifty times, and you didn't answer. You were so lost in thought that you didn't even notice me coming over to stand right next to you. Thank heavens no one came in to attack me."

Phoenix immediately felt ashamed. "You are right. My apologies."

Kenzie rolled her eyes. "Oh my God. It was a joke, Phoenix. Sheesh, you need to lighten up."

"Oh," Phoenix said.

"So, seriously, what's going on with Dante?"

Phoenix stared at Kenzie. They barely knew each other,

and she was supposed to spill her guts?

Kenzie studied Phoenix. "You know what? Save that question. You and I are going somewhere first. Then, we can talk about this Dante situation."

"I don't think—"

Kenzie laughed and opened her office door. "No, Phoenix, I think your problem is that you think too much. Now, let's get out of here."

Phoenix stepped in front of Kenzie, so she could look down the hall and exit first. She let her charge outside, and they got in Kenzie's car. Phoenix didn't say anything until they pulled up to a strip mall where a storefront advertised *Nails, Nails, Nails*.

"What are you doing?" Phoenix asked.

"*We're* getting pedicures."

"I don't think so."

"Oh, come on, Phoenix. My best friend just got home from the hospital and won't be going anywhere for a little while. And I've been spending a lot of time with Sawyer. I love him, but I need some girl time. I thought we could get pedicures and talk about Dante. You're all I have now." Kenzie stuck out her bottom lip.

Dramatic much?

Phoenix didn't blink. "I'm unaffected by your female wiles."

Phoenix didn't tell Kenzie that she actually kind of wanted to talk about Dante. When she thought about it, Kenzie would be the perfect candidate. Phoenix wasn't close to her, and even though she was mated to a shifter, she was human. While Phoenix would listen to her advice, she wouldn't care too much if Kenzie judged her.

"But what the hell? Why not?"

Kenzie clapped her hands. "Yay."

They exited the car and entered the building. Phoenix immediately hated the smell.

Kenzie noted her wrinkled nose. "You get used to it."

"If you say so." This was why Phoenix didn't do girlie things.

A lady stepped up to the counter. "Can I help you?"

Kenzie stepped forward. "Yes, we need two pedicures, please."

The receptionist looked down at Phoenix's feet. "Are you sure?"

"Yes. Why?" Kenzie followed the lady's gaze. "Oh, Phoenix, really?"

"What?"

Kenzie put her head in her hands. "Combat boots? You can't wear combat boots after a pedicure."

Phoenix held up a finger. "Let me remind you, this was your idea."

Kenzie looked up just as the receptionist smiled.

"You know, I think we have something she could wear after she's done. We bought a bunch of clearance flip-flops for things like this. We've just never used them before."

"Perfect," Kenzie said.

Oh, great, Phoenix thought.

"Let me just go and tell the pedicurist to set up," the receptionist said.

Phoenix was getting more uncomfortable, the longer they waited, but when another lady led them back and put their feet in the hot water, she admitted it was wonderful. No wonder women did these all the time. Not that she was

113

going to become a regular, but she could understand the desire to do so. Phoenix could only take so much feminine stuff. Thankfully, their pedicurist left them alone to soak, and they were the only patrons in the salon, so no one was around to witness the rare baring of her feminine side.

"So"—Kenzie wiggled her eyebrows—"tell me what's going on with Dante. I know you've fed him once or twice, but is there something else going on?"

Maybe it was the hot water on her tired muscles or the massage chair kneading her back, but she was lying back against the chair with her eyes closed, and it was like she heard someone else say, "I asked Dante to take me during my next mating heat and get me pregnant."

"Holy shit, Phoenix. When you bring the girl talk, you really bring it."

Phoenix opened her eyes and looked at her companion, who was sitting forward and bracing herself on the armrests. "Sorry, I didn't really mean to just spit it out like that."

"Do not apologize. This is exciting stuff. Tell me more."

Phoenix shrugged. "What else is there to tell? I just said everything."

Kenzie sat back in a huff. "Forget what I said. Your girl talk needs work."

Phoenix sighed. This was why she didn't do stuff like this. Women were hard to please.

"I'm kind of jealous of this whole mating-heat thing. To have days and days in a row that are all dedicated to sex?" The human shivered. "Amazing."

"It's not all it's cracked up to be. One, we can only get pregnant twice a year, unlike you who has twelve times. And, if we're not mated, it really sucks to spend it alone.

Plus, it's hard for us to get pregnant during those two times we're actually fertile."

"But that's only if you're trying to have a baby. Otherwise, you have awesome birth control."

Phoenix lifted a shoulder. "I guess." Phoenix suddenly thought of something, and she sat forward. "Listen, no one knows about my pregnancy plan. No one. You can't tell anyone, even your mate."

Kenzie shrugged. "Sure. No problem," she said. She lay back and closed her eyes.

Phoenix studied her. Was she saying that because she was lying and going to tell Sawyer anyway, or did she really mean it?

Kenzie opened one eye. "What?"

"Are you serious?"

"Of course."

"You don't feel bad, not telling your mate?"

Kenzie closed her eye and reached over and patted Phoenix's arm. "Unlike you, Phoenix, I know how to do girl time. And the first rule of girl time is that stuff stays at girl time. Your secret is safe with me."

Phoenix leaned back and relaxed. "Thank you."

"Your wardrobe, however, is not."

"What?"

"What?" Kenzie was all wide-eyed and innocent-looking.

"You just said..." Phoenix started.

"Lie back and enjoy yourself. You can worry later."

Phoenix hit the settings on her massage chair and smiled. It was kind of nice, having a friend.

FIFTEEN

LEXINE SLAMMED the cupboard door and moved on to the next as she tried to find something to eat when her phone rang. She looked at the display and saw Lucas's name.

Panic came over her whole body, and she lost her appetite. She hadn't heard from any of her new *friends* since the night they'd drugged her, tied her up, and violated her. She'd been waiting for them to contact her, and she knew she needed them to in order for her to take them down. But part of her had been relieved at the same time. She hadn't wanted to speak to that filthy excuse for a vampire. Just thinking about him made her skin crawl.

Lexine cautiously picked up her phone and hit answer. "Hello?"

"Lexine, baby, how are you doing? Going by your blood, I'd say you're shitting your pants."

Lexine stiffened. She hadn't bothered closing the blood connection because Lucas wasn't there. But, apparently, he was close enough to feel her. He had to be near the property.

And she cursed herself for leaving her guard down. She'd foolishly thought that she was safe at home, in the compound. She immediately put up a wall.

Lucas tsked. "Now, now, is that any way to treat your former lover, baby?"

"You don't get to call me baby," she bit out.

"That's not what you said when I was fucking you, doll."

"Yeah, well, I obviously had a moment of temporary insanity." *Asshole*.

"Bitch, you're lucky that I didn't take your blood when I had you in my bed. I should've done it then."

"Yeah, and I should have taken yours."

It would have been really nice if she had the same advantage on him that he had on her. Especially when she hadn't fully recovered. Sterling's donation to her had helped, but she'd need to feed again soon. She was lucky Lucas hadn't killed her.

"Now, now, Lexine, we couldn't risk you getting knocked up, could we? Although…that would have discredited you even more. Damn, maybe I should have let you feed from me."

Lexine almost gagged. "If I had your spawn inside me, I would cut it from my body."

Instead of making Lucas mad, as she'd intended, he laughed.

"Hey, Lexine?" her brother called from the hallway.

"Hold on," she told Lucas. She set her phone against her abdomen to hopefully muffle the sound. "Yeah?" she answered her brother.

Lennox came around the corner, entering the kitchen.

"Have you heard from Mom and Dad? They're not answering the home phone or their cell phones."

A lump formed in her throat. "Uh, no, I haven't." Technically, it was the truth, but she still felt like she was lying. She wanted to shout to her brother that their parents were being held prisoner. And it was all her fault. She'd really fucked up.

"If you hear from them, tell them that I want them to call me."

"Okay."

"Maybe I'll drive over there today."

That was a good idea. Maybe he would discover something. But she didn't want Lucas to hear her encouraging Lennox.

So, she nodded enthusiastically and said, "Do what you need to."

Lennox looked her over. "Are you okay? You've been acting weird for a while now."

"I'm fine," she said, but she really wanted to fall to his feet and tell him everything.

"You're sure?"

"I am."

"Okay. Well, I'd better get ready to go out. I'm meeting Saxon in a bit. Also, you might want to lay off the perfume a little." He gave her one last look and left the room.

She slowly brought the phone back up to her ear and heard Lucas laughing. "What's so funny?"

"Trying to cover up the scent of three guys coming on you? It's good to know we made an impression."

"It's not funny."

"Yes, it is. That, and how your brother is asking about

your parents, and all the while you know where they are. It's hilarious."

"Technically, I don't because you are keeping them prisoner somewhere." And, no matter how hard she had worked to find her parents the last few nights, she'd been unsuccessful.

"Oh, that's right. Darn," he said with absolutely no sympathy in his voice.

She couldn't believe she'd missed that this guy was a sociopath.

"Listen, the reason I called was that I need to know where everyone's going to be tonight. Including brother dearest. We have some work to take care of. And, if you lie to me, your brother will get a visit. But, instead of us running away like we did with the old bat, we're going to attack."

Lexine gritted her teeth. "Fine. I'll tell you what I know."

"That's a good girl."

What a condescending asshole. She wanted to reach through the phone and cut his balls off.

☾

Sterling walked into the kitchen and found Lexine staring out the window.

"Lexine?"

She jumped and turned to look at him.

"Everything okay?" he asked.

"Yeah," she said, sounding exhausted.

He thought about pressing, but the more he pushed

Lexine, the more she closed herself off, so he kept his mouth shut. "You ready to go?"

"Yeah," she said again.

He pulled his car keys from his jeans. "I'll drive tonight. That okay with you?"

"Sure."

They went out to the large garage and got into his vehicle. Lexine seemed almost like she was on autopilot.

It wasn't until they were on the street that he spoke to her again, "Say, I know you need to feed again."

"Hmm?" She turned from looking out the window. "Oh, yeah, I do."

"I'm going to take you somewhere to do that."

"Whatever," she said. She turned her gaze back to watching the scenery go by.

Less than ten minutes later, they pulled up to an estate and rang the buzzer at the gate. A light shone in his face, and he flashed his fangs in the camera mounted there. The doors opened, and Sterling drove through to the front of the large mansion.

He parked among the row of other vehicles on the side. He got out and started heading to the front door before he realized Lexine was still sitting in his SUV. He turned around and opened the passenger door. "Come on, Lexine."

"What? Oh, I'm going in with you?"

"Yes."

"Okay." She stepped out of the car and followed him inside.

Not once did she ask him what they were doing there, which was very unusual for Lexine. Maybe she needed to feed more than he'd originally assumed.

After they walked into the mansion, a beautiful woman dressed in an evening gown came up to them with a clipboard. "Hello, Sterling," she said. She air-kissed him on both cheeks.

"Hello, Francesca."

"Who do you have with you tonight?"

Lexine was finally looking around the room and seemed somewhat intimidated, so he put his arm around her.

"This is Lexine. She works with me."

"Oh. It is nice to meet you, Lexine," Francesca said with a single nod.

"Um…you, too," Lexine said. Then, out of the side of her mouth and in a hushed voice, she said to Sterling, "What are we doing here?"

Of course, Francesca heard her, so she answered, "We are an all-inclusive feeding facility. And, since Sterling brought you here, I'm assuming you need to feed. What is your pleasure? Male or female?"

"I-I don't know," Lexine said, shock all over her face.

"What about you, Sterling? Do you want one of your usuals? Jacinta is with someone, but Kimberly and Amber are both free."

Before Sterling could answer, Lexine said, "Excuse me. Francesca, was it? I need a minute alone with Sterling."

"Of course," Francesca answered with a slight bow. "I will be right over there when you need me."

Lexine finally looked like her regular self and appeared to have snapped out of the trance she'd been in earlier. "What kind of place did you bring me to?" she said with a low voice. She stepped closer and dropped her voice to a whisper. "Did you bring me to some sort of fancy whorehouse?"

Sterling took a step back. "What?" he said a little too loudly. "What are you talking about?" he asked in a lower voice.

"This is an 'all-inclusive facility,'" she said, using air quotes.

"It is," he said, now a little irritated. He would never bring a woman to a place like a brothel. "There is absolutely no sex. In fact, the only touching is done with mouth, fangs, and the area being fed from."

She sensed his anger because she put her hands up. "I'm sorry. I shouldn't have assumed. I've never been to a place like this. I've only heard rumors of their existence."

He was about to ask how she'd never been to one when he remembered that she was a female vampire. Even though there was nothing sexual going on here, the Vampire Council still frowned on feeding facilities.

"Look," he told her, "I know you need to feed, and you don't want to ask your brother or anyone else. I can't feed you again without feeding myself. So, I brought you here."

He hadn't realized that he'd raised his voice back to a normal level until Francesca stepped forward.

"Listen, we understand how awkward this is, Lexine. Why don't you go with Sterling and watch him feed, and then you can feed from him? If we need to repeat the process, then we will." She turned her gaze to Sterling. "Sometimes, it's easier on girlfriends this way."

"Oh, no, she's not—"

"You have a deal," Lexine said.

Francesca smiled, pleased with herself for finding a solution. "This way, please," she said as she turned around to head for the grand staircase.

Once she was a couple of steps away, Sterling said, "This will only slow us down tonight."

"I know, but I'm not feeding from anyone but you," she said adamantly.

He must have given her some sort of look because she sighed.

"Don't read too much into it, Sterling. It's just the way I feel, okay?"

"Whatever you say, Lexine." *Whatever you say.*

SIXTEEN

HUNTER CHECKED his appearance one more time in the mirror. Quentin had told him to dress well, so Hunter had selected his favorite khakis, a blue button-up shirt that he always thought made his blue-green eyes pop, and a black tie. He slicked his dirty-blond hair back and slipped on his polished black loafers just as Quentin texted him that he was outside.

He made himself take the stairs one at a time at a calm, medium pace. He exited the manor and walked down the front path to the street where Quentin was parked. Hunter opened the passenger door and slipped inside.

"Hey," the shifter said.

"Hi," Hunter responded, his tongue dry.

The shifter looked incredible in a leather jacket, and he smelled even better.

Quentin put the car in drive and stepped on the gas. "So, you excited for tonight?"

"Yeah. I'd be more excited if you told me where we were going."

"We're just going to one of my favorite bars. It's a place I go often, so I know a lot of the people there. I think it'll be a good place for you. Not too flashy, nice and laid-back."

"Nice place for me? What does that mean?"

Quentin turned his gaze from the road and looked at Hunter. "You'll see," he said with a big smile across his face, his black eyes shining in each streetlight they passed.

"Cryptic."

The wolf laughed. "I'm not trying to be. I just don't want to give you any unnecessary expectations or doubts."

"Okay," he agreed out loud, but inside, he had even more questions.

It felt like forever, but only about twenty minutes later, they pulled up to an average building in the downtown part of one of the many suburbs.

When they both got out of the car, Quentin came around to Hunter's side and stopped.

"Oh, no, no. What are you wearing?" Quentin asked.

Hunter looked down at his outfit. "You said to dress nice." That was what he had done.

Quentin sighed. "I meant, dress nice like you're going out for the night. Not"—he waved his hand up and down at Hunter's clothes—"dress nice like you're going to church on Sunday."

Normally, Hunter would be able to let this stuff roll off of him, but he felt his cheeks heat. It only got worse when he saw what Quentin was wearing.

The wolf had on dark designer jeans that fit him like they had been made especially for him and black boots, and under his leather jacket, he wore a light-gray V-neck T-shirt. He looked like he was dressed for a night out.

Quentin rubbed his chin and looked Hunter up and down. "I think we can fix this." He stepped forward and started removing Hunter's tie.

Hunter had already been struggling to ignore Quentin's woodsy scent, but now, there was no denying how good the shifter smelled. Hunter looked down at Quentin's neck, too embarrassed to meet his eyes. But the sight of his bare dark skin had Hunter almost licking his lips. He remembered the taste of Quentin's blood last night, and he wanted to taste him again. But, this time, he wanted the shifter to tilt his head and offer Hunter his neck.

Hunter groaned and felt himself sporting wood once more in the presence of Quentin. *Fuck you, penis.* No pun intended.

Thankfully, Quentin was too busy with rearranging Hunter's clothes to notice his reaction.

After Quentin removed Hunter's tie, he unbuttoned the top two buttons of his shirt and pulled it out of his pants. At first, Hunter was panicked because he didn't want the wolf to notice his bulging erection, but then he realized his shirt covered up his crotch, so it was probably a good thing.

Quentin stood back and surveyed Hunter. "Much better."

Hunter looked down. "The bottom of my shirt is wrinkled."

Quentin shrugged. "It's still an improvement. Trust me." He opened the back door of his car and threw Hunter's tie inside. He hit a button on his key fob, and the car beeped. "Let's go," he said as he turned and headed for the entrance.

Hunter followed, feeling self-conscious about his appearance and about his presence there.

As soon as they walked through the door, a group of arms shot up in the air, and their owners made a bunch of noise upon seeing Quentin. Quentin grinned as he returned a wave and took off for his friends.

All the excitement and nervousness turned into regret. He shouldn't have come. Hunter had been in this situation plenty of times—a tagalong as he went out with friends, searching for females to get laid, while he'd rather be at home.

He hadn't known what to expect tonight, but now that he was faced with the situation, he realized that he'd thought it was just going to be him and Quentin. He hadn't known they were going to meet up with friends, with Hunter being the odd man out.

Since he was there, he might as well get a drink. Hunter headed to the bar and ordered a beer. He would quickly drink it, tell Quentin good-bye because he wasn't rude, and call an Uber. He supposed it was a little rude to walk to the bar without Quentin, but the shifter had left him first to join his friends.

Hunter took a seat on an empty stool. The bartender brought him his beer, and he took a drink as he looked around the room and took in the smells. He was surprised. It was filled with mostly guys with maybe one or two females. One of who was in Quentin's group.

That wasn't what surprised him though. There were humans, shifters, and vampires in the room. He hadn't known there was a place where all three hung out. It was only recently that the shifters and vampires had made a truce.

A guy came up and sat next to Hunter. The place was busy but not so busy that he had to sit right next to him. The male was human and ordered a rum and Coke.

After the bartender stepped away to make the drink, the male said, "How's it going?"

Hunter looked around and pointed to himself. "Are you asking me?"

The male laughed. "Yes." He held out his hand. "I'm Mark." The male was average height for a human with blond hair and brown eyes.

Hunter shook his hand. "I'm Hunter."

Marked looked Hunter up in down in a way that made Hunter squirm in his seat. "Hunter. Hmm…it suits you."

Uh… "Thanks."

The bartender set Mark's drink down, and Mark took a sip. "So…I've never seen you in here before. Are you new around here, or are you recently out?"

Hunter didn't quite understand the question. "Um…I grew up in the area. I'm here with a friend."

Mark raised his brow. "A friend or a *friend*, friend?"

Hunter was still confused by the whole conversation. "A friend."

Mark took another drink and smiled. "Hmm…I'm not sure if that's a good thing or not. I can't get a good read on you. Usually, my radar is spot-on."

Now, their exchange had taken a turn that Hunter didn't comprehend. He was about to ask Mark what he meant when he felt a warm, large hand rest on the back of his neck. Under his shirt, not over.

"He's with me," Quentin said from behind him.

It was a possessive move, and once again, his dick

thought it was a fine time to stand up and make itself known.

Mark noticed his boner and smirked. He looked over Hunter's shoulder to Quentin. "Oh, he's all yours"—he glanced at Hunter's groin again—"apparently. It's a shame though because I'm a good time," Mark said. He dropped off the stool and moved on to someone else.

Quentin filled the now-empty seat and let go of Hunter's neck. "I was wondering where you went. I thought you were right behind me."

"Sorry. I decided to get a beer first," he lied.

He didn't want to start a fight with the shifter. One, they were in public, and, two, he really didn't know the male well enough to start an argument.

"Well, grab your bottle, and come with me. I want you to meet everyone."

Hunter forced a smile. "Sure."

Quentin got off the stool and turned toward his friends but waited for Hunter. Hunter followed, but when he reached Quentin, Quentin put his hand on Hunter's lower back and directed him to his friends.

As they headed over, Hunter reminded himself that Quentin had made no promises that they were doing something alone. It was Hunter's own assumption that had disappointed him. He owed it to Quentin to try to enjoy himself. The hand on his back did make it easier to give the friends a try.

They reached the group, and Quentin introduced them, keeping his hand on Hunter's back. "This is Mason, Noah, Levi, Zoey, and Isaac."

All five of them were shifters, but they smiled genuinely at Hunter.

"Guys, this is Hunter."

"Hello," Hunter said. He couldn't help but smile back.

"I'm going to get a drink," Quentin said. "I forgot while I was over there. Does anybody else want anything?"

"I'll take another," Zoey said.

"Got it." Quentin turned and headed back for the bar.

Hunter felt uncomfortable, being left alone with people he'd just met. He'd never been great at small talk, but they seemed to welcome him without any prejudice and had no problem being left alone with him.

"So, how did the two of you meet?" Isaac asked.

"We kind of work together."

"So, you're a Guardian?" Isaac asked.

"Guilty."

"Cool," said Isaac.

"Ooh," Zoey said. "This is the first time Quentin has ever brought a guy, and he's a Guardian. When he does it, he goes big."

Hunter was confused again. "What do you mean, brought a guy? He's never brought friends here before?" He couldn't deny that he felt a little delighted at this news.

"Oh, he's brought friends, but he's never brought *friends*. You must be special, Hunter."

There was that emphasis on friends again. Hunter changed the subject because he was getting tired of not knowing what was going on.

"So, how do you all know Quentin?"

"Isaac and I went to high school with him," Mason said.

"Yeah, I'm the resident straight friend," Isaac said.

Zoey laughed. "And I'm the resident lesbian. Quentin actually introduced me to my mate."

"And I'm Quentin's ex," Noah said. He held up a hand in front of him. "Don't worry though; we are just friends now. Besides, I have a new boyfriend," he said as he put his arm around Levi.

"New boyfriend?" Levi said. He leaned toward Hunter. "We've been dating for over two years."

Hunter was trying to keep up with the conversation, but his mind was reeling with all the information he'd just taken in. "I'm sorry, but are you telling me that Quentin's gay?"

Everyone lost their smiles and looked awkwardly at each other.

Zoey put her hand on Hunter's arm. "Hon, you do know you're in a gay bar, right?"

Hunter didn't know what kind of face he made, but it must have been notable.

"Oh, hon, you had no idea, huh?"

Noah shrugged. "Sorry, dude, we thought you knew because we thought you were one of us."

Hunter wasn't gay. *Am I?* Suddenly, he saw his reactions to Quentin in a whole new light.

Just then, Quentin returned with three drinks. He gave one to Zoey and set another beer in front of Hunter.

"Sorry it took me so long. The bar suddenly got a rush of customers at the same time I went up there." Quentin looked up from the table and took notice of the tension in the group. "Uh-oh, what did I miss?"

Zoey took pity on him. "Quentin, I think you and Hunter need to talk."

SEVENTEEN

ON A MISSION, Phoenix let herself into the Guardians' compound. In light of their new relationship, Dante had told her that she didn't need to knock anymore. In fact, he'd given her a key to make it easier for her to come and go.

Phoenix heard some noises coming from the television room, but she didn't run into anyone on her way upstairs to Dante's room. When she reached his door, she knocked and waited for him to answer. When she didn't hear anything on the other side, she opened the door to see the bedroom was empty.

She felt a little deflated upon the absence of Dante. Kenzie had given her some advice on what she should do tonight that might make it easier to get to the sex part with Dante.

Phoenix had pretty much told Kenzie everything. At first, she'd been hesitant, but then she'd remembered everything Kenzie had gone through to keep the shifters a secret from the humans, and Phoenix had known that she could trust her. Besides, Kenzie had way more sexual experience than Phoenix, so if she was going to get advice from anyone, it should be the human who knew what she was talking about.

But, with Dante not around, she was starting to lose her steam and her nerve. Maybe she should go find him. He was probably in his office. But, once she got there, would she go through with her plan downstairs, or would she drag him back up to his bedroom? Now, she was overthinking.

"Hey, you're here," Dante said from behind her.

She jumped.

Some sentinel she was.

She turned around. "Yes," she said, nervous now that he was in the room.

"Sorry about that. I had some paperwork I needed to finish up." He studied Phoenix now. "What's going on, Red? You seem…preoccupied."

Phoenix glanced behind him. "Can you shut the door?"

"Sure," he said. He did as she'd asked. "What's up? Spill."

It was now or never.

She took a deep breath and said it all at once, "I-want-you-to-get-naked-and-let-me-explore-your-body."

Dante cocked his head. "I'm sorry, but you're going to have to repeat that. You said that way too fast."

"I want you to get naked and let me explore your body," she said slower as she winced.

She understood that she felt awkward and anxious, but she didn't understand why.

Do I think Dante will say no? Doubtful, as the whole thing had been his idea in the first place.

Am I worried Dante will take advantage of me once he is naked? No, absolutely not. He would never do that.

Am I embarrassed? Okay, so maybe she was. It wasn't every day that she asked if a male would get naked and let her touch him all over. But that wasn't totally it either.

Am I worried that he will judge me on my skills? Yep, there it was. She was worried that he would find her lacking.

But what did Kenzie tell me?

"Guys are totally different than women. If you take Dante's clothes off and ask him if you can touch him, he's just going to be happy that you're touching him. He's not going to worry about what you do as long as you are putting your hands on him."

When Phoenix had pointed out that her ex-boyfriend had cared and cheated on her, Kenzie had tried to explain that, if a male really cared about a female, he would never cheat on her for something like that. Instead, he would talk to his girlfriend and try to figure out what they could do to work on the problem. Together.

So, Phoenix had been obligated to add that Dante wasn't her boyfriend, and she wouldn't know if he cared about her.

Kenzie's response had been, "Girl, he's going to give you his baby, isn't he?"

So, Phoenix tried to take all the positive reassurance Kenzie had given her and tell herself that it was going to be a good night as she waited for Dante to respond to her.

"Are you sure about this?" he asked.

Kenzie was wrong.

He held out his hands. "I am totally sure about this. I just want to make sure you are. This is kind of a big step."

Okay, so maybe Kenzie was right.

"Yes. Ken—a friend told me that I would be more comfortable when it came time for us to have sex if I got to know your body better. Then, maybe I wouldn't be so scared of it." She thought about what she'd said, and just in case he misunderstood, she added, "Scared of sex. Not scared of...*it*." Although she was a little afraid of the big, bad *it*.

Dante laughed and pulled her close. He cupped her face, and his gorgeous brown eyes searched hers before he kissed her.

She didn't have much experience with this, but she was pretty sure Dante was an awesome kisser. She loved the way he tenderly sought out her tongue and explored her mouth. And, when he sucked on her bottom lip and let his fangs run over it, her knees pretty much melted out from under her.

After the kissed ended, Dante asked, "How do you want to do this?"

"Do you mind if I undress you?"

He held out his arms. "By all means, I'm yours."

Dante was wearing a white T-shirt and jeans with bare feet. She decided it was better to start with the top and move down.

She walked behind him, reached for the hem of his tee, and slowly pulled it over his head, not paying attention to where it landed. Dante was a beautiful specimen of a man. He was muscular with smooth skin. His back was strong and defined. She wanted to touch him but hesitated.

What had Kenzie told her again?

"Now, I wouldn't normally tell someone to treat someone else like an object, but in this case, it might help you a little. Forget about what Dante is thinking. Forget about what you're thinking. Just feel. Feel with your hands, and feel with your mind."

Phoenix touched Dante's shoulders. His skin was soft, but the muscles underneath were hard and strong. She moved her hands south, down his back, touching him everywhere.

She gradually walked around to his front. Dante had his eyes closed, which was kind of a relief. Maybe Dante was just feeling, too. His chest was also smooth but firm. He was absent of any chest hair. He was just strong pecs and small brown nipples. His oblique muscles stood out against his hips, giving him a sexy V-line that would bring out the drool in any heterosexual female.

He could be on the cover for a romance novel, except for a long scar that started from one shoulder and ended on the opposite hip. It was harder to touch his front where he could look at her at any moment.

Stop thinking. Just feel.

She lightly touched his chest, adding a firmer touch as she moved her hands around, and then she got bolder. She traced his scar from hip to shoulder and back down again. She liked it on him. It added to his overall appeal, and she wanted to know where he'd gotten it. But she didn't want to ruin the moment with talking.

She moved on, circling around his nipples and then dragging a fingertip over one.

Dante hissed, but his eyes stayed closed, and his arms remained at his sides.

She did it again to see if she'd get the same reaction, and she did, but it seemed like he was trying not to make any noise. She liked it though. She felt a little...powerful. She wasn't new to the feeling. She felt powerful when fighting. But this was different. It was sexual power.

She looked to the button on his jeans. Now, the big guns. Or, more accurately, the big gun.

She'd seen Dante's penis outlined in boxers, and she knew he was far from small.

She unbuttoned the top of his jeans and slowly lowered the zipper. She could tell Dante was already at least semi hard under his boxer briefs, but she tried to ignore it as she encouraged herself to continue.

Just feel.

She pushed Dante's jeans down to his ankles, and he lifted one leg and then the other as she removed them. Now, he stood in his underwear, and there was no hiding the Coke can he kept in his pants. His boxer briefs outlined the whole thing.

She gave Dante a little push backward, leading him toward his bed. He didn't protest or question what she was doing, and she cherished that he trusted her. When his legs hit his bed, he sat down. She then gently pushed him back until he was lying down.

She brought his arms up over his head, but it was Dante who grabbed on to the rungs of his headboard.

Before she removed his underwear, she looked at his legs, letting her bravery build up a little bit more. He had barely any hair on his legs either. She lingered as long as she dared because she knew Dante must be getting antsy.

She paused and took a deep breath again.

Don't worry about Dante. Just feel.

As she reached for the top of Dante's boxer briefs, it almost felt surreal. *Am I really doing this? Is this really happening?*

As her fingers touched the skin on the side of his hips

and then his legs as she dragged his underwear down, she knew that this was definitely real.

She kept her eyes on his boxer briefs until she removed them and tossed them off to the side. It was only then that she looked up at his penis and sucked in her breath. When she'd said Coke can in her head, she meant it. Only it was longer.

Most females would probably love his dick. Phoenix might not date, but she hadn't been living under a rock. She'd heard plenty of size conversations among women. Although it wasn't as big of a deal as most men would believe. It wasn't a deal-breaker for most women, just something to be appreciated and admired.

Phoenix debated on how to approach it. She didn't know if she should stand on the side of the bed or if she should get on the bed beside him. She finally decided on the bed and went around to the other side to climb on. Dante's head turned slightly as he felt the bed move, and he registered where she was.

Phoenix crawled toward Dante and sat on her knees when she reached him.

She had to steady her breathing as she felt her heart rate picking up. It was probably hard to imagine that Phoenix had had sex before with two different men, but she never touched a penis with her hands. She was never interested in them before.

But she found that she wanted to touch Dante. She wanted to know if he felt the same as he did on the rest of his body. His groin had some hair, and his penis stood out among the little he had. It lay on his belly, big and long enough to almost reach his belly button.

She swallowed. She had no idea how she was ever going to fit it inside her.

"Don't think about sex yet." Another direction from Kenzie. *"If you worry too much about the future, you're going to get caught up in your head and ruin it for yourself. Just feel."*

Phoenix tentatively used the first two fingers of one hand to touch him. Dante didn't move, but his penis jerked, and she squeaked as she moved her hand away. When she realized that Dante wasn't going to go anywhere or do anything, she touched it again. It jerked again, but this time, she was ready for it.

She applied more pressure and began touching him from base to tip. She noticed his breathing had changed, and he pretty much held his breath anytime she came to his head. Kenzie had warned that it was the most sensitive part of the male anatomy.

The human had also told her a few other things.

Phoenix wrapped her hand around Dante's penis, amazed that her fingers didn't even touch her thumb. She squeezed him, and Dante sucked in a breath. She then pumped her fist up and down once.

Dante had tried to whisper, but she heard him mutter, "Oh, shit."

Phoenix smiled, feeling dominant and enjoying it. She loved Dante's reaction to her. She needn't worry about him not liking what she did.

She pumped her fist a few more times, admiring the way Dante's hips came off the bed even though he seemed to be trying to keep them still. His knuckles were white from clutching the headboard so tightly.

She kept up the movement, watching as Dante lost

control, but she didn't stop. She knew he wouldn't hurt her, and she liked seeing this side of him.

People accused Phoenix of always being so in control of herself, but Dante was the same way. He was forever the leader, guiding his fellow Guardians.

Phoenix didn't stop what she was doing to Dante until a huge groan and a loud curse left his mouth. His already incredibly hard penis stiffened even further, and his cum shot out of him as he orgasmed. It landed on his belly and chest in an amount that surprised her.

She hadn't realized there was that much when males came. And, for a fleeting second, she thought it would be just that much more likely to get her pregnant. It kind of fascinated her that this was all she needed to make a baby.

With her other hand, she touched the white fluid with her fingertips, amazed to find it a little sticky. Then, because she'd heard plenty of stories about blow jobs, Phoenix brought her fingers to her lips and sucked on them.

She swore he tasted like cinnamon.

EIGHTEEN

"WHY DON'T we go sit over there?" Quentin said to Hunter, pointing to an empty booth in the corner.

"I think that's a good idea," Hunter agreed.

They grabbed their beverages and made their way over to the circle booth in the corner. They both sat with Quentin putting several feet between them, so they could look at each other.

"So, I obviously missed something while I was getting us drinks. What happened?"

Hunter didn't know how to answer right away. He didn't want to sound like he was accusing the shifter of anything or that what he'd found out was a bad thing because it wasn't. Hunter had simply been surprised.

"Your friends seem to think I'm your date. I told them that I'm not. Am I?"

"Do you not want to be my date because you're unsure of where we stand? Or because you're not gay?"

The look on Quentin's face was serious, and instinct told Hunter that how he answered was very important.

"Well, to be honest, I'm not sure if I'm gay or not. Like I told you the other night, I had kind of come to the conclusion I was asexual because I'd never been attracted to females or males. You know, asexuality is a real thing, right? I actually did quite a bit of research on it. It didn't quite fit for me though because I, uh...like to pleasure myself. So, then you entered my life, and I didn't really know what to think."

Quentin nodded, so Hunter continued, "I was shocked when they told me that you were gay though. Although it makes sense why there are mostly guys in here. I guess I always thought that gay bars were..."

"More flamboyant?"

Hunter winced. "No, just more lively. It's so tame in here."

"Well, this is a bar, not a nightclub. Just like straight bars and nightclubs, there is a difference. I like it here because it's easier to hang and talk with friends. Nightclubs can be more for hooking up sometimes."

"That makes sense."

"Look, I'm sorry I didn't tell you beforehand. It's just that I didn't want your view to be prejudiced before you even walked through the door. It's almost harder with guys right out of the closet than straight guys. It was for me."

"For you?"

"Yeah, I was kind of like you. I coasted through high school, dating the head cheerleader who wanted to stay a virgin until marriage. It never occurred to me that it didn't bother me until I started hanging out with Noah. I was the perfect boyfriend for her, and she was the perfect beard. I just didn't know it until Noah asked me why I didn't even want to have sex with my girlfriend. The rest of the pieces fell into place. I broke up with my girlfriend and started dating Noah."

Hunter cleared his throat. "So, do you think I'm gay?"

Quentin tilted his head. "Would you have a problem with it if you were?"

Hunter gave the question truthful consideration. "I'll be honest. Yes, and no."

Quentin raised his brow, apparently surprised by his honest answer. "How so?"

"Well, I say yes because vampires are old-fashioned, as you probably already know. I can only imagine how my family would react. And I have no idea what the Vampire Council would do. Hopefully, my position as a Guardian wouldn't be threatened.

"I say no because, while I might be accepted for being the way I am, I've always wondered what everyone was talking about when it came to sex. Especially when feeding. So many of my friends love to feed when having sex. It really ups the sensations. I've never felt it. I only feed because I need to. I always thought that maybe I just had to wait to meet that special someone. I just didn't know that someone would be a him instead of a her."

Hunter caught the deer-in-the-headlights look on Quentin's face.

"I'm sorry. I didn't mean to imply that you are stuck with me for the rest of my life or that we have to date or… jeez." *Way to go, Hunter. Scare the guy off.* "I was just trying to explain how it feels to be me."

Quentin scooted closer. "So, that night we were assigned to each other…I've been wondering about that. You seemed like you wanted to get away from me. Was that because I was gay or—"

"Oh, no. That was because of my reaction to you. I didn't know what was happening, and I didn't want to scare you away or have you think I was weird."

Quentin laughed and moved closer until they were right next to each other. "Never," he said. Then, he kissed Hunter.

Holy shit, was his first thought.

He'd kissed and been kissed before, but it had never felt like this. Quentin's mouth was larger than any females' he'd previously made out with. His tongue was forceful and dominant, and his beard scraped Hunter's face. Most significant was that Hunter was hard in two-point-five seconds, something that had never happened in the presence of females.

The difficult thing was that Hunter had no idea what to do in this situation. He'd never kissed a male before. Thanks to society, he knew what to do with a woman, but there was no guy talk about making out with another guy.

It was a good thing that Quentin knew what he wanted because he used one hand to guide Hunter's fingers to his cock while Quentin wrapped his own around Hunter's.

Hunter almost came in his pants. That had never happened to him, not even in high school.

Hunter slightly pulled away. "We have to stop," he said between breaths. When Quentin frowned, he clarified, "Otherwise, I might make a mess."

Quentin grinned and moved his hand away but not before he kissed Hunter again. "Damn, you taste good."

Hunter realized he still had Quentin's erection in his hand and blushed as he drew his hand away.

The wolf took pity on him and said, "Come on, let's go back to the group. I'm sure they have all kinds of theories about what we are talking about."

Turned out, no one said anything to either of them. They just welcomed them back. And, now that everything was out in the open between Hunter and Quentin, it was definitely true that they were on a date.

Quentin touched him whenever he had the chance, it seemed, and if another male came up to introduce himself to Hunter, Quentin made sure that the male knew exactly who Hunter had arrived with and who he was going home with. Hunter just wasn't sure if that *going home* was going to be Quentin dropping him off or if something more was going to happen.

When it was closing time, Hunter didn't know what he was going to do for the rest of the night. For him, it was like the middle of the afternoon. There were still several hours before the sun came up.

They said good-bye to Quentin's friends and got in his car. As they left, Hunter could tell that Quentin was taking him home by the direction he was going. The vampires lived in St. Paul, whereas the shifters, both wolf and cat, lived on the Minneapolis side.

Hunter looked over at Quentin several times. *Am I gutsy enough to let the wolf know I want more than just a kiss in the back of a bar?*

He thought back to the girls he'd dated. He wouldn't have thought twice about it, but now, he realized it was because he hadn't really cared if they turned him down or not. But he didn't want Quentin to reject him.

"So, did you have fun tonight?" the shifter asked.

"I did. Your friends are great. And they didn't care that I was a vampire."

Quentin smiled at him before turning his eyes back to the road. "In my experience, shifters are less prejudiced than the other way around."

Yeah, Hunter had heard the same thing.

They drove the rest of the way in silence, and as they grew closer to the compound, Hunter knew he was losing his chance to make a move. He had been so busy ruminating in his head that he hadn't even realized they had arrived until Quentin parked and opened his door to get out.

He left the vehicle running, so Hunter didn't take that as a good sign.

Hunter got out of his own side of the car as Quentin walked around. Before Hunter could say anything, Quentin pulled him close and kissed him again. It felt different because he was taller than the wolf, which was more apparent with both of them standing. He had to lean down to kiss the male but not as much as any female he'd kissed.

Quentin thrust his tongue in Hunter's mouth, and Hunter took the opportunity to suck on it. He couldn't believe how good Quentin tasted. He wanted to kiss him all night. Hunter rubbed his erection against Quentin, shocked for a second when he encountered another hard-on.

This male-on-male-kissing thing was going to take some getting used to. Hunter grabbed Quentin's dick and squeezed. He wanted to see the male naked. He almost came in his pants again, just thinking about it.

Hunter groaned, and Quentin ended the kiss.

Hunter reached for the wolf again, but Quentin put his arms up to stop him.

"I think that's enough for tonight."

Hunter was confused. "Why? I thought you liked it."

Quentin smiled. "Oh, I do." He stepped forward, touching Hunter on his chest. "But you just came to some conclusions tonight. While you think everything is all figured out right now, part of that is the honeymoon phase. Tomorrow, you're going to wake up, and you might feel the same. But you might also feel differently. I don't want you to regret anything we did tonight, okay? I don't want you thinking that I took advantage of you. *I* don't want to think that I took advantage of you."

Hunter opened his mouth to protest, but Quentin shook his dark head.

Hunter closed his mouth, and the shifter smiled.

He kissed Hunter one last time and walked around to the driver's side. He rolled down the passenger window as he put his car in park. "To be continued," he said with a grin before he sped off into the night.

NINETEEN

DANTE SLOWLY OPENED his eyes to see Phoenix kneeling next to him on the bed. With half-lidded eyes, he watched her as she touched his belly where he'd come all over himself, and then she slowly brought her fingertips to her mouth and sucked on them.

It took everything in him not to groan, afraid that he would scare her.

She glanced over to his face, and a guilty look crossed over hers.

He released his grip on the headboard and put a hand on her arm. "Hey, you can do whatever you want with me."

She smiled, and all the guilt melted away.

He looked down at himself. "I should probably go clean up though." His semen was starting to get cold.

"Oh. Oh, I'm sorry," Phoenix said as she started to get off the bed. "I'll go get a towel."

"Don't bother. Just grab my shirt off the floor," he told her. It was closer and already dirty anyway.

She grabbed his tee off the floor and brought it over to him. He held out his hand, but she shook her head.

"Do you mind if I do it?"

Surprised but feeling lucky, he told her, "Sure."

She used his T-shirt to gently wipe his chest and stomach off. When she was done, he took it from her and threw it in his closet where he'd put it in his hamper later.

When he looked back at Phoenix, she was frowning at his groin.

"What's wrong?" he asked.

"You're still hard. How is that possible?"

What kind of losers has she been with? "Well, I find myself pretty much hard whenever I'm around you."

"But you just orgasmed."

He chuckled again. "It doesn't matter." Since she didn't seem to mind that he was naked and it might be a good thing for him to stay this way for as long as possible so that she'd get used to him, he put his arms behind his head. "Besides, I've always been a two-times-in-a-row kind of guy."

Phoenix hissed. Like a cat.

Dante felt his eyes widen. "Holy shit, did you just hiss at me?" he said the words out of shock, but he was worried that she'd think he'd said them out of anger. He brought an arm down and cautiously grabbed her hand. "I didn't mean to worry you. Just because I can come twice in a row doesn't mean I would ever do that to you if you were not comfortable with it."

Here he'd thought that they'd made a breakthrough tonight, and he'd just set them back. Him and his big mouth.

"I wasn't trying to brag or anything. I apologize."

"What?" she said, confusion on her face. "Oh no," she said with a laugh. "I'm not worried. Just a little…um… uh…" She scrunched up her nose, pursed her lips, and grunted. "I'm jealous, okay?"

"Jealous?"

"Yes," she said, shaking his hand off hers and throwing her hands in the air.

"But…why?"

"I keep picturing you coming twice."

"So?"

She gave him a dirty look.

"Oh. I get it. With other—" He was going to say females but stopped when her eyes narrowed. He grabbed her hand again and pulled her on top of him. He rolled them over until he could look down at her face. "I'm sorry. I can't change the past."

She sighed, and some of the anger left her face. "I know. I keep thinking about that first time I offered to feed you. 'When I feed, I fuck,' you said."

Dante closed his eyes and winced. *Damn.* He opened his eyes and made sure to meet hers. "When I said that, I was mad. I'm sorry. I should have never spoken those words to you. And you know that's not true. I feed from you all the time, and we don't have sex."

Phoenix looked away from him. "Yeah, but that's probably only with me."

Huh?

It took him a second, but he finally figured out that she felt insecure.

Oh, Phoenix.

Dante was stunned as hell, but this wasn't about him. "Hey."

Phoenix continued to stare at the ceiling.

"Hey," he said again. "Phoenix, look at me."

She met his eyes reluctantly, according to how long it had taken her to meet his gaze.

"It's not true. You're not the only one, okay? As my position as a Guardian, I actually do it quite often. I can't have civilians get attached to me because I'm a Guardian. Not trying to brag. By the way, it's my position they're attracted to, not me. The point is, I said that feed-and-fuck thing because I was angry. I was feeling vulnerable, and I took my resentment out on you. I'm sorry."

"Apology accepted," she said somewhat halfheartedly.

Then, because he felt words would no longer do him justice, he kissed her. Gently but thoroughly, trying to let her know that he meant what he'd said.

He broke the kiss when he started to rub against her, and he remembered he was still naked.

"Dante?"

"Yes?"

"I want you to have sex with me while you feed from me."

He put his forehead against hers and groaned. He wanted that so badly, but he couldn't let her do something like that out of jealousy. When they made love, he wanted it to be because they both wanted it and for the right reasons.

"Soon, Red," he told her.

"But I'm feeling good, and I think I'm ready," she said as she arched against him.

He lifted his head and looked at her. Crucial moment

here. He couldn't say no because she would definitely feel rejected. But he refused to agree to have sex with her and have her regret it later. He needed a perfect compromise.

"I don't think you're ready for that yet."

She opened her mouth, and he held up a finger.

"But I would love to make you feel good in another way."

She considered this. "Like how I made you feel good?"

"Yes. A little tit for tat."

She frowned.

"But not because I owe you. I've been wanting to do this forever."

That seemed to make her happy because she smiled. "Okay. But I don't know if anything will happen. You know, like me having an orgasm."

"Why don't you let me worry about that?" Dante said as he got off the bed. He went and grabbed his jeans and slipped them on.

"Why are you getting dressed?"

"I'm just putting my jeans on," he told her as he walked back over to the bed. "I know you said you're ready, but just in case you start to feel nervous, I want you to know that I'm not naked."

"Okay," she said, not arguing with him. Maybe she realized that she wasn't quite as ready as she had thought she was.

"Can I undress you?"

She bit her lip. "Yes?"

"Everything or bottoms only?"

She thought about this for a few seconds. "Bottoms only, please."

He nodded and knelt on the bed, parting her legs. He leaned forward and kissed her again. He could tell that she was nervous, so he kissed her until some of the tension left her body. When he went to break the kiss, she pulled him back and kissed him again.

He moved to end their kiss a second time, and she let him this time. He lifted up her shirt, only to the bottom of her ribs and kissed her belly. He kissed the middle and the sides until she started to melt under him.

Only then did he undo her pants. He got them unzipped and kissed her lower. Over her hips and her pubic bone, using his lips, his tongue, and his teeth. Her breathing got heavier and heavier, so he slowly pulled her pants and underwear down her legs and off her feet.

He kissed each sole and then moved up her calves to her knees. He kissed each leg as he moved higher. As he reached her thighs, he gradually spread her legs and looked upon his prize.

She was pink and wet and covered in red-and-black curls to match her head. She had more hair than the vampires he'd been with and definitely more than the few humans he'd fucked, who shaved themselves bald. But he liked it. It was so…Phoenix. There was no other way to describe it.

He kissed up her thighs, and when he reached the juncture in her legs, he heard her take in a breath, as if she was waiting for what he'd do next. He gently parted her lips and licked inside her.

Fuck, she tastes good. Spicy and hot.

It took Dante several seconds to realize that Phoenix had a death grip on his hair. He thought maybe he'd gone too far, but instead of pulling him away, she pushed him back between her legs. That was all he needed to go to town and feast on her.

She made mewling noises as he ate her out. He made sure not one part of her was neglected. He licked inside her, he sucked on her lips, and he paid extra special attention to her clit.

When he felt like she was ready, he slid his middle finger inside her and immediately groaned against her pussy. She was tight on one digit. He couldn't imagine what she'd feel like wrapped around his cock.

One thing was for sure. They'd have to do this many times until he made sure that she could take him without any pain. She might be sore and tender after they had sex, but he didn't want her to hurt.

Dante began to fuck her with his finger as he sucked on her clit. He wanted her to get a little taste of what it would feel like for him to be inside her. She dug her nails into his scalp, and he couldn't help but smile. She was so into what he was doing; she didn't realize that she was practically drawing blood.

Dante pushed his finger in as far as he could without causing her discomfort and bent his finger up toward him to rub on the spongy area inside her that he knew would make her come.

He released her clit, wishing he had two mouths as he kissed his way over to the top of her inner thigh. He sucked on her there, feeling for her pulse to make sure that he would miss her artery and hit her vein. When he was sure that he was where he needed to be and that Phoenix was getting closer to coming, Dante sank his fangs into her leg and sucked on her delicious blood.

She'd said she wanted to have sex while he fed from her. He figured this was pretty damn close.

Phoenix was practically riding his hand, so he withdrew his fangs and licked her closed. He barely even touched her clit again, and she exploded, coming all over his finger and squeezing him so tightly that he was sure it was turning blue.

Her orgasm went on and on, and Dante again cursed the lazy fucks who'd had sex with her. Their loss was his gain though because he got to be the first one to make her come.

When he was sure her orgasm had waned, he withdrew his finger and moved beside her to collapse on the bed. He grabbed one of his pillow shams and placed it over her naked body, cursing himself for not thinking of finding something to cover her with before they'd started.

"Holy shit," she said between pants. She slowly regained her breath.

Dante looked at her and smiled. "Yeah," he agreed.

She pushed the pillow off her lap, rolled on her side, and curled up to him. "So, when can we do that again?"

TWENTY

LEXINE LIGHTLY PUSHED on the gas pedal, keeping the car at ten miles per hour, as she moved closer to her target.

After feeding from Sterling again a few nights before, she felt more like herself and back to her normal strength, physically and mentally. She had spent all day coming up with a plan in between the forced naps that she made herself take. She wasn't going to go into any situation weak again.

The first step of her plan was to hire a private detective. There were a few vampire private eyes she could have hired, but she'd ultimately decided to go with a human. Lucas and the others would find a human less threatening, and a human could go out during the day. She needed to find out where her parents were being held. Someone from Lucas's group had to own property or had to be related to someone who owned property where they were keeping her parents. She didn't really think anyone in the group would keep her parents at their own homes, but she had looked anyway. There had been no trace of them.

Lennox had gone to their parents' home and hadn't found anything. Lexine had thought about going out there, too, but she already knew who had taken her parents. She had hoped that maybe Lennox would find something that showed they had been kidnapped and report it to Dante. But Lucas and his gang were smart. There were no signs of foul play or anything amiss.

So, now, Lexine had moved on with her plan. She inched her way toward Steve's house, hoping to find him and Analeigh there. She didn't technically live there, but she spent most of her nights at her boyfriend's. Lexine was hoping for a two-for-one deal.

She was driving at a snail's pace because she didn't know if Lucas would be there. She did not need him sensing her. She doubted he was at the house. But she wasn't going to assume anything.

She was at the end of their street now and couldn't see any other vehicles parked outside besides Analeigh's. Lexine mentally high-fived herself, feeling like something was finally going her way.

Lexine drove past and parked a block away among a group of trees that partially hid her car. She put on her black cap, black sweatshirt, and leather gloves. Then, she made her way through Steve's neighbors' backyards until she reached the back door to his garage. The fool never locked it. Lexine listened for sounds on the other side, hoping that maybe the two of them were still sleeping. The darkness beyond the windows was a good sign.

After waiting several minutes, Lexine felt it was safe enough to go in. She opened the garage door just enough to slip inside. As she approached the door to the house, she listened intently. She could be wrong, but it sounded like there was a rhythmic smacking on the other side.

Lexine practically rubbed her hands together in glee. They were fucking, and she couldn't have asked for a better distraction. It was even better than if they had been sleeping.

Once again, Lexine turned the knob without any trouble. The idiot didn't lock this door either.

She entered the dark galley kitchen and tiptoed toward the back of the home. The house was ranch-style with the kitchen and living room in front and the master bathroom all the way at the end of the hall in the back. Their sex sounds grew louder as Lexine got closer. Hopefully, Analeigh and Steve would never hear her coming.

When she got to the bathroom, Lexine went inside. Steve's home was older, built before en suite bathrooms had become really popular, and she hoped one of them would come in there to clean up after themselves.

She searched the mess on the bathroom counter for Analeigh's perfume and sprayed herself with it, hoping the post-sex haze and the fragrance would cover up her scent. Then, she hid behind the door to wait.

Lexine really wanted to bust in on them fucking, but she wasn't dumb. Even though she was a Guardian and had training, it was two against one. She wasn't going to risk ruining her plan because she let her feelings overrun her common sense.

That was how she'd ended up in this situation in the first place. If she hadn't agreed to the gang's plan to try to separate the shifters and the vampires, in her hopes of getting Phoenix away from Dante, she never would have gotten involved with this group. If she didn't make this right, Dante would never see her as a romantic partner.

Lexine listened as she heard the squeaks of the bed frame speed up, the headboard making an almost constant bang against the wall. She heard a male groan and then nothing. It seemed Steve was a selfish lover, as she hadn't heard any female moans.

"Sorry, love. I'll get you next time." Steve's voice floated into the hallway.

"That's okay. I'm good."

Lexine made a face at the back of the door, betting that Analeigh was lying. But whatever; it wasn't her relationship.

"I'd do it right now, but we're supposed to meet everyone in less than an hour."

Lexine's ears perked up. Could everyone be the *everyone* she'd come to know? Were they planning something tonight? Was Lucas going to call her and quiz her again? *Shit.*

She quickly took out her cell and made sure it was on silent before Lucas did call her, alerting Steve and Analeigh that she was in the house. Her phone was on vibrate, but even that could be heard, so she switched to silent.

She cursed herself as she put her phone back in her pocket because she almost missed Analeigh respond, "I'd better grab a shower then. You made quite a mess on me."

Lexine tried not to gag or picture what Analeigh was talking about. And she really hoped she wouldn't accidentally touch anything organic in nature when she took Analeigh down.

She heard Analeigh in the hallway, so Lexine slowed her breathing as best she could so as not to be heard. Analeigh flipped on the light in the bathroom and closed the door behind her. She let her robe slide down her shoulders just as she looked up into the mirror and saw Lexine behind her.

"Shouldn't have crossed me, bitch," Lexine hissed as she put one hand over Analeigh's mouth and her other over the front of her neck, squeezing Analeigh's pulse points.

Analeigh clawed at the gloves around her neck and made a high-pitched muffled sound, but soon, she collapsed against Lexine as she passed out. Lexine gently laid her down on the bathroom rug, so there was no noise to alert Steve that something was wrong. It was hard because she really wanted to drop her, letting her fall on her face and break her nose.

Lexine grabbed a clean washcloth on the shelf behind the toilet and got it wet. Thankfully, Steve thought Analeigh was in the bathroom, getting ready for the night. Lexine washed the area behind Analeigh's knee to make sure it was clean because she didn't know what the two of them had done in the bedroom.

Then, Lexine bent over and sank her fangs into the area, aiming for the popliteal vein. It was a relatively large, deep vein, so it was easy to quickly feed from, although a very unusual spot to do so, which was why she'd picked it. She needed to do this fast, and she needed a spot where Analeigh wouldn't obviously look. Even with the healing properties in their saliva, it could be difficult to heal a wound one hundred percent. It also helped that the area was on the back of her body. When Analeigh woke up and inspected herself, she probably wouldn't think to look there.

Lexine quickly took just enough blood in order to sense and get a read on Analeigh before she withdrew her fangs.

She didn't want to take any more than she needed because she didn't want Analeigh to guess that she'd lost blood.

Lexine closed the bite mark, taking as much time as she could spare to heal it as completely as possible. Then, she put soap all over the back of Analeigh's knee to hopefully wash off her scent. There was a chance Analeigh wouldn't remember seeing Lexine in the mirror, so she wanted to remove all traces of herself if possible. Lexine used the washcloth to remove the soap and threw the wet cloth on the counter. For added measure, she sprayed the same perfume she'd sprayed on herself earlier on the back of Analeigh's knee. Then, she turned Analeigh over onto her back and threw the discarded robe over her.

Lexine stood and turned on the shower, so Steve would think his girlfriend was in there and to help cover the sound of her footsteps. Then, she headed for the bedroom to seek her next mark.

She made her first mistake as she entered the bedroom, expecting to see Steve lying on the bed. She should have checked the same behind-the-door hiding spot she'd just used, but instead, she looked around the room and stood there, confused that she didn't see him. She hadn't heard him walk past the bathroom.

She looked at the closet right before she heard the door shut behind her, and an arm wrapped around her throat and another around her waist.

Fuck.

Apparently, she hadn't covered her presence as well as she would have liked to.

Even though Steve was a male, he didn't have the fighting experience that Lexine did. He expected her to try to wiggle out of his grip, but Lexine put her chin down, wedging it between her neck and Steve's arm. Then, she took the arm around her waist and bent his thumb back until it either broke or went with her. Once she pulled the lower limb away from her body, she used Steve's own height against him. She pushed her butt into his body and leaned over, and Steve started to lose his balance. Then, she flipped him over until he landed on his back.

Steve made an oomph sound as all the air momentarily left his body, and then he moaned.

Lexine lifted a booted foot to smash into his face, not caring that she wasn't supposed to leave a trace of herself here, and brought it down on him. Except he moved, and she only got his collarbone instead. It made a satisfying crunch as it landed on his clavicle, and Steve bellowed with pain.

Her second mistake was assuming that, since he was in pain, he wouldn't be able to fight her as strongly. But rather, he seemed to up his ante, his injury pissing him off in the process. He grabbed on to her ankle with his good hand and pulled her leg out from under her so hard and fast that she landed on her back, hitting her head. She groaned as she saw stars.

Steve quickly crawled over her and wrapped his fingers around her throat. Even with one injured side, his uninjured side was squeezing hard enough that her vision started to dim.

"Fucking bitch. You should have just left us alone," Steve said as he squeezed harder.

Then, out of nowhere, Lexine heard a roar, and Steve was ripped off her body. She rolled over and started coughing as she tried to regain her breath. Her throat burned as she sucked in air, and she knew it would take a few days to heal.

When she finally felt like she had enough air in her lungs, she paid attention to her other senses and realized who had saved her. It was Sterling. Her blood link to him was open, and he was pissed.

She quickly turned to see Sterling in a sitting position with his legs crisscrossed over Steve's waist. Sterling slowly choked him out with both hands around Steve's neck.

Lexine tried to get to her feet, but her legs were unsteady, so she half-crawled, half-walked as she rushed over to Sterling. She grabbed on to Sterling's hands. "You can't kill him!"

She couldn't let Sterling take a life in defense of her. She'd gotten herself into this mess. She could not let Sterling take this on his conscience. But he was in a daze and ignored her.

"Sterling, you can't kill him," she said again. She went around to Sterling's back and tried to pull him away. It was like trying to move a house. *Think, think, think.* She had to do something.

She bit Sterling on the ear and shouted, "You can't kill him. He's knows where my parents are. They've been kidnapped."

That finally seemed to get through to him, and he let go of Steve. Steve slumped over onto his side, but at least Lexine could see his chest rising and falling.

Sterling jerked his body out of Lexine's embrace.

She briefly glanced at his face, and the anger there almost had her cowering in the corner. But Lexine still had a mission to finish. She wasn't going to let Sterling stop her.

She rolled Steve to his back, and since he already knew she'd been there, she leaned over and drank from his neck. She took more than she had from Analeigh because the asshole had tried to kill her. Something she hadn't even been planning to do to him. She wasn't here to see him die. She'd only come for his blood.

When she was done, she licked the wound closed but didn't bother healing him. When he woke up, she hoped the fucker's neck hurt as much as hers did.

She sat up to see Sterling watching her.

"What the fuck is going on?"

TWENTY-ONE

"I COULD ASK you the same thing. How did you find me?" Lexine asked, trying to deflect Sterling's question.

He didn't answer her question, just like she hadn't answered his query.

"Why did you drink from him? And what's up with the unconscious female in the bathroom? When did your parents get kidnapped?"

He could see a look pass over Lexine's face as she realized that he wasn't going to let this go.

Lexine had snuck out of the house before everyone else was up, so he had tracked her here. When he'd come upon her lying on the floor as some asshole tried to choke the life out of her, he'd seen red. And, if she even thought about lying to him, she was going to regret it.

She sighed. "I need to be able to track him and the female in the bathroom. The rest, I'll tell you once we get out of here. It's not safe."

She stood up and started to leave the room, but Sterling clasped her wrist and didn't let go. If Lexine needed to track the asshole, then Sterling was going to be right there with her. He picked up the male's arm and struck him on the inside of the elbow. As he took deep pulls, trying to take as much blood as possible in a short amount of time, he felt Lexine trying to break free of him. He tightened his grip. There was no way he trusted her not to flee once he let go. When he took enough, he dropped the male's arm and stood. Sterling spit on the male's chest before walking out of the room.

Sterling then dragged Lexine into the bathroom where he did the same thing with the female, minus the spit. She hadn't tried to kill Lexine. At least, going by her lack of injuries, he doubted there had been any sort of struggle.

Once that was done, he and Lexine left the house through the backyard to get to their cars. Sterling had parked his SUV right behind her car when he pulled in.

"How did you find me?" she asked again, pissed.

He couldn't believe she was the one who was pissed. He'd just saved her ass back there. "I tracked you."

"How?" she demanded, yanking on her arm but giving up when she realized he wasn't going to let go.

"I put a GPS on your car."

He could see the wheels turning in her head, and she was angry with him for tracking her car.

"Okay, that got you to this location. How did you find me in the house?"

"Your phone."

"You asshole," she said as she tried to fight off his grip.

He pushed her against the side of his SUV and pressed his body against hers. "I'm the asshole? You are obviously up to something, but you won't tell anyone or ask for help.

You almost died tonight, Lexine. If I hadn't tracked you here, you would have died. And you're angry with me? I don't think you have that right."

She lifted her chin. "I don't think you have the right to track me down. I'm going to make sure you never do that again."

He shook his head. "You and your stupid pride. You can't even admit when you're wrong. And I'm sorry, honey, but you can use a different car and you can turn off your cell phone, but you can't get rid of your blood. And, if that's what it takes to see that you're safe, then that's what I'm going to have to do. And seeing as how you drank enough for both of us tonight..." Sterling used his hand that wasn't holding on to her wrist to bend her head to the side.

He expected her to fight him even more, but she didn't fight him at all. It was like all the fire had left her body. It was one thing to take her blood when she was mad and getting in his face, but with her like this, he couldn't do it. He felt too much like a predator, and she was his prey.

He let go of her wrist and used his vehicle to push himself away from her.

He couldn't understand what happened next or why it happened, but Lexine flung herself at him. She beat on his chest with her fists as she started sobbing. Sensing that she needed to get this out, he let her use his body to vent her frustration.

It went on for some time until she collapsed against him, and the same arms that had hit him now burrowed into his back as she buried her face in this chest. Without hesitation, Sterling wrapped his arms around her and stroked her hair over and over.

She sniffled against him a few times, but the crying seemed to have stopped when she looked up into his eyes. He expected to see sadness and vulnerability there, but instead, he saw raw heat.

She had never looked at him that way.

"I'm still mad at you," he told her.

"I'm still mad at you, too."

That was enough for him to let go of her and back away again, except she grabbed on to his shirt and pulled him down to kiss her.

He knew he should end this, but while she had vented her feelings, his were still brimming on the surface. How dare she scare him like that. Didn't she know how much—

She bit his lip, and Sterling lost what was left of his self-control. He pushed her back against the side of his SUV and took her mouth. He cupped the back of her head and pushed his tongue inside her mouth. She moaned against him, which only made him kiss her harder.

He wanted her so badly, and apparently, she felt the same because she unbuttoned his jeans and pushed her hand in to grasp his cock. He reached under her sweatpants and cupped her bare ass. He ground his cock against her as much as he could with her hand still enveloping him.

He wasn't sure who did what next. All he knew was that they both went from dressed to Lexine wearing only one leg of her sweats while his pants were pushed around his knees. Lexine grabbed on to his neck and jumped up, wrapping her legs around his waist. Sterling pushed her butt against the vehicle and thrust inside her.

Neither of them seemed to care that they were outside

where anyone could walk or drive by. The big trees only blocked so much, but at the moment, it didn't matter.

They were in a frantic rush. There was no other way to describe it, except as him pounding into her over and over again.

She dug her nails into his back and ass and told him, "More," and, "Harder," as if he even thought about slowing down.

Then, she moved one of her hands to the back of his head and pushed it into her neck. "Do it, Sterling."

He kissed her there and sucked until she moaned, but he didn't do the one thing he was dying to do. He couldn't forget the way she had just stood there earlier.

"Do it, Sterling. I want you to. I want you to fucking bite me. Take my blood. I want to be inside you, the way you're inside me."

Fuck if those weren't the most erotic words ever spoken to him, and Sterling struck. He hesitated for a moment after his fangs were inside her neck, but she moaned so loudly and clenched her pussy around him, so he knew she had been truthful when she said she wanted it.

He sucked on her as he thrust inside her.

"Oh my God, I'm going to come," Lexine said into his ear. "Oh, please, don't stop. Right there. Oh, *fuuuuck*," she cried out as she convulsed around him.

Sterling withdrew his fangs and licked and sucked on her neck while he waited for her orgasm to finish. When he could tell that she was nearing the end, he pushed inside her once, twice, and three times before he came in a rush, too.

He withdrew from her body and set her feet down on the pavement. He kissed her again as he slid his hand between her legs and pushed two fingers inside her, so he could feel himself there. She was wet with his cum, and he pushed it further inside her. He used the rest to rub over her clit, and she clutched his shirt and gasped into his mouth.

He wanted to fuck her again and tell her that, this time, he wanted her to take his blood even though that was not a possibility. She wasn't his mate, and right now was the wrong time to even think about a baby. She was caught up in a mess so deep that he feared she wouldn't get out of it.

Sterling continued to use his fingers and thumb until she came again. Only then did he withdraw his hand. He brushed his fingers against her lips and kissed her one last time, so they could taste themselves together.

He broke the kiss and pulled up his pants. He bent down and helped Lexine get into hers.

As she slid her foot inside her shoe, he said, "We should probably get out of here. You said it wasn't safe."

He almost regretted his words because her post-orgasmic look changed to one of panic.

"Let's go," he said. "We'll meet somewhere, and you're going to tell me everything."

"Okay."

"Everything," he reiterated.

"I know," she said with just enough irritation to make him smile. "But you're not going to like it."

"Honey, I haven't liked it from the start, but at least I will no longer be in the dark."

TWENTY-TWO

"I THINK we're going to have sex tonight," Phoenix told Kenzie.

Kenzie whipped her head up from her computer at work. "What time are you supposed to meet him tonight?"

"I usually go around sundown, but tonight, he actually asked me to come around five."

"Why didn't you tell me sooner?" Kenzie asked in a panic.

It had been several days since Phoenix and Kenzie started becoming friends and several days since Phoenix had taken Kenzie's advice. Every night since then, she and Dante had been intimate. Intimate as in, she had given him a hand job, and he had gone down on her. She figured they'd been doing that long enough, and it was time to move on to the final step. Her mating heat was about a week away, but that was just a guess. They didn't come exactly six months apart. It was only a general time difference in between. She could technically get it tomorrow. Some women were more regular but not Phoenix.

"What's wrong?" Phoenix asked.

"What's wrong? You can't be serious."

"Yes, I am."

Kenzie pointed to the clock on the wall. "You've known about this all day, yet you didn't tell me until almost noon. We barely have time left," she said as she started stacking papers and putting her stuff away in a rush.

"Time for what?"

Kenzie stood up and pushed her chair in, all the while looking at Phoenix like she was nuts. "To go shopping."

Phoenix was confused. "Shopping for what?"

Kenzie stared at her with a deadpan look.

"What?"

"You aren't serious, right? You're just joking with me."

Humans. Women. Both. Phoenix would never understand them.

"I seriously don't know what you are referring to."

Kenzie came around her desk and pointed to Phoenix. "Girlfriend, your clothes."

Phoenix looked down at her outfit. "What's wrong with my clothes?"

"Nothing. As long as you're not a bag lady standing on the corner, begging for money."

She gasped from the insult.

"Phoenix, babe, you have a banging body. Banging." Kenzie held up her hands, making okay signs with her index fingers and thumbs. "But you hide it under your hideous clothes."

Phoenix felt herself getting warm from Kenzie's compliment but instantly tried not to think about it. Her body was what had caused her problems when she was younger.

Phoenix had started dressing like this to hide her body. Back when she had been vulnerable and couldn't take care of herself.

Although she wasn't that naive young girl anymore. Dante had made her see that already. And maybe even Kenzie had helped her realize that, too.

So, maybe Kenzie was right. Now, Phoenix was so used to her clothes and dressing the way she did that she hadn't realized there was anything wrong with them.

"Look," Kenzie said, "I get that you have some…things that make you dress the way you do. But, if you would let me, I would love to help you shop for some clothes that would look nice on you yet were still modest."

Phoenix hesitated.

Kenzie folded her hands together. "Please, please. It would be so fun."

Phoenix raised her brow.

"Okay, it would be fun for me."

She still wasn't sure. "I don't know."

"Well, how about we go and get lunch, and you think about it? Then, I will take you to all my favorite stores."

Phoenix stood and looked at the human's clothes. "Uh…"

Kenzie showed way more skin than Phoenix was comfortable with.

Kenzie waved her off. "You don't have to dress like me. I promise, I'll make you look very nice. I mean, you are going to bone Dante, right? At the very least, you need some sexy lingerie."

"Holy crap, Kenzie. Does Sawyer know you talk like this?"

"Why do you think he mated with me?" Kenzie went to her office door and opened it. "Come on. Let's get you stylin'."

☾

Phoenix flopped back on the chair in the dressing room area. "Kill me now."

"Oh, stop it, you big baby," Kenzie said. "I only had you try on a few things."

Phoenix looked at the piles of clothes. *Piles.* The yeses, the noes, and the maybes. "You're nuts, you know that?"

"Nah, I just like shopping."

"Can we please be done now?" Phoenix begged.

Kenzie smirked and held up two articles of clothing on her fingers. "Only if you promise to wear the bra and panties I picked out for you."

"Uh-uh." Phoenix purposefully shook her head. "No way."

What Kenzie had picked out could scarcely be classified as a bra and panties. The bra barely covered her nipples, and her ass hung out of the underwear.

"Bra and panties, my ass. Literally."

Kenzie smiled. "I would never make you wear something that didn't look good on you."

"The answer's still no. Nope. Nada. Not going to happen."

Kenzie sighed and gave Phoenix her innocent big eyes again. "Well, I guess we're going to have to do more shopping."

Phoenix grunted, snatched the lingerie out of Kenzie's

hand, and stomped out of the dressing room. "Fine, but I'm not getting the maybe pile!" she yelled over her shoulder.

She heard Kenzie laugh all the way to the purchase counter.

The lady looked up as Phoenix approached.

"Hello. Are you ready to check out?"

"Yes, but I left all the clothes I'm going to purchase back in the dressing room." She held up the bra and underwear, leaned forward, and lowered her voice. "I'm supposed to buy these with my clothes, but if you could accidentally set them aside, so I don't bring them home, that would be great."

"Don't even think about it," Kenzie said as she dropped all the yes clothes onto the counter. "She's buying them," she told the lady. "And, if she doesn't stop fighting me, I'm going to make her wear them out of the store."

"Bitch."

"Brat."

"I don't like you right now."

"The feeling's mutual," Kenzie replied, unfazed.

The saleslady laughed at them as she rung up Phoenix's clothes. After Phoenix handed over her credit card and paid, she and Kenzie grabbed the bags and headed out to the parking lot.

"I can't believe I agreed to this," Phoenix said as they put her purchases in the trunk.

Kenzie shut the trunk. "Have I steered you wrong so far?"

Phoenix reluctantly said, "No."

"Wow, that was easier than I'd thought. I'd thought I'd have to pull that no out of you."

"I'm not that bad."

Kenzie snorted. "Anyway, I know what I'm doing here. I might not be the brightest bulb on the tree, but I do know what I'm talking about when it comes to relationship stuff."

Phoenix's shoulders slumped. "I know. I'm just nervous."

"Come on. Let's go, and you can tell me all about it."

They got in Kenzie's car.

"So, tell me why you're nervous," Kenzie said. "Besides the obvious."

"What if I don't like it?"

"You've liked everything else so far, right?"

Liked it was an understatement.

"Yes. But what if I don't like sex as much as I like oral sex? What if I can't have an orgasm? Or worse, what if I don't like it at all? Dante's big. What if it hurts?"

Kenzie put her hand on Phoenix's arm. "How big?"

Phoenix rolled her eyes. "Does it really matter?"

"Yes."

"Fine. The first time I saw it naked, I thought of a Coke can but longer."

"Holy shit, girl, you hit the jackpot."

"Yeah, maybe, if I were you. You like sex. I'm terrified as hell. What if he rips me in half?"

Kenzie laughed, but when she looked over at Phoenix's serious face, she stopped. "I'm sorry. I shouldn't laugh. I know you're freaked out."

"I am."

"Okay, remember what I told you the other day about just feeling? You have to do that tonight, too. If you start to panic, you'll add pressure to yourself, then you'll add pressure to Dante, and then back to you. It'll be a vicious cycle.

And, if you're all tense, you're going to be tense down there, too."

Phoenix threw her head back against the seat's headrest. "I know."

"Look, you need to get out of your head. You need to stop worrying about your ex-boyfriends. They were losers. Dante is just going to be happy that you're naked and willing. Trust me. You are going to make him happy just by showing up."

"You really think so?"

"I know so. By the way, does Dante know it's the big night?"

"No."

"Damn. You are totally going to make his night."

"God, I hope so."

TWENTY-THREE

DANTE LOOKED up at the clock in his office. Almost five.

He lathered his face, neck, and hands with sunscreen and then grabbed his black jacket and wide-brimmed black hat. He wished it were the middle of winter tonight, so it would already be dark or at least make the place they were going to stay open longer. But he couldn't control Mother Nature or the company's hours.

He reached the front door just as Phoenix knocked and stepped through.

Wow, he thought upon seeing her outfit.

Under normal conditions, she was dressed casually and quite conservatively. But, for Phoenix, she was dressed practically provocatively.

She was wearing a V-neck black sweater that matched the dark streaks in her hair, making the red stand out. The top was not tight but not loose. Her dark blue jeans were the same. Both hugged her curves, and Dante was afraid he wouldn't make it through their date.

Phoenix, on the other hand, looked nervous. She pulled

on her top—not realizing that, when she tugged it down, her gorgeous cleavage made an appearance. "Does it look bad? It does, doesn't it? I tried to tell Kenzie it didn't do anything for me, but she insisted. I should go home and change."

Upon hearing her rambling, he realized that he hadn't said anything out loud. He'd just been staring at her, gawking like a teenager. "You look beautiful." His big, dumb brain finally made his mouth form something useful. "Please don't go home and change."

"Are you sure?" She looked down at herself, noticed her cleavage being exposed, and let go of her sweater. "Oops."

"Yes, I'm very sure," he said as he stepped closer to her.

She sniffed the air. "Why do you smell like coconut?"

"It's my sunscreen. Are you ready to go?"

At this, she lost some of her edginess. "Go?"

"Yeah, we're going out tonight."

She looked toward the stairs and then back at him. "But I thought...aren't we...don't you..." She grunted. "Never mind. Look, I'm not much of a going-out person. Maybe I should just go home."

Dante laughed. "No way. I had to plan this a week ago. We're going. Besides, you don't even know where we're going."

"You said, going out. So, I'm assuming you mean, like, to a club or something. Then, we can get drunk and dirty-dance all over each other. But I don't drink—at least not to get wasted—and I definitely don't dance."

Dante put his hands up. "Whoa, whoa, whoa. Phoenix, you act like I don't know you. When I said going out, I meant, going out of the house. We've been hanging out here, watching *Game of Thrones* and making out like teenagers. I haven't even taken you on a proper date. Therefore, we are going out tonight."

She looked like she was in pain.

Dante sighed. "What now?"

"*Weeeell*, I'm not really a dinner-and-movie girl either."

Dante laughed. "Again, Phoenix, it's not like I just met you. Have a little faith. I know you're a unique female. Now, will you please trust me, so we can go?" He put his hand behind her back and led her to the garage.

She seemed preoccupied again. He hoped she wasn't worried about their date.

"What's wrong, Red?"

She hesitated but only for a moment. "What did you mean by I'm not a regular female?"

"You said it yourself. You don't like drinking and dancing or dinner and a movie."

"That makes me sound hard to please."

He put his arm around her and tugged her close. "Nah, you're just different."

Her shoulders tensed.

"But I like that about you."

Her shoulders relaxed.

"And I'm ninety-nine percent sure that you're going to like where we're going tonight."

She let herself lean into him. "Now, you've spiked my curiosity. Lead the way, oh wise one."

Dante stopped at the door to the garage and kissed her. "I would love to, but you have to drive. At least until the sun goes down. I'll ride in the back."

They climbed into the SUV with illegally tinted windows, Phoenix in the front and Dante in the back.

"I feel like your chauffeur," Phoenix said.

"Sorry about that," Dante said as he pulled up the address on his phone.

"Or I could just kidnap you and have my way with you."

He looked up and met her eyes in the rearview mirror. He liked this more playful side of her. She was really starting to come out of her shell.

"You don't have to kidnap me to do that," he said with a smile.

He looked back down at his phone and hit Navigate. He leaned over the front seat and put his phone in the holder reserved for things such as this. As he went back to his own seat, he brushed his lips across her cheek.

He put on his seat belt and told her, "I'm ready whenever you are."

Phoenix opened the garage door, and they headed down the driveway and then out to the road. When they arrived at their destination, a big brick building, Saxon and Tegan were standing outside.

Phoenix parked and turned around to look at him. "You asked those two to come along? What are you up to?" she asked as she handed him his phone.

He pocketed it and smiled at her. "You'll see. Let's go inside."

Dante quickly said hello to Saxon and Tegan as he headed for the building as fast as possible. Thankfully, he was only out in the sun for a few seconds. But, even if he needed to feed sooner, it'd be worth it.

The three shifters followed him inside, and Phoenix finally saw where they were.

"Paintball?" she said, her voice full of amazement.

Dante took off his cap and smiled at her. "Yep. You and I are going to kick these twos' asses."

Saxon grinned. "I don't think so. Right, Tegan?"

"Right. I've been brushing up on my shooting skills." She pretended to point both fingers and shoot, and then she blew at the tips of her fingers.

"Not fair. I just found out," Phoenix said.

"I have a feeling, you'll do just fine," Tegan told her.

At that point, a guy came out from the back. Dante told him the name for the reservation he'd made. They were shown to all their equipment. Suits, goggles, guns, paintballs, and so on. After they were ready, they split into their groups.

"How are we going to do this?" Dante asked Phoenix.

This was her day, and he wanted her to decide on their plan of action.

"Okay, here's what I'm thinking…"

She leaned forward and laid out her idea, and she made sure to add what she felt were their opponents' weaknesses. When she was done, they high-fived and went to opposite sides of the room.

They had the room for two hours, and they used it the whole time. Dante and Phoenix were good, but so were Saxon and Tegan. In the end, Phoenix and Dante barely won, but the important thing was that they'd all had fun, especially Phoenix, if the ear-to-ear grin was anything to go by.

By the time they got cleaned up, it was almost eight at night, closing time, and just about the time the sun went down. When they walked out of the building, the sky was dark with a sliver of red on the horizon.

Saxon and Tegan said good-bye to him and Phoenix.

After the two of them were alone, Dante put his arm around her and guided her to the SUV. "Hungry?"

"Starved."

"Good. Me, too." He held out his hands. "Keys?"

She took them out of her pocket. "I can drive again."

"Nah, I already risked my life once tonight."

She laughed and pushed him away. "You'd better watch it, or your life really will be in danger."

"I'm scared."

"You should be. Now, feed me."

Dante got behind the wheel, and Phoenix slid in beside him.

"Where to?"

"Burgers. I need meat."

"Sounds good to me," Dante said.

He headed for the nearest Five Guys. They got a few stares when Dante ordered five burgers, and Phoenix ordered three. But he was used to it, and he figured Phoenix was, too, because she didn't even bat an eye.

They ate their first two burgers each in silence; they were so hungry. Dante had had no idea paintball was such a workout. He might have to bring Phoenix there again.

The thought had him pausing and setting his fourth burger down. He'd never really thought about what would happen after she went through her heat. He supposed a part of him had assumed that they would keep up this thing they had started. But he had no idea what Phoenix was thinking. Would she want to continue in a relationship? Or would he simply be her baby daddy, and she wouldn't need him anymore?

She licked her lips after she took an especially big bite, and it made him think of how she would bite her lip when she came. He couldn't imagine, after the way she responded with him, that she would want to go back to a platonic relationship. At least, he really hoped she wouldn't.

She ate some fries and then stuck her finger in her mouth and licked it off. He pictured her doing something similar to him. So far, the oral sex had been one-sided, which was okay with him. He loved making Phoenix come. But he couldn't help but picture her going down on him.

And, now, he had a hard-on.

Without looking up from her food, Phoenix asked, "Is there a reason you're staring at me?"

Whoops.

He hadn't realized he'd been staring. He'd been so lost in his head, watching her.

"Sorry." He smiled when she looked up. "I was just thinking about some stuff."

"All good things, I hope."

"Mostly good things."

She pointed to his food. "Are you going to finish that last burger?"

He looked down and picked up the one he'd been eating. "I'd planned to."

She stared at him, her green eyes looking at him with big pools of sadness.

"Fine. You can have half."

She grinned. "Thank you," she said, already cutting it apart.

"Faker."

She looked up at him. "It got me what I wanted, didn't it?"

"I believe it did."

She smirked.

"Maybe you're more of a dinner girl than you originally thought."

She tilted her head. "Maybe I am. Or maybe I just am with you."

He smiled at her, feeling good about their future.

They finished all their food and picked up their garbage.

"Come on, Red, let's go."

He still had a big night planned for her.

TWENTY-FOUR

PHOENIX FOLLOWED DANTE INTO THE GUARDIANS' compound, feeling nervous. She'd felt relaxed and comfortable after paintball and dinner, but now, her concerns were back. What if this sex thing went horribly wrong? What if it was so bad that Dante changed his mind about getting her pregnant?

Of course, Dante never even said that was what they were going to do. It just seemed like they had led up to it, and tonight was the night. Especially with the date. Why else would Dante have done something special for her tonight?

As Dante led her upstairs, they passed Hunter, who barely noticed them. He seemed to be preoccupied with his own thing. Phoenix was grateful because, if she later ran out of the mansion from humiliation, she didn't need anyone else to witness it.

When they reached Dante's room, she shut the door behind them.

"Hey, should we turn on *Game of Thrones*?" he asked, walking toward his TV, oblivious to her turmoil.

"No."

Dante turned around and frowned. "No?"

"No," she whispered, not knowing what else to say.

His look turned to one of concern, and unexpectedly, she questioned everything.

What am I doing here?

He was beautiful, both inside and out, and she had no right to ask him to sacrifice his whole world for her. She was damaged goods. He should be with someone who could give him everything he deserved. She was wasting his time, and she suddenly realized how selfish she was for taking advantage of his good heart.

Phoenix took a step back. "I think I should go."

"Did I do something?" Dante asked as he strode toward her until she put a hand out to stop him.

Of course he would blame himself.

"No!" she practically shouted. "You're...fricking perfect. I'm the fucked up one." She put her head in her hands, not wanting him to look at her. She should really turn around and flee like she had the first time she let him feed from her.

She didn't hear Dante move closer and didn't know he was right in front of her until he pulled on her hands. "Phoenix."

She didn't budge.

"Hey. Red. Look at me, please?"

It was the *Red* that did it. She dropped her arms and looked at him.

He cupped her face and ran his thumbs over her cheekbones. "We don't have to do this, you know. I don't want you to feel like you are being forced to do anything you don't want to do."

She shook her head. "You don't understand."

His brown eyes looked so lost, and she felt guilty for putting that look there.

"Can you explain it to me?"

"I *want* to have sex with you."

Dante smiled, but his eyes still looked sad. "Okay, Red, you're going to have to help me out here. I'm confused."

She looked down—at least the best she could since he was still touching her face. "What if I mess it up? What if you don't want to do it again?"

"Oh, Red, no matter what, that will never happen. Haven't you ever heard the old saying that pizza is like sex?"

She met his eyes. Now, she was confused. "Huh?"

"Pizza's like sex. Even when it's bad, it's still pretty good."

She raised her brow.

Dante laughed. "At least for guys."

Kenzie had told her that sex was different for men than women.

"My point is, no matter what, I'm going to like it because *I'll get to be inside you.*"

A delicious shiver spread down her spine at his words.

"Plus, you're not the only one who is feeling pressure. I think sleeping with you is more pressure than sleeping with a virgin. I want to make it enjoyable for you more than anything. I'm not trying to make you feel worse. I just want you to know that we're in this together."

She put her arms around his neck. *What did he just say to me?* "I'm going to like it because you'll be inside me."

"Fuck," Dante said before he lowered his head and kissed her.

He worked her mouth until she was jelly in his arms, and then he stepped away, taking her hand and leading her to the bed.

"Undress me, Red."

Phoenix slowly removed Dante's clothes, like she had the first time she touched him. After she removed his shirt, she leaned into his chest and inhaled. He had sweat off all the sunscreen and smelled like Dante again. Cinnamon, musk, and male. She kissed his neck, nipping him there with her canines, and went to work on his pants.

Once his pants were removed, she wrapped her fingers around him, but unlike the last few nights, he put his hand over hers, stopping her.

"Not tonight." He kissed her. "I'll barely last as it is."

She let go of him and touched him on his chest as he slowly removed her pants. He bent down and helped guide one pant leg over her heel and then the other. He pulled her close and inhaled between her legs, like she had done to his chest minutes ago.

He looked up at her. "Can I take your shirt off?"

She almost said no, but she and Dante had been through a lot. He'd already seen her breasts when he healed them, so she nodded. This was the first time he had asked if he could remove her top, sensing she had issues with her upper body.

Dante stood and carefully pulled her sweater over her head before letting it drop next to her.

"Damn, Red."

Phoenix looked down at the bra and panty set that Kenzie had made her wear. It was red and lacy and barely covered anything. "I didn't pick it out. It—"

He put his finger over her lips. "You look…stunning. I am the luckiest son of a bitch alive right now."

She couldn't have stopped the blush and grin that spread across her face if she tried.

Dante sat on the bed and pulled her between his legs. He ran his hands up her thighs to her hips and leaned forward to kiss her on her chest above her breasts. She held her breath as she waited to see what he would do. He moved up her neck and kissed there again before moving back down to her chest. But he never kissed her breasts, and he left her bra covering her. She didn't know whether to be relieved or disappointed, but for now, she was going to go with relieved.

He slipped his fingers under the waistband of her underwear and pulled them down off her legs. She kicked them aside and looked down at Dante's naked body.

They hadn't been naked at the same time until now. Dante was always very aware of her being comfortable and not misleading her, so he made sure one of them was always wearing pants.

This was a turning point in their relationship. As if Dante was thinking the same thing, he looked at her until she nodded her okay.

Dante scooted further back on the bed and took Phoenix's hand. He led her forward, so she was straddling him. "I want you to direct how this goes," he said. "You get to control everything. No pressure."

She moved up, so her opening was right over his penis. "Will you help me put you inside me?"

Dante took her hand in his, grabbed his dick, and then placed it at her entrance. She was starting to feel nervous again but for a different reason. He was so large, and she was afraid it would hurt. She knew that Dante had been preparing her the last few nights to help her get used to him, but they hadn't been doing this very long. What if they needed more time?

"Relax, Red."

"Easier said than done."

Dante used his free hand to pull her down and kiss her. He always knew what to do to make her feel better. So what if it involved kissing a lot? She loved kissing him.

Before she knew it, she felt Dante rubbing his cock through her slickness. She felt like it was now or never, so she sat back up and slowly pushed down on him. She immediately felt him stretch her, but it didn't hurt. She continued on and on and on until she was seated firmly on him.

She had never felt so full in her life.

Experimenting, she rotated her hips a little. Dante groaned. She squeezed down on him, and he cursed.

Hmm... She could get used to this.

Except she realized that, after he was inside her, she didn't really know what to do. She'd never been the one in control.

Dante must have sensed her dilemma because he placed his hands on her hips. "Rock your hips. Move up and down. Do whatever you want, Phoenix. I promise, no matter what, it'll feel good."

She leaned over and took his mouth again, and she moved over him. At first, slowly and tentatively, but as the friction their bodies created started to feel good, she increased her pace. Soon, she had to break their kiss because she was finding it hard to breathe.

She had an arm outstretched on each side of his head as she rode him. "Does it...always...feel this...good?" she asked him.

He shook his head. "Good. But never...like this." He dug his fingernails into her hips. "I don't...know...how much...longer...I can...last. Fuck."

The veins on his neck stood out, and it only turned her on more.

Dante moved one hand from her side and pushed it between them. His fingers aimed right for her clit, and Phoenix moaned. The feel of him touching her there with him inside her was like heaven.

He continued to touch her as she moved her pelvis on his over and over, unrelenting in her movements.

Oh God. Could she...would she actually be able to come like this?

Her body answered her by climaxing around Dante so hard that she was nothing but a worthless heap of shifter when she was done. Thankfully, she had felt Dante's release right before she collapsed on him.

She was so content to lie there that she felt herself beginning to doze. She didn't know if she'd ever felt so relaxed in her life. She gathered enough strength to lift her head and look at Dante. His eyes were closed.

"Dante?"

"Hmm?" he said as he began rubbing her back.

"Did I do okay?" The only reason she asked was because she already knew the answer, and she was feeling a little smug.

Dante looked at her, his eyes half-lidded and stress-free.

"Red, you were fucking phenomenally well. But don't move yet."

Phoenix's eyes widened as his semi-hard cock, still inside her, went full mast.

"I want to feel you come all over me again."

TWENTY-FIVE

HUNTER SAT in front of the wolf-shifters' mansion, wondering who was going to be assigned as his partner tonight yet, at the same time, not giving two shits one way or the other. So far, a different shifter every evening had either come out the door or come to pick him up, and every night, he found himself feeling more and more miserable.

Hunter hadn't seen Quentin since the night they had their date.

No, he took that back. It hadn't been a date. It had been hanging out. Because, if it had been a date, Quentin wouldn't have just disappeared after that, never to be heard from again.

Or maybe he would have.

Maybe Hunter was that lousy of a date. The wolf-shifter alpha had told him there was some family emergency when he called Hunter to tell him he'd be getting a new partner. But for Quentin not to say anything to Hunter—no phone call, no text—could only mean one thing. Quentin wasn't interested, which really pissed Hunter off.

Fuck you, Quentin.

Fuck him for making Hunter feel things and then disappearing. Fuck him for not caring enough to drop a line. And fuck him for putting Hunter in this situation with no one to talk to.

After Quentin had left, Hunter had realized he had no one else to talk to about his whole maybe-gay situation. He was disappointingly alone right now.

Hunter pulled out his phone for what was probably the one-millionth time since he'd gone out with Quentin. His notification bar was mockingly empty. It might as well be putting the middle finger up at him.

Just then, his phone rang, and he cursed the split second of joy that bloomed in his chest before he saw it was Ram.

"Hello?"

"Hey, where are you?"

"Wolf-shifters'. Waiting for my partner."

"Good. Someone called into the tip line about seeing something about ten minutes from your location. Can you check it out?"

"Sure. Does Dante know?"

"Nah, he's busy fuckin' the cat. We decided it wasn't worth bothering him unless you discovered something. You know how it goes. Most of the time, these tips are bogus."

"Right. Of course."

"You okay, man?"

No. "Can I ask you a question?"

"Shoot."

"If a...someone asked you to hang out for the night at a bar with their friends as a casual thing and then kissed you, would you think it was a date? Would you think you would hear from that person after that?"

Ram chuckled. "Girl problems?"

"Yeah, something like that."

"Hmm. I guess I would say that, since it was never specified as a date, then it wasn't a date. And, since it wasn't a date, that person didn't owe me anything. A kiss is just a kiss. If she dropped down on her knee and asked me to marry her, it would be a totally different thing. But a kiss? Nah, man."

Hunter dropped his head, feeling bad for expecting so much out of Quentin. Ram was right. Quentin had never promised Hunter anything.

"Yeah, that makes sense. Thanks."

"You're welcome. And don't worry. Whatever chick you're doggin' will forget about your ugly mug as soon as the next guy kisses her."

Hunter laughed nervously. Of course Ram would assume Hunter was the ditcher and not the ditchee.

A movement out of the corner of Hunter's eye caught his attention.

A shadowy figure was coming down the dark path to his car.

"Hey, my partner is here." He turned his head toward his window, so whomever he was assigned with tonight would see he was on the phone. "Can you text me that address?"

"Yep. Already done," Ram said as Hunter's car door opened.

Hunter swore he smelled Quentin, just like every other night since he'd last seen the wolf, and he told his brain to shut the hell up. "I'll call you if we find anything important."

"Later."

"Later," Hunter said. He moved his phone from his ear and hit End.

"Something important come up?" Quentin asked.

"Holy shit," Hunter said as he jumped. He'd been so lost in his head that he'd forgotten someone had gotten in with him. Upon hearing Quentin's voice, Hunter about had a heart attack.

He wasn't prepared for this. He'd been missing the shifter, but now, he was mad at Quentin and mad at himself for caring. He didn't know how to act, feeling like a teenager who had had his first kiss, and that was without all the other confusion upon seeing Quentin for the first time in several days.

Ugh. When had he turned into such a pussy?

He needed to suck it up. There were real problems out there. His love life was not that important.

Quentin raised an eyebrow. "You okay?"

"Yeah. Yeah. We, uh…have an address we have to go check out. Tip-line call." Hunter pulled up his text messages and found the address. He was grateful he'd driven tonight. It would give him something to do besides fidgeting in his seat.

"Sounds good," Quentin answered.

Hunter put his car in drive.

They traveled for a few minutes before Hunter sucked up his hurt feelings and asked, "Everything okay with your family?"

"What?"

"Uh, Damien said you had a family emergency."

"Oh, uh…yeah, everything's okay." Quentin looked away from Hunter and out his window.

Hunter was trying to be the bigger man here and not let his hurt feelings ruin anything. But Quentin couldn't even talk to him. The shifter was acting like Hunter had screwed him over.

Whatever.

Hunter gripped the steering wheel until his knuckles turned white, but at least he didn't say another word to Quentin. He would keep it professional. They had a job to do after all. That was the only reason they were here.

Too bad his heart and his dick didn't agree with his head.

Thankfully, Ram was right about the distance away, and Hunter and Quentin arrived in just under ten minutes. They each exited the vehicle and made their way up to the front of the house. They were in shifter territory, so Hunter let Quentin take the lead.

After knocking on the door, a little old cat-shifter couple, who had to be close to a thousand, answered. There was no way they'd seen anything, going by the thickness of both their glasses.

"Hello, sir, ma'am," Quentin said. "We got a call about a tip?"

"Huh? Speak up, young man," the male said.

"George, I told you to put in your hearing aid," his mate said, loud enough to alert the whole block.

So, it seemed like the elderly couple probably hadn't heard anything either. Hunter was feeling let down. This was his last shot at a positive evening, and it looked like it was a bust. He needed to get out of there. He couldn't stand next to Quentin and pretend everything was okay.

Hunter took out his phone and held it up. "I need to take this," he told the couple.

"Whaaat?" they both said.

"I need to take this," he practically shouted. He looked at Quentin. "Can you handle this?"

Quentin looked down at Hunter's black screen and back up at Hunter.

Hunter quickly put his phone against his chest, so Quentin couldn't see that he was lying.

Quentin shook his head in disappointment. "Yeah, I got this."

Hunter took off, back toward his car, not even bothering to pretend to answer his phone.

A couple of minutes later, Quentin joined him, slamming his car door closed.

"Hey, be careful," Hunter said, gunning the gas.

"Sorry," Quentin said with no hint of remorse in his voice.

Hunter drove, not knowing where he was going, feeling his anger get stronger and stronger, the more he tried to repress it. He glanced over at Quentin, whose jaw twitched as he stared straight ahead.

Finally, Hunter couldn't take it anymore. "What the fuck is wrong with you?"

Quentin whipped his head around to look at Hunter. "What the fuck is wrong with me? What the fuck is wrong with you?"

And what was he supposed to say to that? *I've only known you less than a month, but I missed you while you were gone.*

Yeah, right because it was obvious that Quentin hadn't missed him.

"I asked you first."

Quentin didn't answer, and the two of them stared at each other until a horn honked, jolting Hunter's eyes back to the road just in time to miss hitting a semi whose lane he had wandered over to.

"Holy shit, you're going to kill us," Quentin said. "Pull over there." He pointed to a park. "We obviously have a few things to say to each other, and I'd rather not die in the process."

Quentin was right, and Hunter pulled off the road and into the parking lot. The night wasn't cold, but it was still cool outside, so the park was blessedly empty. Hunter opened his door, got out, and headed for the nearest tree to rest his back against, sliding down to the cool ground. He couldn't stay cooped up in his car with Quentin.

The shifter came and sat beside him. Neither one spoke as they stared off into the darkness of the night. After almost crashing, Hunter had lost a lot of his steam. He was still upset, but it didn't seem worth dying over.

Hunter spoke first, "Look, I don't want to fight. I don't even know why you're mad at me."

"Why don't you start by telling me why you're mad at me?"

Hunter barked out a humorless laugh. "Do I have to?"

Quentin looked him right in the eye. "Yes."

Hunter exhaled. *Why not add humiliation to the list of things wrong with tonight?* "I'm more mad at myself than at you." He put his head back against the tree and stared up at the empty branches. "I was disappointed to find out you were gone. And then, when I didn't hear from you…" He shrugged. "I don't know." He lifted his head and made a sound of exasperation. "I've never felt like this before. I'm a mess of emotions, and quite frankly, I don't like it." He looked at Quentin. "The thing is, I know you never promised me anything. I guess I just thought we had…I don't know…some sort of connection. That was my bad to assume that. I shouldn't project my feelings onto you. I promise, I will try to be more levelheaded tonight and from now on."

Quentin stared at Hunter until he said, "Fuck being levelheaded," and he grabbed Hunter behind the neck and pulled him close.

Quentin kissed him like he was dying to taste him, which was just fine with Hunter because the feeling was mutual.

Hunter shoved his tongue in Quentin's mouth and pushed the shifter to the ground. He shoved his hands under Quentin's shirt and ripped it over his head. Quentin's beautiful dark skin was covered in a dusting of curly dark hair and topped by brown nipples. Hunter put his mouth to one and sucked.

Quentin arched underneath Hunter and rubbed his cock against the vampire's. Hunter wanted to feel it in his hand. He'd only ever held his own, and he wanted to know what Quentin's felt like.

But then Quentin rolled Hunter over, so he was on top. He sat up and practically tore off the button to Hunter's jeans as he opened them and pushed them down. Quentin grabbed Hunter's dick in his hand and squeezed. Hunter moaned.

Quentin leaned down, and Hunter knew exactly what

the shifter was going to do. Hunter sat up and quickly covered himself. At least, he did the best he could with Quentin still holding him.

"What's wrong?" Quentin asked.

Hunter blushed. "I don't—" He rolled his eyes at himself. "I feel like I've been waiting my whole life for this. I don't want the first time we do this to be angry sex. Or angry oral sex."

Quentin's face softened, and he cupped the back of Hunter's neck again and pulled him in for a kiss. Hunter tasted blood and realized that he'd bitten his lip in the excitement earlier.

Quentin pulled away. "Fuck, do you taste that good everywhere?"

Hunter blushed again and shrugged. He knew vampire blood was sweet compared to human and shifter blood, but he had no idea if his semen would be different. "I don't know. I've never tasted myself."

Quentin grinned. "Let me find out and let you know."

Hunter groaned. He wanted that so very much. "But—"

"Hunter, I'm not mad. I'm very, very not mad. Now, lie down, and let me suck your cock, like I've been dying to do since I saw you in the conference room."

Hunter sucked in a breath but only lay back onto his elbows. He wasn't going to miss this opportunity for the world.

Quentin gently lowered his mouth to Hunter's dick, but he didn't touch it with his mouth. He blew on the tip and stroked Hunter with his hand until a drop of pre-cum emerged. Quentin grinned down at the liquid, as if that was what he'd been waiting for, and then he put the head of Hunter's cock in his mouth and sucked.

"Holy fuck. Holy fuck, holy fuck," Hunter said as he watched Quentin slowly suck more and more of him down.

Quentin put all of Hunter in his mouth and then gradually suctioned his lips as he brought his mouth back up. He released Hunter and blew on his tip again. This time, his breath combined with his saliva was cool on Hunter's penis, and a shiver ran down his spine.

The wolf met Hunter's eyes, and he could see that they had shifted—no white of sclera left. Hunter was really looking at part of the wolf now.

It might scare someone to know a predator was that close to one's junk, but it only turned Hunter on more. He felt himself leak more. He was afraid he was going to come too soon.

Quentin lowered his mouth again, licking the seam where his pre-cum had appeared and swallowed. And, apparently, the shifter was done with all teasing because he began to work over Hunter's cock like no one had done before.

Hunter tried to watch as Quentin deep-throated him, but it felt too good. Hunter collapsed back against the grass. Soon, he felt his impending orgasm, and he knew it was going to be different than any other. When he exploded, he heard Quentin groan and actually heard him swallow. Hunter came so hard and so fast that he was afraid he'd pass out. It was better than any female going down on him.

Quentin continued to suck him until he drained Hunter dry, and there was nothing left for him to give. The wolf then lay next to Hunter and kissed him deep, making sure Hunter could taste himself on Quentin's tongue.

Quentin pulled away. "What do you think? I think you taste better than I ever dreamed."

Hunter smiled. "I think that I can't wait to taste you. In more ways than one," he said as he lightly ran his finger across Quentin's neck. "And I think I'm definitely not asexual."

Because that was by far the best orgasm he'd ever had.

TWENTY-SIX

"I WANT you to be on top," Phoenix told him.

Dante hesitated. "Are you sure?" He was a lot bigger and didn't want her to feel like she was being forced in any way.

"Yes, I want to feel you all over me."

He wanted the same thing.

"Damn, Red, you know just what to say to get what you want."

Dante rolled them until Phoenix was on her back, and Dante was over her, but the best part was that he was still inside her.

"Ooh," she said.

He immediately went on alert. "Are you okay?"

"Yes. You just feel different now."

"Good different? Or bad different?"

Phoenix laughed and put a finger between his eyes to smooth out his frown. "Good different. Please don't worry so much about me."

"That's like telling the sun not to rise." He kissed her.

He began to pump slowly inside her. She was swollen from their first round of sex and because she didn't normally do this sort of thing. But, thankfully, she was wet from her desire and his.

He moved a little faster when she moaned into his mouth, and he was sure she was feeling good. He left her mouth and kissed her cheek and then down the side until he reached her neck.

He sucked on the skin there, wanting to taste her more than he'd ever wanted to taste anyone. He'd tasted her before, but he'd never had his fangs inside her while *he'd* been inside her.

Phoenix pushed on the back of his head and said, "Bite me, Dante."

"Are you sure?" he said against her neck. "I'm not due to feed yet."

She grabbed a section of hair and pulled. "Quit asking me if I'm sure. I want the whole vampire experience. Now, bite me, Dante."

He growled at the way she'd said his name and struck. He sucked gently as he fucked her, wanting to make it last as long as possible. He wanted to live here. Inside her pussy and inside her vein.

As he drew her blood into his mouth, the taste along with the tightness of her around his cock meant that he would not last long. He didn't want to come without Phoenix though. She deserved this after the assholes she'd dated before.

He knew she needed to be touched down below, or she needed to taste his blood. God, he wanted her to suck on him, but it felt like cheating. Dante had just decided to give up on her neck in order to get a better angle to reach her clit when she used her cat canines to bite his shoulder.

He loved that Phoenix wasn't being timid and was going after what she wanted in bed. Dante knew he should give her a little time, but everything—her blood, her snug wetness, her courage—had him thrusting into her harder and faster. He was going to have to apologize to her when he was done, but she felt amazing.

But then Phoenix surprised him as she beat him to the finish line. She came around him, squeezing him so tightly that he was afraid his dick was briefly going to lose circulation.

He had the good sense to close her vein before he orgasmed and momentarily lost control of his motor skills.

Wanting to be as far inside Phoenix as possible, he grabbed one of her legs and put it over his shoulder, opening her up to him as he pounded out his release. He pushed into her and held his body there while he poured himself inside her.

When he came back to himself, he let go of her leg and put his forehead to hers. "Please tell me you're okay. I kind of lost myself there for a while."

"Is that because of me?"

Duh seemed like the only appropriate answer.

"Yes, Red, it's because of you."

She ran her hand down his chest. "Wow. I've done that to a guy before."

Dante started laughing so hard that he rolled off of Phoenix and started coughing.

She sat up and looked down at him. "What's so funny?"

"You."

She puckered her brow. "Me?"

He put his hand on her hip. "Yes. You really have no clue the power you could have over the male population if you wanted to."

"Is that a good thing or a bad thing?"

"It's a good thing because you don't. I like you clueless and innocent."

She crossed her arms. "Yeah, well, I don't know if I like that."

He pulled her down to lie on his chest. "I'm glad you don't use your looks for evil."

She traced her hand down his scar. "How did you get this?" she asked.

He looked down at himself even though he knew what she was talking about. "My father."

Phoenix gasped. "What?" She leaned up on an elbow to look at him.

He shrugged. He supposed it sounded like a big deal to someone who'd never heard the story before. "Did you know my father was the previous leader of the Guardians?"

"No."

"He was." A lock of her red-and-black hair fell down around her shoulder, so Dante picked it up and twisted it around his finger. "He was kind of a hard-ass. He started grooming me to take over for him when I was little. He was teaching me how to spar, and he cut me. This was before my conversion, so I didn't have the ability to heal like I do now."

"That's horrible."

"It is what it is. It taught me the valuable lesson of getting out of the way. Believe me, he never cut me again."

"I don't like to think of you being hurt."

Her words melted his heart.

"Same here. Why don't we watch some more *Game of Thrones* and forget what my dad did?"

"Is your father no longer alive?"

"He died over ten years ago."

"Okay," she said as she lay back down. "I'm ready to watch."

"Why did you ask?"

"Because, if he wasn't already in the ground, I was going to put him there myself."

Dante kissed the top of her head. "You need to work on your romance," he said with a laugh.

☾

Hunter and Quentin were back in Hunter's car, on their way to their next destination, but Hunter wanted to be back at that park, finishing what they had started. Quentin had told him they had taken too much time already, and they were supposed to be working.

But, if they were back at the park, they wouldn't have to finish their conversation from earlier. He didn't want to fight with Quentin or be hurt, but he wanted to know why Quentin hadn't contacted him. He knew he couldn't avoid it forever.

Hunter opened his mouth when Quentin said, "I'm sorry I never called or texted you. I was dealing with a lot of stuff."

"Your family emergency?"

Quentin snorted. "More like family shit. My sister…

she's...well, she's a drug addict. My mother and father have been trying to get her help for years. We all thought that moving back to Minneapolis might help her, get her away from her crowd. But she's like a heat-seeking missile. She finds the shittiest druggies and becomes their new best friend."

"She doesn't appreciate the help, I take it."

"She hates it. She hates me. She thinks I became a cop and a sentinel to be a kiss ass, but that's not true. I like being a protector. She doesn't get it."

Hunter had almost forgotten about Quentin's day job since he'd been spending so much time out in the field, doing his sentinel thing.

"She always dares me to arrest her. I fucking should, too. But then I look at my mother, and I just...can't. It would break her heart."

Hunter grabbed Quentin's hand. "I'm so sorry."

Quentin looked over at him. "Yeah, me, too. But I doubt she'll ever change because she doesn't want to."

Hunter squeezed his fingers around Quentin. "I'm sorry I didn't call or text you either. I know it's a two-way street, and I shouldn't have waited for you to make the second move."

Quentin smiled. "It's okay. You're forgiven. I wouldn't have been fun to talk to anyway. I feel like my sister brings out the worst in me. She's always feeling sorry for herself, but I don't understand why. She came from a good home with good parents. She had everything she could have ever wanted. But she keeps insisting that life is so tough. Tell me about it, lady, I'm a fucking homosexual, sentinel, and police officer. I think I know the meaning of tough." He shook his head. "Nope, we're not talking about her anymore. She's already ruined enough of my week."

"Okay, I understand. But, if you ever need to talk, I'm here."

Quentin smiled again. "Thanks." He turned his eyes to the windshield. "So, where are we headed again?"

Hunter sighed. "Another tip. Let's hope this one turns out better than the last."

TWENTY-SEVEN

THERE WAS a knock at Sterling's bedroom door.

"Come in," he said, already knowing who was on the other side.

He swiveled around in his desk chair as Lexine walked into his room.

"I think I know where Lucas is going to be soon. I'll stay back, so you can sneak up on him. We'll find out where my parents are"—she punched a fist into her open palm—"and then you can take the fucker out."

Lexine and Sterling had been methodically finding all of her old group of friends and taking their blood to track them. They were hoping to find her parents or Lucas. Thankfully, they hadn't had any problems since the first night when Sterling rescued Lexine. They had managed to obtain their blood by knocking out each one, so they wouldn't know it was Lexine who'd attacked them.

But the Steve guy had to have warned the others. Except Lexine hadn't heard from Lucas, whom she was expecting to call her at any moment. Lexine thought it was luck, but from what she had told Sterling, he figured the asshole was up to something. After all, despite the fact that they had gotten everyone's blood and were able to track them, none of them had led Lexine and Sterling to her parents or Lucas himself.

"Why do you want to kill him when you haven't wanted to kill any of the others?"

Not only had she *not* wanted to kill any of the others, but she had also insisted on it.

"He and his friends should go in front of the Vampire Council when this all goes down," he said.

"Because he's their leader. We'll never be able to take the rest down without him out of the way."

She had to realize that was a lame excuse.

"Which we can do if we drag him in front of the Council."

She shook her head. "No, we have to get rid of him."

Sterling rubbed a hand down his face. "You can't even say the word. If you can't say that we should kill him, how are you actually going to kill him?"

A look of pure rage flashed across her face. "Trust me, I'll be able to do it."

"When are you going to tell me what he did to you?" Sterling had gotten Lexine to spill most of her story to him, but he could tell that she had left something out just by her attitude toward Lucas.

"Never." Her eyes widened as she realized her slip. "I mean, he didn't do anything to me." She shrugged a shoulder. "Nothing more than the others did anyway."

She was such a liar.

"You know I don't believe a word that comes out of your mouth, right?"

A look of sexual prowess came over her face, and she dropped to her knees. Her hazel-green eyes sparkled as she crawled over to Sterling. "Then, why don't you kick me out?"

Because he was a glutton for punishment.

She unbuttoned his jeans and lowered the zipper. She took out his cock and stroked it with her hands. She looked him in the eye and licked her lips.

He knew why he hadn't kicked her out. He knew why he hadn't gone to their leader, the Council, the king and queen, or even her brother. Because, while she was in love with Dante, Sterling was foolishly in love with her. He would do almost anything for her.

It pissed him off that she had that power over him.

He grabbed her white-blonde hair and wrapped it around his fist. He tugged her head back until it hit her shoulders, exposing her neck. "Someday, you are going to tell me what he did to you."

Any other female would be scared of his mood right now but not Lexine. She laughed and bit her lower lip.

He pulled harder until he drew her body partly away from his, but she just tightened her grip around his dick.

He leaned down and kissed her, almost violently. She might have this unwanted control over him, but she wasn't his boss. He grasped her lower lip between his teeth, scraping her with his fangs, and he slowly released it.

She was panting, and the room was filled with the fragrance of her arousal.

He sat back in his chair, bringing her head with him. "Put me in your mouth, Lexine."

She didn't even hesitate, sliding him between her lips. He pushed her head down, still holding on to her hair, and she took him to the back of her throat. She tried to slightly bring her head up, but Sterling didn't let her. Instead of getting mad, she smiled and sucked harder.

He yanked her head up and off him, and she released him with a pop. She still had blood on her mouth from the scrape and licked her lips.

"Again," she said.

He pushed her head back down over his cock. She sucked him in again, and this time, when he brought her head up, she scratched him with her fangs. There was a bite of pain, but if he were honest, he liked it, and it only turned him on more.

He stood, bringing her with him, and kissed her. He tasted her blood and his blood on her lips. He let go of her hair and pushed her pants off her hips. He released her mouth, swung her around, and pushed down on her back. "Hands on the desk, and stick your ass out."

He knew they were stupid for doing this here. All it would take was someone getting too close to his door, and they would smell the sex coming from the room. Fraternizing wasn't necessarily frowned upon, but it would raise a lot of questions. Questions Lexine wouldn't want to answer.

But, right at the moment, he couldn't manage to give a fuck what someone else thought, and obviously, Lexine felt the same, as she did exactly as he'd told her. She even wiggled her ass at him when he wasn't fast enough.

He grabbed her hips and slammed into her.

Lexine moaned so loudly that he was convinced someone was going to come knocking on his door at any second, but they would just have to wait while he finished fucking Lexine.

He clutched her hips and relentlessly pounded into her. He knew he was taking out his frustrations with his feelings on her body, but the thing he'd learned about Lexine since that night he followed her was that she liked sex a little rough. That only made him want her more.

He let go of her hips and put his hands on the desk on each side of her body. He continued to drive into her as he used his nose to move the neck of her shirt over before pushing her head to one side. He didn't even bother asking anymore. He just sank his fangs into her shoulder. She responded by taking a hand and pushing his head down further toward her.

She shoved back on him with each thrust, fucking him as much as he was fucking her. He felt her pussy start to quiver around him as her breathing became erratic.

"Please," she said. "Don't stop. Don't stop."

Not even if someone held a gun to his head would he stop.

He held off his own orgasm until he felt the beginning of hers. He wrapped his arm around her waist so that he stayed inside her as he emptied himself into her.

They both collapsed on his desk, and Sterling realized he still had his fangs inside her. He slowly withdrew and licked her wound closed. He winced when he saw the bruise on her shoulder and pulled her shirt back up to her neck.

Sterling stood all the way up and pulled out of her pussy. He watched some of his cum slide out of her body and down the inside of her thigh. He used his first two fingers to wipe it from her leg and used his other hand to turn her around. "Open," he told her.

She opened her mouth and sucked his fingers into her mouth, like she had done with his dick just a short time ago. She didn't even hesitate to swallow. He really wanted his blood in her when they had sex, but that was irrational, so he settled for the next best thing.

He pulled his fingers from her mouth and went to his bathroom to grab two hand towels. He walked back over to Lexine and nudged her to sit on his desk. He put the towel between her legs and used the other to clean himself up.

He went into his closet to put it in the dirty clothes, and then he buttoned up. He took a couple of deep breaths. He was frustrated with himself for reacting to her. She'd purposely given him head to distract him, and he'd let her to the point that they'd had sex. He really needed to get his head on straight when it came to this female. She was already going to leave his heart in shreds; he didn't need her doing the same thing to his head.

Sterling walked out of the closet just as Lexine was pulling her pants up.

He took her towel, threw it with his, and then sat back down at his desk. "Tell me more about your plan."

☾

Lexine sat on Sterling's bed and told him about a vampire-only event at a nightclub, Pulse, at the end of next week.

"How are they going to do that?" he asked.

"It's invitation only. Didn't you get yours?"

217

As Guardians, they were probably on the top of the list.

Sterling rose from his chair and went over to a small table by his bedroom door where a stack of mail sat. He stood with his back to her, and she scanned his body, pausing to admire his spectacular jean-clad ass. She should really put a mirror on the ceiling, so she could watch him move in and out of her. She'd never understood that appeal before, but now, it made sense.

She didn't know what to make of this turn in their relationship. Until recently, they'd pretty much just been coworkers. Now, they were having sex. The night Sterling had followed her and fucked her against his SUV was a total surprise. Tonight had been a total surprise. Sterling was always so soft-spoken and compliant. He never challenged Dante. He might question their leader but never challenged. She'd had no idea Sterling had such a dominant streak.

She squirmed on his bed, her sexual arousal rising again, despite the fact that he had just screwed her and given her one hell of an orgasm.

She really, really liked having sex with Sterling, and it confused the hell out of her. She loved Dante. *Didn't she?* Yes, she'd had sex with Lucas before she found out what an asshole he was, but that had been more of a distraction from her broken heart. With Sterling, she actually liked being with him.

The scary thing was that she'd seen the cat-shifter arrive tonight, and Lexine knew Dante was screwing her now. But she had felt…well…nothing upon seeing Phoenix go into Dante's room tonight as she made her own way to Sterling's room.

The whole thing frightened her because she had

pictured her and Dante together for so long. She didn't know what she was going to do if they didn't end up together.

"Here it is," Sterling said as he turned around.

His gray eyes met hers, and she could tell he was still upset with her. She hated this guilt she felt when it came to him, but she couldn't tell him what Lucas had done to her. He already felt sorry for her because of her feelings for Dante and his relationship with Phoenix. She didn't need Sterling to pity her, too.

"So, how are we going to do this?" he asked.

TWENTY-EIGHT

PHOENIX WAS PACING Kenzie's office again. No matter how hard she'd tried to stop or how much Kenzie had threatened her, she couldn't keep her body still.

She needed fresh air.

She glanced over at Kenzie. But Phoenix needed to stay here and watch over the human.

Maybe Sawyer would switch with her earlier than scheduled. Kenzie was his mate after all.

"Okay, I give up," Kenzie said from her desk.

"Huh? What?"

"You're driving me nuts. Something is off with you today."

"I'm sorry," Phoenix said.

"Is everything okay with Dante?"

Phoenix smiled and stood still for the first time in the past hour. "Yes. Better than okay actually."

"Hmm. Well, you're obviously distracted. Your distraction is affecting my concentration, so we might as well get out of here early. Thank God I have a light day."

"Sorry," Phoenix said lamely again.

"Meh. We all have bad days. Let's go get something to eat since I worked through lunch."

Phoenix and Kenzie walked out of her office. They passed by several people with Phoenix barely paying attention. She was just concentrating on getting out of the hotel.

When they passed by one of the usual security guards, Kenzie said, "Whoa, that was weird."

"What was?"

"You didn't see it?"

"No. What?"

"Bill smiled at you and totally checked you out. Before today, I could have sworn he was a robot. That man doesn't do anything but stand against the wall and scowl."

"Oh."

Kenzie rolled her eyes. "'Oh,' she says."

Once outside, they went to Kenzie's favorite restaurant, which was a couple of blocks away.

They walked inside, and when they got away from people, Kenzie leaned forward. "Did you take a sexy pill today? Every guy on the way here was checking you out." She stepped back and scanned Phoenix. "Or maybe it's the new clothes I picked out for you." She snapped her fingers and fanned a hand in front of her face. "That's right. I'm that good."

"I think you're hallucinating," Phoenix said. "I didn't see anyone checking anyone out."

"Whatever. You're in denial." The two of them approached the counter to order. "What do you want?" Kenzie asked Phoenix.

"I'll just have a salad."

Kenzie turned to the cashier and ordered their food, and then she spun back to Phoenix. "Oh my God, you're dying, aren't you?"

Phoenix scowled at her. "No, I'm not dying. Why would you say that?"

"Because you are not a just-a-salad girl. You usually eat three times as much as I do. And I'm pregnant."

Phoenix shrugged. "I'm not hungry, okay?"

Kenzie looked worried. "I was joking about you dying, but seriously, are you sick?"

Phoenix did a mental scan of her body. "I don't feel sick. I'm a little warm, but it has been warmer outside lately."

Kenzie put the back of her hand on Phoenix's forehead, and Phoenix batted it away.

"You're warm, but you're not fever warm," Kenzie said as their food was brought to the counter.

The two of them went to a table, took a seat, and ate their food.

Kenzie looked at her phone as they were finishing up. "Say, we have an hour or so to kill before Sawyer's done for the day. Since I'm not going back to work, do you want to go to Naya's with me?"

Phoenix barely held in her groan. So far, she had managed to avoid going with Kenzie to see Naya and her babies. Phoenix hadn't seen them since the hospital. She'd even managed to get out of Naya and Vaughn's welcome-home party.

"Sure."

Kenzie raised her eyebrows. "That's a lukewarm response if I ever heard one."

What was she supposed to say to that?

Phoenix couldn't tell Kenzie that it depressed her to be around the new family. Even with Dante promising to take her during her heat, that didn't change how Phoenix felt because she wasn't pregnant yet. It lessened the blow, but the envy was still there. It was hard enough, being around Kenzie almost every day, but that was easier because she wasn't even showing. Naya and Vaughn's babies were going to be right there in front of Phoenix.

Not wanting Kenzie to feel bad or deny Kenzie from seeing her best friend, Phoenix said, "We'll go. Like you said, I'm off today."

Kenzie beamed. "Wait until you see them. They are *soooo* cute."

Phoenix could hardly wait.

Vaughn woke from a deep sleep, sweaty, disoriented, and horny as hell. He put an arm out and felt for Naya, but her side of the bed was cold. He sat up and looked around. The blinds were closed, and the alarm clock said it was still daylight.

Lately, Vaughn and Naya had been sleeping all wonky hours because of the babies. They didn't really have a sleep schedule anymore.

Vaughn got out of bed, adjusted himself in his boxers, and wiped the sweat off his bare chest. *Damn.* There was morning wood, and then there was morning wood. He didn't know why he was so hard.

He glanced in the special crib Naya had purchased to keep the babies beside her when she slept, but it was empty.

Vaughn frowned. She was supposed to wake him when both babies were up. He didn't want her feeling like she needed to do this alone.

Vaughn opened his bedroom door and was hit with a wave of lust. A shot of pain sliced through his groin.

"Fuck."

There was a female shifter in the house, and she was in the beginning stages of heat. No wonder he was so horny. He thought maybe it was because Naya wasn't cleared to have sex yet, so it had been a while since they had done the deed. But this heat thing was going to be a shitstorm if he didn't get whoever was downstairs out of his house.

Stupid biology didn't care that he was mated and in love with someone else. It would demand he try to impregnate the female in heat.

Vaughn stumbled down the stairs because his hard-on was starting to throb—and not in a good way.

He heard voices coming from the living room. Naya's and Kenzie's. But that didn't explain who the female shifter was.

"Naya," Vaughn called as he started coming around the corner.

"Shh. The babies and Phoenix are sleeping," his mate said as he entered the room.

Kenzie's eyes widened at his appearance. "Holy boner. Jeez, Vaughn, is that thing licensed?"

Vaughn ignored her. "Phoenix. Phoenix, get up."

Naya stood. "What's wrong?"

Vaughn had to catch himself when he doubled over.

Naya cried out and grabbed his arm. "Vaughn, you're scaring me."

He smiled at his mate. "Don't worry, baby; I'm not going to die. Phoenix is in heat. And we need to get her out of here." Another blast of pain went through him. "My body is just responding to hers. It wants me to...you know... mate with her."

Naya stood up straight. "Over my dead body."

Vaughn laughed through his pain. Man, he loved his mate.

He glanced past Naya to see Kenzie jump out of her chair, on full alert. She sat next to Phoenix and tried to shake her awake.

"Holy shit, this explains why all the guys on the street were checking her out." She paused, as if she realized how that sounded. "Not that Phoenix isn't pretty. I didn't mean it like that. It was just that every guy was practically panting as she walked by."

Vaughn waved her off. "We all know what you meant."

Kenzie shook Phoenix harder. "Phoenix, get your ass up."

No movement, except for when Kenzie moved her.

Vaughn stood up straight, took in a deep breath, and got out his future alpha voice. "Phoenix Kaplan, this is your future alpha talking. Get up. Right. Now."

Phoenix flew into a sitting position on the couch, hitting her head against Kenzie's.

"Motherfucker, that hurt," Kenzie said.

Phoenix held her head and looked around the room. Her eyes were slightly glazed. "Ugh, it's so hot in here," she said as she started to take off her shirt.

"No!" the three of them yelled.

"Come on, Phoenix, let's get you out of here," Kenzie

said as she helped the female up.

Phoenix struggled on her feet, so Naya went to help.

Kenzie looked over at Vaughn. "Can you call Dante and warn him that I'm coming?"

"Dante?" Naya asked, confused.

"Yes. I don't have time to explain. Just let him know I'm coming."

"But you're not supposed to be alone," Naya pointed out.

"Shit," Kenzie said.

Vaughn waved her toward the door. "I'll call Dante to tell him you're on your way. Then, I'll call Sawyer and tell him to meet you there."

"I'll help you to the door," Naya said. "I wish it were night, so I could go with you."

Vaughn grabbed his cell. "Yeah, I'm sorry, too, Kenzie. But the farther I stay away, the better."

Kenzie smiled at them. "No problem, guys. Thanks for your help."

Vaughn took his phone upstairs and made his phone calls. He had no idea what was going on with Phoenix and Dante, but Dante apparently was not surprised when Vaughn called him.

He was just hanging up the phone with Sawyer when Naya walked into their bedroom with the baby monitor since the twins were sleeping downstairs.

"Are they gone?" he asked.

"Yes," she said, putting the monitor on the dresser. "And the babies are still sleeping. The commotion didn't bother them in the least."

He breathed a sigh of relief. "Good."

Naya moved closer to him, and he held up his hand.

"Baby, you gotta stay away from me. It'll be a while before the effects from Phoenix wear off, and you know I've already been having a hard time with staying away from you as it is."

Naya smiled that secret smile that she reserved only for him and pushed her long dark hair off her shoulder as she walked closer. Vaughn backed up until he hit the bed and fell over.

"Don't you remember what last night was?"

Vaughn tried to think. He had worked last night, but that was all he could come up with. "No."

She wiggled her eyebrows at him. "I went to the doctor."

This had him sitting up with concern. "Are you okay?"

"I'm more than okay," she said as she stalked toward him and whipped off her shirt. When she reached the bed, she pushed her pants and underwear off with one quick movement.

Vaughn was pretty sure his penis was going to fall off if he didn't get some relief soon. If he hadn't already been hard from Phoenix's hormones, he would have been going full mast now.

God, his mate was beautiful.

Vaughn swallowed. "Does this mean, you've been cleared for sex?"

Naya pushed him back on his elbows and grabbed his boxers. "It does."

Vaughn dropped onto the bed. "Hallelujah," he rejoiced to the ceiling.

This news couldn't have come at a better time.

TWENTY-NINE

RIGHT AFTER SUNDOWN, Dante opened the front door to see Kenzie rushing to him. Phoenix was coming up the walkway at a slower pace behind the human. She looked beautiful as the setting sun hit her red-and-black hair, making the crimson color glow. He loved her new clothes and how she was no longer hiding her body.

"Here are her car keys," Kenzie said, holding them out for Dante.

"Hello to you, too."

Kenzie chuckled. "We don't have a lot of time. You'll see…or smell…or whatever it is you do."

Dante scratched his head. "Yeah, I don't know if vampires are affected the same way as shifters."

Kenzie snorted. "*Yeeaahhh*…the humans we passed today sure looked affected."

What humans?

He must have shown how he felt on his face because Kenzie added, "Don't worry; nobody hit on her. The permanent scowl on her face pretty much threatened every male within ten feet. She didn't even notice."

"Good to know."

"So, listen, I don't know how this works exactly, but she's been hot and antsy almost all day. On the way here, she started making noises. Not sure what that means. I don't know the stages, but I wanted to let you know."

"Thanks," Dante said just as Phoenix reached the door.

She pushed Kenzie out of her way and pressed her body right up against his. She wrapped her arms around his neck and rubbed herself against him. "Take me upstairs, Dante."

He could sense her pheromones, and to say his body was already ready to go was an understatement. Maybe vampires were affected after all. It was a good thing he had warned the other sentinels that they might want to leave for the night and move to another floor for a few days—far away from Dante's room.

He looked over Phoenix's shoulder to the human, who raised her brow.

"Well, I'll just be off then. Good luck."

Phoenix jumped up on Dante, and he had to catch her bottom as she wrapped her legs around his waist. Her keys dug into his hand from her weight.

"You drove her here. Do you need a ride?" Dante managed to ask even though all he wanted to do was hurry to his bedroom.

Kenzie looked behind her. "Nope, Sawyer's here."

Phoenix started sucking on Dante's neck, not concerned at all that they were in the open where anyone could see them or that Kenzie was standing right there.

"Bye," Kenzie said as she shut the door behind her.

Dante was already halfway to the stairs.

He raced to his room while Phoenix kept kissing him everywhere she could reach. He slammed his door shut and set her on the ground as he tossed her keys on his nightstand.

She started stripping off her clothes the second her feet hit the floor. Even her bra came off, and without her clothes, Dante could smell her arousal even more. Once her clothes were gone, she moved onto his shirt because it seemed he wasn't fast enough for her.

He'd never seen her act this sexually forward.

"Are you always like this when you're in your heat?"

"I don't know. I'm usually drugged up and out of it."

"What?"

"Yeah, unmated shifters take medicine, so we don't have to suffer through the effects."

"That's unfortunate."

She had already removed his shirt, and he helped her with his pants.

Once they were both naked, she grabbed his cock. "Fuck me, Dante."

He picked her up again, like he'd carried her upstairs. "Who could refuse that command?" he said to her as he lifted her and slid her down on his dick. "Fuck me," he said upon feeling how hot and wet she was.

"I'm trying," she said, rotating her hips on him.

Dante stepped toward his bed and laid her down. At that moment, her hormones flared. He'd thought they were strong before, but it was nothing compared to now.

She cried out, and it wasn't in pleasure.

He straightened and looked down at her. "What's wrong?"

"Oh my God, it burns."

"What does?" he asked, his voice practically shaking. He was starting to worry.

She put her hand above her pelvic bone. "Here," she said as she moaned in pain.

"Shit," he said as he started to pull out.

She clutched his back, digging her nails in. "No, you don't understand. I need you to come inside me. It's the only way it'll lessen."

It didn't seem right. Having sex with her while she was in pain.

She met his eyes. "I'm serious, Dante. I appreciate your concern. But I need you to fuck me right now. That's the only way you can help me. Otherwise, it'll only get worse. Listen to your body."

His head was tormented, but he took her advice. Normally, seeing a female, especially Phoenix, in pain would be enough to deflate him, but he was still hard as a rock. His body knew what she needed.

Dante began to cautiously move inside her.

She moaned again, but this time, it was partially from desire. "More."

He thrust harder inside her, studying her face as he moved. He continued and felt himself getting close. But, while she gave the impression she was enjoying herself, she wasn't close to an orgasm. Dante had really learned her body the last few weeks. He knew when she was ready to climax and when she wasn't.

He adjusted himself, so he could use his hand to help her along, but she held him close.

"No," she told him.

"No?"

She shook her head and thrust her hips up. "I just need you to come."

He hated to disappoint her.

As if she knew how he was feeling, she pulled his head down and kissed him. When she released him, she said, "Please, trust me."

He put his forehead on hers, needing to see her face as he did what she'd asked. He increased his pace and pumped into her. He concentrated on how amazing she felt rather than his worry for her. He loved her pussy, and that was the final thought he had before he came, emptying his seed inside her.

His release seemed to trigger hers, and Phoenix came and came until she made him come again. The whole thing lasted several minutes, and it amazed Dante.

After his second orgasm, her body seemed to calm a little.

He withdrew from her and lay down next to her. "Wow. You're right."

She turned on her side and snuggled into him. "About what?"

"Everything."

She chuckled. "Just Mother Nature trying to ensure the next generation gets made."

He slid an arm underneath her neck and pulled her onto his chest. "About that? You do realize, if we make a baby, it'll only be half-shifter. The other half will be vampire."

He felt her smile against his chest where she turned her head and kissed him. "I know. And I'm okay with that. I want your baby, Dante." She yawned. "I need to sleep. You should, too. We have a lot of this ahead of us."

"Yeah," he said, agreeing with her.

But his mind was still reeling on her-wanting-his-baby statement. He'd thought she just wanted *a* baby. He hadn't realized that she wanted *his* baby.

He kissed her forehead to tell her that he wanted the same thing when her heavy breathing told him she was out.

Dante smiled and slowly drew his body from next to hers. They were lying sideways on his king-size bed, and if she was going to sleep, he wanted her to be more comfortable. He pulled his comforter and sheets down and picked her up and moved her. She was so out of it that she didn't even notice.

Dante got into bed beside her and pulled her close once again. He had already gotten a full day's sleep, but he didn't want to leave her side. He didn't know when she would need him again. He pulled out a book to read while he waited.

It turned out to be sooner than he'd thought.

Over the next ten hours, she needed him—repeatedly. He hadn't known that he could get it up and have sex so many times in a row, but each time her heat flared, his body would respond. He had been worried that, since he wasn't a shifter, it wouldn't affect him the same, but thankfully, it did. He did not want to disappoint Phoenix.

When they weren't having sex, Dante had managed to keep them fed, hydrated, and rested. Thankfully, he didn't need blood anytime soon, and he had kept his fangs away from Phoenix. He figured Phoenix would probably need all the blood she had in her body to conceive.

Dante had fallen asleep after their last sex session but now woke again with a hard-on and Phoenix's body heat beside him. She groaned in her sleep, and he knew she needed him again.

He brushed his lips across hers as she opened her eyes.

She smiled up at him and spread her legs.

Dante settled between them and pushed inside her. She was so swollen now from all their lovemaking that he was afraid he would hurt her, but she cried out in pleasure. He couldn't believe they would be doing this for several days.

Dante rolled so that Phoenix was on top. "Ride me, Red."

Phoenix smiled coyly at him and sat up on his hips. She moved her body without any hesitation. One thing he could say about her heat was that all her reservations seemed to be pushed aside.

But, even with that, she surprised him when she grabbed his hands and placed them on her breasts. Her beautiful, full breasts that he'd only seen one other time in a completely nonsexual way.

She threw her head back, holding her palms over the backs of his hands as he caressed her breasts, and rode him. She had a stunning look of pure bliss on her face, and Dante felt like a king because he was the one who'd put it there.

Suddenly, she lifted her head and looked down at him. "I want your blood," she said seriously.

Dante tilted his head and exposed his neck. "Whatever

you need, it's yours." He would give her practically anything.

He thought she would use her claws to cut him and drink his blood from that wound, but she leaned over, opened her mouth, and bit him. It was a combination of pleasure and pain as she sank her teeth into his shoulder. It wasn't the best way to get a lot of blood at once, but she didn't seem to care as she sucked on him while she burrowed her teeth in further. He was going to have one hell of a mark, but he didn't care.

He came with a roar and poured himself inside her. Once again, his climax initiated hers, and she bucked her hips as she orgasmed. She released his neck as she shook over him. Like many times before, her body continued to contract around him until he came again.

She collapsed on him and buried her nose in his neck over the bite that she had given him. Dante rubbed her back as she settled on his body. He was still inside her but didn't bother to pull out.

"What time is it?" she asked after a few minutes.

Dante looked over at the clock. "Almost six thirty in the morning. Why?"

"I need to check in," she murmured into his neck, her voice sleepy again.

"I think Vaughn probably took care of that."

She didn't answer.

"Phoenix?"

A soft snore slipped past her lips. She'd already fallen asleep.

THIRTY

PHOENIX WOKE UP, feeling refreshed, alive, and needing to use the bathroom. She rolled away from Dante and stretched like one did after a long sleep.

How long have I been out? It felt like a long time. Yet, as she sat up, she noticed that her body felt almost back to normal.

That's strange. She didn't understand how she could feel so rested without needing to have sex again.

She looked at Dante's alarm clock. It read ten to seven. She'd only been sleeping for twenty minutes?

Phoenix grabbed her phone out of her jeans on the floor and turned on the display. Her battery was almost dead, and when the time showed up on her screen, she felt her heart stop.

Her phone said it was *6:52 p.m.*

P.M.

Six. Fifty-two. P.M.

She'd been sleeping for over twelve hours.

She scrambled from the bed and went into the bathroom. She hadn't even woken because of her heat. She'd woken because her bladder was full. As she used the facilities, she tried not to panic, but it was like a sense of doom was settling over her.

She'd only been in heat for about twelve hours. She'd only been having sex for about ten. This was not right. She should be in heat for days.

She washed her hands and looked up into the mirror, willing her heat to rise again. Not even a spark. Instead, her appearance taunted her. She was naked, which didn't bother her. It was her obviously flat stomach that made her heart sink.

Not only was her heat over, but her womb also hadn't swelled from her body taking all it could from Dante to try to get pregnant.

Phoenix felt like she couldn't breathe, and she walked backward until she hit the wall. Not knowing what to do, she sank down until she hit the floor. Once again, her body had betrayed her.

Even though it was more difficult for shifters to get pregnant than humans, most eventually did. She'd known that her chances of getting pregnant during her first attempt were on the low side, but she hadn't even finished her heat. Her body hadn't even made it through a whole day without quitting.

Phoenix put her head in her hands and cried.

She didn't know what she'd done so wrong. She didn't think she was asking too much to be a mother.

She didn't know how long she sat there, curled against the wall, but she smelled him before she felt him.

Dante put his hand on her upper back. "Phoenix, what's wrong?"

She shook her head as she rested it against her crossed arms that lay over her bent knees. She didn't want to tell him. She was embarrassed, and it was as if saying it out loud would make it more real.

She heard Dante shift his weight as he sat down beside her. "Red, you're scaring me."

Phoenix lifted her head and let it fall back against the wall, not caring if she hurt herself. She didn't look at him as she said, "It's over, Dante."

Out of the corner of her eye, she saw him turn toward her. "What do you mean?"

"My heat. It's over."

"How is that possible? I thought it lasted longer."

"I don't know, okay!" she yelled.

Dante flinched, and she immediately felt guilty. It wasn't his fault that her body was a disappointment.

She stood and glanced down toward him but not at him. "It's over. I have to go," she said as she marched out of the bathroom.

She heard Dante get up and follow her.

She grabbed her clothes and began yanking them on.

Dante grabbed her hand, forcing her to look at him. "Phoenix, you don't need to leave."

She scanned his body, ignoring the bite mark on his shoulder and noting his now-flaccid penis. It was like a slap in the face. She knew Dante had no control over her heat and his reaction or non-reaction to her hormones, but seeing him soft like that was another way the universe was telling her that it was over and done with.

She couldn't be around him. She couldn't be around anyone. She needed to get out of there.

She shook her hand free. "Yes, I do. I need to go."

She quickly finished dressing while Dante picked up his clothes and followed suit. She couldn't let him stop her or follow her.

She seized her car keys from his bedside table and took off down the stairs. Dante wasn't far behind, but she had one thing in her favor that evening.

She stepped outside into the setting sun, knowing Dante couldn't follow her. Racing for her car, she heard Dante yell her name as she hit her key fob and hurried into her vehicle.

She put it in drive and hit the gas. She drove home and prayed no one would be there for a little while at least.

When she arrived, several cars were in the driveway, but thankfully, no one was in the bunkhouse. Phoenix grabbed some workout clothes and went to the bathroom to turn on the shower. It might seem weird to bathe before she headed downstairs to work off some of her feelings, but she needed to be clean.

She needed to wash Dante's scent from her body and his seed from between her legs. She didn't need either as a reminder.

Once she was done scrubbing her body until it was raw, Phoenix grabbed her iPod, put in her earbuds, selected her hard rock playlist, and cranked her music as Tool filled the silence. She headed for the basement and got on the tread-mill, cranking the speed up and hitting Start.

Exercising helped her focus a little. So, she'd been dealt a horrible blow. She really wasn't any worse off than she had been a month ago. Now, she realized the level of hope she'd had that her future would change, but that was neither here nor there. She had to face the fact—like really and truly face it—that she would most likely never have children.

It seemed so much more real now than it had before, but that was probably only because she hadn't realized how much hope she'd had stored away until it was taken away from her.

But she could get over this. She would have to get over this. Life was a fickle bitch, but there was nothing she could do about it.

After the treadmill, Phoenix lifted weights and then did some yoga. She knew she was trying to work herself into exhaustion, so she could fall into a dreamless sleep and forget all about her failed heat. It was going to be pretty hard to do when she'd just slept for twelve fricking hours.

And, now, she was getting upset all over again.

Just as she used the bottom of her shirt to wipe the sweat from her forehead, there was a tap on her shoulder, and Phoenix jumped. She pulled out her earbuds and pivoted to see Tegan standing there.

"Sorry. I called your name, but you didn't hear me."

Seether blasted from Phoenix's earbuds as they hung from her hand. "Yeah, I had my music loud. What'd ya need?" Hopefully, something fast because she still didn't feel like talking to anyone.

Tegan hesitated, and Phoenix guessed that she had picked up on her volatile mood.

"Um...Dante's here."

Phoenix shook her head. *No way.* "Tell him I'm not here."

"I already did because I didn't realize you were home at

first, but he saw your car. He's upstairs, and he refuses to leave until you come back."

Phoenix was suddenly mad at Dante for coming there, and it felt good to have someone to turn her frustrations on. She turned off her iPod and tossed it on the workout bench before pounding up the stairs.

She marched toward Dante, who was sitting and talking to Saxon.

When he spotted her, he stood and told Saxon, "Excuse me," before striding toward her. He looked determined and not the least bit intimidated by her anger.

Dante gripped her hand, not bothering to say anything to her, and dragged her outside. He walked her away from the house before he dropped her upper limb and faced her. "What the fuck is up with you leaving like that?"

"What do you mean? I told you, it's over. My heat is gone."

"Yeah, but we're not over."

Phoenix didn't say anything, just stared at Dante, not letting any emotion cross her face. She couldn't let him know how much it hurt to be with him now. It would be a stupid reminder of everything she couldn't have.

Dante huffed. "Oh, I see. When you said it was over, you meant, more than just your heat. You meant us, too."

Phoenix shrugged, as if it were no big deal.

Dante dropped his arms. "So, now that you didn't get pregnant, you're going to build that big, bad wall you had around yourself back up, huh?"

"You don't know what you're talking about."

"Oh, I don't, do I? I know I've been trying to rip it down for a while now, and I thought I had succeeded. You know, you don't have to do this alone, Phoenix. I'm here for you. We can try again in six months."

She snorted. *Yeah, right.* She was not going to go through this again. "I don't think so."

Dante laughed, but she knew he didn't think the situation was funny. "So, you're just going to give up?"

Phoenix raised her chin. "It's not giving up. It's facing reality."

Dante shook his head. "You know, I'm disappointed in you, Phoenix. I thought you were stronger than this."

She growled at him. "I am strong, you asshole." That was why she was doing what she was doing.

"You're not acting like it, Red."

"Don't call me that." She was saying things to hurt him, and she felt bad. She really did.

But, if she gave Dante any sign that she cared, he would pounce on it.

Dante just shook his head again, unfazed by her bitchiness. "I see how it is. I'll tell you what. I'm going to give you some time to deal with what happened today. I understand you're hurt and devastated and that now is not the time to try to reason with you. But know this; I will be back."

She crossed her arms across her chest and snorted. "Is that a threat?"

Dante stepped closer to her, wrapped an arm around her waist, and pulled her close. He pushed his lips against hers. It was a closed-mouthed kiss but was still full of passion. "No, Red, it's a promise," he said as he let her go. He turned his back to her and went to his SUV. He climbed in and drove away without looking back at Phoenix once.

She knew this because she watched him the whole time.

Furious with everything, she ripped off her clothes right there for anyone to see and shifted into her cat. Since working out hadn't helped, she ran toward the woods, hoping to hide.

Hide from what exactly, she didn't know. Her human side, Dante, reality, or the emptiness that had settled in her heart. Maybe all of it. It was certainly easier that way.

THIRTY-ONE

LEXINE SAT at the corner of the kitchen island, relaxing with her feet up, eating strawberries, and watching Sterling. He sat at the kitchen table, reading over some document, in a white T-shirt, jeans, and bare feet.

When had bare feet become so sexy? How had Lexine lived with someone for years and never realized how gorgeous the man and his feet were?

She shoved a strawberry in her mouth and wondered if Sterling felt the same thing about her. Did he even know she was looking at him?

"Hey, Lexine. Hey, Sterling," Lennox said from behind her.

She looked over her shoulder and watched her brother walk into the room. "Hey," she said back.

"Hey," Sterling said without looking up from his paperwork.

Her brother went to the fridge, opened it, and shut the door. "Where are my strawberries?" he said as he turned around.

Lexine had just taken another bite and tried to swallow it before he noticed. It wasn't completely chewed and hurt a little going down. She tried to hide her bowl and fork under the counter, but Lennox saw her.

"You little snot," he said as he tried to swipe her food.

Lexine jerked away, laughing, until she moved too far and winced as she pulled the muscles of her aching vajayjay. At the same time, she dropped several pieces of fruit on her lap.

Lennox frowned. "What's wrong?"

Lexine reached down to put her food back in the bowl as she said, "Nothing. I'm just sore." She whipped her head up. "From working out," she quickly added.

Sterling didn't lift his head, but she saw the cocky smirk on his face.

Figures. It was his fault she was like this.

Sterling hadn't bothered to leave when Phoenix was in heat. Instead, he'd tied Lexine to his bed and fucked her all night. At the time, she'd loved it. Loved it so much she hadn't thought about Dante and the cat-shifter all night, but now, her fricking vagina was practically on fire. She didn't know how shifters did the whole heat thing. She'd only experienced it for a night. Rumor had it, shifters were in heat for days.

Lennox was still scowling at her, so she put the bowl on the counter.

"Grab a fork. I'll share."

"No, I'll share because they were mine in the first place."

"Ah, but I'm the one who cleaned and cut them up."

Her brother didn't respond, but he got his fork and didn't try to take the strawberries away from her.

"Sterling, you're not saying much, man," Lennox said.

Sterling looked up for the first time. "Sorry. Just looking over some stuff."

"That's a lot less fun than the night before."

"What do you mean?" Lexine asked.

"Rumor has it, Dante wasn't the only one getting it on all night."

"Let it go," Sterling said as he looked back down, dismissing the conversation.

Her brother wasn't going to be deterred. "I don't think so. Apparently, the female was a real screamer."

Lexine willed her body not to show any reaction, but her face began to heat despite her restraint. "Oh, yeah?"

"Yeah, Morgan said she heard them all night." Lennox furrowed his brows. "I'm surprised you didn't hear them. You didn't go out last night, did you?"

Stick as close to the truth as possible. "No, I was here, but I didn't hear anything." It was sort of accurate. She hadn't known she was a screamer and hadn't heard herself.

"What was it like?" Lennox prodded.

Sterling sighed and set the papers down, obviously seeing that her brother wasn't going to go away. "Like right after you go through conversion times ten, okay?"

"Holy shit," Lennox said. "I was a damn hornball after my conversion. No wonder your lady friend was screaming."

Sterling's mouth was set in a grim line. He obviously didn't like her brother talking about her like that even though he had no idea it was her.

Lennox didn't seem to realize that Sterling was getting pissed. "Wow."

"What's wow?" Hunter said as he joined them in the kitchen.

"Lennox," Sterling warned.

But Lennox just talked right over him, "Were you here last night? Apparently, Sterling here got it on with some girl who was of the vocal variety. Did you hear them?"

Hunter shook his head. "No, but I wasn't here all night."

"Did you have to go out and find a piece?"

"What?" Hunter said at the same time Lexine said, "Lennox, come on, a little tact. We're not pieces of ass."

In his true fashion, Lennox ignored her and answered Hunter's question, "Dante's female shifter. She was in heat. Didn't you feel the effects of it like Sterling did? He said he'd never been so horny in his life."

Sterling held up a finger. "That isn't what I said exactly."

Lennox waved him off. "It's what you meant," her brother said as he turned back to Hunter, who was frowning. "So, is that what it was like for you?"

Hunter looked uncomfortable. "Uh…"

"Lennox, leave him alone," Lexine said.

Her brother rolled his eyes. "I just want to know what it's like. Can't blame a guy."

"Um, yes, I can," she retorted.

Giving her the finger, Lennox walked over to Sterling and nudged his shoulder with his hand. "Who is she? Maybe you'd like to share, or does she have friends?"

Lexine made a gagging noise. "Gross," she whispered under her breath.

Sterling looked up at Lennox. "I said, let it go. She's none of your business, and I'm not sharing her with *anyone*."

Lexine got a little tingle inside her belly, but that only lasted for a second before Lennox leaned over and read Sterling's paper.

"Transfer papers? To California?" Lennox straightened. "What the hell, man? Are you leaving us?"

The little tingle inside Lexine's belly turned to a rock.

Hunter looked surprised. "You're moving? But it won't be the same. The king and queen are here."

Sterling glanced at her but then quickly turned his eyes back to her brother and Hunter. "There are rogue vampires everywhere that need policing. Besides, I'm just exploring my options. Nothing is definite yet."

She didn't understand why he would do this.

The garage door opened, and Dante walked into the kitchen. Everyone turned to look at him, forgetting about Sterling's situation for the moment. He looked distraught and stressed out, but Lexine found that she didn't care.

That wasn't right. It wasn't that she didn't care; she did. She just cared like a friend would, but she didn't care like she would have a month ago.

Sterling stood. "You okay, boss?" His voice was full of concern.

And, with everything else, why was it that all she could think about was how Sterling had ordered her around in bed last night? He had definitely been in charge there, but you wouldn't know it now by his submission to Dante.

Dante went over to the liquor cabinet, grabbed a drink, and leaned back against the counter. "Honestly, I don't know." Dante rarely drank, always saying he should be a good example.

Lennox tilted his head. "Wait a minute. What were you doing out? I thought that whole heat thing lasted for days."

Dante took a sip of his drink. "It's supposed to. Apparently, something happened, and it only lasted about half a day."

"Ooh, is your female okay?" Lennox asked.

Dante took another drink. "Nope. And I really don't think she's my female."

"What happened?" Hunter asked.

Dante didn't answer. He just took one last swig of his drink, downing it all. He put his glass in the dishwasher and turned back to them. "What are all of you doing here? Shouldn't you be working?"

Lexine and Sterling were supposed to be out in the field, but there didn't seem to be a point when they had a plan to go after Lucas in a few days. But they couldn't tell Dante that.

"Yeah, Sterling and I were just getting ready to go."

"What about you guys?" Dante asked Hunter and her brother.

"It's my night off," Hunter said. He cleared his throat. "I was going to go out, but if you need me—"

Dante waved him off. "No, go. Have fun. Someone should."

"I was going to head out in a few," Lennox said. "I have to meet up with Reid." He raised his brow. "Do you want to come with? Reid's cool."

Reid was the tech guy for the cat-shifter sentinels.

"No, thanks. I should probably catch up on paperwork."

He rubbed the back of his neck. "Listen, I'm sorry I haven't been around much lately. I know I've been preoccupied, and you haven't seen me much when I'm not working. I apologize."

"That's okay, Dante," Lexine said. "We understand."

Everyone but Dante stared at her like she'd grown horns.

"What? Was I lying?"

Hunter looked away first. "No, Dante, Lexine is right. We understand, and if we really need you, we know you'd be there."

Dante headed to the hallway and slapped Hunter on the back. "Thanks."

Once their leader was gone, silence filled the room.

"Well, I'd better go," Hunter said. "Later."

"Later," the three of them answered.

Lexine stood slowly so as to take care of her tender bits. "Listen, I have to go talk to Dante for a minute. I'll be right back."

"Okay," her brother said. "I'll probably be gone when you get back. I'll see you in the morning."

"Okay," she said.

Then, she glanced over at Sterling. His mouth was set in a hard line again.

"I'll be back," she told him.

She went down the hall to Dante's office and knocked on the door.

"Come in."

Several minutes later, she left the office and walked back to the kitchen. Sterling had put on his boots and was sitting with his transfer papers, but this time, he had a pen in his hand. He wasn't writing, but it wasn't a good sign.

He looked up when she entered.

"Do you want to get out of here?" she asked.

Sterling stood and glared at her. "Everything okay?"

She didn't know what he meant. "Yeah."

Sterling stared at her, as if he thought she was going to say more, but she didn't know what else to say.

He nodded, as if he'd given up on something. "All right, let's go then."

"After you," she said.

Sterling headed for the garage. As soon as the door opened and Sterling was out of eyesight, she grabbed his paperwork and threw it in the garbage.

THIRTY-TWO

HUNTER PARKED in the hotel lot and walked inside to the front desk. After registering and getting his key, he meandered his way over to the bar. He looked around and saw it wasn't busy, and Quentin wasn't there yet. He took a seat at the bar and ordered a drink.

He'd taken the first swallow when he felt Quentin's warm hand on his back. He smiled as he turned to look at the shifter. There was a moment when he thought Quentin might kiss him but instead took a seat next to him. Hunter was relieved and then ashamed for his relief. He knew he shouldn't care what others thought, and he mostly didn't. He just couldn't get past worrying about what might happen if the Vampire Council found out.

He tried telling himself that he shouldn't have to lie about who he was for the sake of keeping his place in their society, but he sadly was not there yet. There was a large chance the Council wouldn't do anything anyway, and he should just let it go, but there was that nagging doubt in the back of his mind that wouldn't shut up.

"How are you?" Quentin asked.

Despite his reservations, Hunter couldn't help but feel almost giddy inside about getting to spend the night with Quentin. "Good, now that you're here. And you?"

Quentin smiled. "Same."

The bartender approached them, and Quentin looked at Hunter.

Hunter shook his head. "You can help me finish mine."

Quentin turned back to the bartender. "Nothing for me. Thanks."

The two of them took turns sipping on Hunter's drink. They made small talk and tried to act relaxed, but anyone around them had to feel their excitement and anticipation.

Hunter knew he was dying to get up to the hotel room he'd reserved, and he was pretty sure Quentin felt the same way. They hadn't done anything intimate together since that night in the park. It seemed rather ridiculous that two grown males couldn't find quality time to be alone together, but when both of them lived and worked in large groups, it made things harder than it should have been.

They'd had moments alone, but Quentin had insisted they were going to take their time being together and take things slower. He'd said there would be no more rushed blow jobs in an empty park while they were supposed to be working.

Instead, Hunter had made do with rushed self-hand jobs while he pictured the first moment Quentin had put him in his mouth.

After they finished the drink, they slowly got up from the bar and walked casually to the elevator. As casually as possible when it felt like they both wanted to bolt through the lobby and up the stairs, taking them two at a time.

The elevator doors opened, and a mother and daughter exited before Hunter and Quentin got on. Hunter thought they'd have the elevator to themselves, but a man in a suit got on after them while he talked on his phone. He immediately turned his back to them and went into the corner, too busy with his conversation to even nod hello.

Quentin smiled at Hunter when he met his eyes. The shifter put the back of his hand against his and rubbed his index finger along Hunter's. It was such a minor intimacy, but he was growing hard, and his jeans began to tent out.

Quentin smirked as Hunter adjusted himself. He looked over and saw that Quentin also had an erection. Despite being able to smell their arousal with his advanced sense of smell, it was nice to be able to see physical proof, too.

The elevator opened to their floor, and the pair of them went to the room. Hunter slid the key in the slot and felt like it took forever to turn green. He turned the handle, and the second the door was open, Quentin pushed him inside and against the wall and kissed him.

Hunter opened his mouth to Quentin's tongue, wanting to devour the wolf. He wanted things he had never felt with another being before. Hunter opened Quentin's pants and shoved his hand in, wanting to feel the evidence of Quentin's desire for Hunter, and he noted Quentin's lack of underwear.

Hunter enveloped Quentin's cock in his hand and made a fist around him. Hunter swallowed Quentin's groan and squeezed again. He could die happy right now, knowing he made this male feel this way.

Although he really hoped he lived for a long time because they had a lot more exploring to do.

Hunter pushed Quentin just enough to get the shifter's feet moving. Hunter then maneuvered them over to the single king-size bed in the room. He broke the kiss and pushed back on Quentin until he sat on the bed.

Hunter got on after him and straddled him, wanting to be close. In the past, when he'd been with females, Hunter had been the one straddled, and his mind played a trick on him for a second, like he'd somehow done a role-reversal thing. Hunter respected females, but he didn't want to be one. Hunter had to remind himself that there was no male or female situation in this room. It was two people who wanted to be together, and that was all that mattered.

Hunter kissed the side of Quentin's mouth and worked his way down the wolf's neck. Quentin's short beard was also something Hunter had to get used to. He was used to soft, flowery skin. But Quentin was rough and woodsy. Masculine.

Hunter wouldn't have traded it for the world. It was such a turn-on.

He hit the collar of Quentin's shirt, so he sat back enough to drag the shirt up and off the male, and his eyes went to Quentin's now-bare neck.

His skin was stunning. Hunter had the complexion of a pasty-white, well, vampire, while Quentin's was a beautiful golden brown. Hunter slowly brought his hands to Quentin's neck and caressed him.

"What are you thinking? You have the most serious expression on your face," Quentin said.

Hunter looked into his lover's eyes. "I was thinking of

how gorgeous you are and that I'm afraid, if I kiss you again, I won't be able to resist tasting you." Hunter subconsciously licked a fang.

"Open your mouth."

Hunter did as he had been asked.

Quentin used his thumb to feel along Hunter's fangs. "They're so sharp."

He then pressed his thumb hard against one fang. Hunter felt the pressure, and then the taste of Quentin's blood dripped onto his tongue.

"Suck," Quentin said.

Hunter did, his eyes practically rolling back in his head. He had never tasted anything as good as Quentin. He didn't know if it was because he was a shifter or if it was because he was male, but at the moment, the *why* didn't matter.

Quentin pushed his cut against Hunter's tongue and then dragged his thumb from Hunter's mouth. "That's enough for now." Quentin put a hand on Hunter's hips. "You can put yourself inside me," the wolf used his other hand to finger Hunter's fangs, "when I can put myself inside you," Quentin said as he thrust his erection against Hunter's ass.

Hunter kissed Quentin again, and the two of them fell back against the bed.

"You are such a tease," Hunter told him.

Quentin smiled. "I'd like to think of it as foreplay."

"You're very good. You should write a book."

"I can see it now. *How to Turn Your Vampire Lover On.* National best-seller."

Hunter laughed and sat up. He smiled at Quentin and

moved down his body until he was at Quentin's feet. He grabbed the wolf's pants and pulled them down his legs.

Quentin stopped him before he got to his knees. "I want you naked, too."

Hunter grinned at Quentin. "Okay, but I'm warning you. I'm not nearly as sexy as you."

Quentin smiled, but he growled at Hunter. "I'll be the judge of that."

Hunter stepped back and stripped off his clothes, putting on a show. His skin might not be as gorgeous as Quentin's, but Hunter knew he had a nice body. He was in fighting form for his role as a Guardian, and he took pride in his physique.

Quentin growled again—this time, with hunger in his eyes. "Get your ass over here."

Hunter's dick bobbed as he stepped closer to Quentin, and once again, he pulled on the shifter's pants. This time, Quentin didn't stop him.

Hunter knelt in front of the bed and grasped Quentin behind the knees, pulling his cock closer. Hunter took Quentin's hard-on in his hand and studied it. Quentin was slightly larger than him. He would be intimidated, except he already knew his own dick was big. Quentin was just bigger.

Hunter leaned forward and kissed the tip, slightly sucking it into his mouth. Almost immediately, he tasted Quentin's pre-cum. This was definitely a first. Hunter had had no idea what to expect and was surprised at how salty Quentin tasted.

Quentin groaned and thrust his hips up.

Hunter looked at Quentin, who had his eyes closed. "I

just want to warn you; I've never done this before, so…you know…I might not be any good."

Quentin blinked at Hunter, his eyes turning wolf, and said, "If you keep doing what you're doing, I'll be in heaven. But it really doesn't matter, baby. Just knowing that I'm the first guy you've blown and that you want to do this has already made my night."

And those words made Hunter's night. He leaned forward and took Quentin in his mouth. He had assumed that having a dick in his mouth would be awkward and uncomfortable, but Hunter didn't feel that way in the slightest.

He thought about what he liked when getting head and tried to do the same to Quentin. He sucked on him, creating friction that had Quentin groaning and clutching his hair. He alternated this with kisses that he placed on each side of his penis. The hardest thing was he really wanted to take Quentin all the way down, but his gag reflex needed some work. Quentin didn't seem to mind though. Everything Hunter did had him reacting in one way or another.

One thing he noticed was that, whether or not he was enjoying going down on Quentin, his jaw was no longer interested because it was getting sore. Also, fangs were a bitch, as he tried to avoid scraping Quentin's cock, much less with the rest of his teeth. The next time some male complained about not getting head from his female, Hunter was going to smack him. BJs were a lot of work.

Hunter could tell Quentin was getting close, and he could feel his own arousal spiking. He really wanted to make this orgasm good for the shifter. Quentin was driving his hips up in small thrusts, as if he couldn't control himself, and Hunter had to fight not to smile and to keep doing what he was doing.

Quentin said something above him, but Hunter was unable to make out the words. He continued to suck Quentin in as far as he could take him.

Quentin spoke again, "Fuck, I'm going to come. If you want to back away, you'd better do so now."

The sun beating down directly on his head wouldn't be enough to drag Hunter away.

Hunter had been warned about the knot that would form in the wolf's penis. He knew his mouth couldn't handle that much girth, so he moved his lips to the tip and sucked.

Quentin arched up one last time and poured himself into Hunter's mouth. He couldn't quite swallow fast enough, and he felt some of Quentin's seed escape his mouth. The wolf was briny and woodsy, like his scent, and Hunter loved tasting him.

THIRTY-THREE

PHOENIX STOOD in front of the Guardians' compound again, there to feed Dante, like she had a little less than a month ago. But so much had changed since then.

She rubbed her thumb over the key Dante had given her, staring at it. It didn't seem right to use it to go in. She and Dante hadn't talked much since her failed heat, and it seemed like a violation for her to walk into his home, unannounced.

The truth was, she was early to feed Dante. It hadn't been a month yet, but she was afraid that Dante would feed from someone else if she didn't get there first.

It probably made her sound like a crazy person since she'd been blowing Dante off for the last week. After all, why would she want to feed him if she was evading him? But she just couldn't stomach the image of him feeding from another female. And, now that she'd had these encounters every month, it had satisfied her cat's need for skin-to-skin contact that all shifters required. She didn't want that with anyone else.

And what about picturing him having sex with another female, Phoenix? her stupid brain taunted.

That was just something she was going to have to not think about.

Phoenix pocketed the key and raised her hand to knock on the door.

☾

Dante smelled her before she even rapped her knuckles on his bedroom door. The scent of sunshine and female cat-shifter tickled his nose and hurt his heart.

He threw his book on the bed as he stood and said, "Come in."

The door opened, and the sight of Phoenix walking into his room caused him to close his eyes and hold his breath for a second. She'd been all but avoiding him since he confronted her a week ago after her heat. He'd thought that she just needed time, but he could see now that the old Phoenix was back. He had tried to prepare himself to see her again, but he realized it was going to be harder than he'd thought.

Dante opened his eyes, met Phoenix's eyes, and sighed. "Why are you here, Phoenix?"

☾

Phoenix thought that was obvious. "I came here to feed you."

"It's not time for me to feed yet." Dante's eyes were hard.

She had never seen him like this. At least, not toward her.

She lifted her chin, trying to not let his mood affect her. "I know I'm early, but I figured, why not?"

He lifted an eyebrow, clearly not believing her bullshit.

"So, that's it? You came here to feed me, and then you're going to go back home and hide?"

She scowled. "I'm not hiding."

"You're not, huh? Okay then, tell me what happened to you when you were younger, Phoenix. Why don't you like your breasts being touched? Why don't you even like taking off your shirt?"

It took all of Phoenix's strength not to flinch at his words.

Dante shook his head in disappointment. "I can feel your panic. It's so thick."

What did he mean by feel?

She didn't get to ask because he continued on, "I thought I'd made it clear that you could trust me. That I was here for you. That I would do anything for you. But, no, one failed pregnancy attempt, and you have raised that wall you erected around you back up. I spent a lot of energy trying to tear it down, and now, I think it's higher than it was before. But then it was never truly down, was it? I just found a small hole in it and wiggled my way in. But, now that I can't give you what you want, you've pushed me out and sealed that hole with reinforced steel. For one of the bravest people I know, you sure are a coward, Phoenix."

She clenched her fists. "What the fuck do you know about it?"

Dante threw his hands up in frustration. "Nothing.

Because you won't tell me. That's what I'm trying to get across to you."

She hated being called a coward, but she just couldn't go back to the way things had been before. She couldn't handle the hurt and disappointment, which had only doubled when she started bleeding—the shifter equivalent of a period—a few days ago. It had been light, but it was still another blow she hadn't needed.

"Well, maybe I'm not as strong as you. I can't get my hopes up, only to have them thrown in my face."

Dante closed his eyes and sighed. When he opened them, he looked at her. "You just don't get it. Don't you think I'm disappointed, too? I know this was all your idea, but I wouldn't have gone along with it if I hadn't wanted a child with you. I'm sad, too, that you didn't get pregnant."

Phoenix was shocked.

"I see that you didn't think of how I might feel. You only thought about yourself. I never took you for selfish, Phoenix. What you don't realize is that we could comfort each other. We could be in this together. But you have your heart so hidden, I don't know if you even know how to find it."

"That's not fair," she said in a low voice.

"Are you fucking kidding me?" Dante roared. "What's not fair is you giving yourself to me, only to take you away."

She took a step back. "I didn't do that."

"Oh. So, you used me then. Everything we did together was fake on your part? Great. You've succeeded in making me feel worse."

She held on to the one thing she could give him. "But I want to feed you, Dante. No one is making me. I want to do that for you."

Dante's brown eyes filled with anguish, and Phoenix shook her head.

No. Please.

It was as if all the anger had left his body, and he had given up. "Phoenix, I can't feed from you any longer."

She knew it wasn't what he wanted. She didn't understand why they couldn't at least have that together. "Why?"

Dante collapsed back to sit on his bed and put his head in his hands. "Because I can't do it anymore. I can't…I just can't do it anymore, okay?"

"But…"

Dante dropped his arms to his thighs and looked at her. "I'm not saying, we'll never see each other. We have to work together sometimes, and we'll see each other at social functions. I would like to think we are friends. But I can't go back to the way things were. It's over."

Another female might have curled up in a ball and cried but not Phoenix. She was getting pissed. She didn't understand why they couldn't have the feeding thing. It had worked for them before.

"I don't get it, Dante. *I can't* isn't a reason. We had a good system down. There is no reason we can't do that again."

"No."

"Just no?"

"Yep. No."

"Why? I came here to be honest with you. I think you can do the same for me. You talk about hiding. Who's hiding now?"

Dante jumped up from the bed and charged toward her.

☾

Furious, Dante got in Phoenix's face. "Why? You want honesty?" he yelled.

Phoenix narrowed her eyes. "Yes."

"Because I can't just pretend like nothing happened," he roared. "When my fangs are inside you, *I* want to be inside you. I know what it feels like to come inside you. I know what it's like to feel you come so hard around me. I want you so fucking bad. I want you under me, your legs wrapped around my waist, while I'm pumping inside you. I want to hear you scream as I feel you come around my cock again and again."

He took a step back, and his whole body seemed to sag.

His voice now soft, he said, "You're like an addiction to me. Your blood has become like an addiction to me. Now, I know how good I feel when I'm inside you, and I can't go back to just drinking your blood. Because, after it's over and you leave, I'll be alone. You're telling me I can have you, Phoenix, but not the way I want you. That's why I can't do this anymore. Addictions aren't healthy, and this half-assed being with you will only make it worse. You can't give me what I need, and I guess, in the end, I can't give you what you need."

Phoenix visibly swallowed, and he almost relented when he saw the agony on her face. But he couldn't give in. He loved her, but he couldn't sacrifice his own happiness for hers, especially when she wouldn't really and truly let herself be happy. They would both end up resenting each other, and then they'd be worse off than they were now.

Turning her away was the hardest thing he'd ever done, but it had to be that way.

"I'm here if you ever change your mind," he foolishly added. *Man, don't I have any pride?* "But know that I'm not going to wait around forever. I care about you, Phoenix, but if you don't want me, then I have to move on."

Phoenix just looked at him. He had no idea what she was thinking. Her blood in him was like a blank line of nothing.

"I hope, someday, you find someone who can make you happy." He only wished that male were him. He stepped around her and opened the door to his room. "I think it's best if you go now."

☾

Phoenix slowly pivoted on her heel and headed for the open door. She felt so...empty inside. She took one last look at Dante before she left, but he wouldn't meet her eyes. She slid the key from her pocket and put it in his palm, and then she walked down the stairs and out of the compound.

She had never felt so numb. Ever.

This thing with Dante was done. This was why she hadn't wanted to get involved with him in the first place. She knew it would end in disappointment and heartache.

Damn, she hated being right.

THIRTY-FOUR

LEXINE AND STERLING entered the nightclub, Pulse, on a mission. They were going to find Lucas tonight, and she was going to find her parents.

"Are you sure he'll be here?" Sterling asked.

"I'm ninety-nine percent sure. Like I said, he hates the vampire-shifter alliance. He wouldn't miss an opportunity to have so many vampires in one room, so he can spew his filthy lies."

Sterling's eyes rounded. "Lies? Weren't you on his side not that long ago?"

Lexine winced. "Yes," she admitted since she'd confessed everything to him already. "I was foolish, and I regret ever getting involved with them. I already told you all of this."

"I just don't understand the change of heart."

She opened her mouth to tell him that he was the one who had changed her mind. It had started when the elderly Mrs. Howard almost got hurt, but Sterling was the one who had truly made her see things differently.

"I just have, all right?" she said instead.

"All right. Let's go find this asshole."

Lexine rubbed her hands together. "Let's."

The plan was for the two of them to track Analeigh, Steve, Michelle, Mathis, and Dani, whose blood she and Sterling had stolen. There was no way Lucas wouldn't come without his entourage, and they would use them to find Lucas. Once they located the group, who would hopefully all be together, Lexine would lure Lucas away from the group when he sensed her nearby. Once she got Lucas away from the group, Sterling would sneak up behind him and take his blood. Once Sterling could track Lucas, then she would be able to find her parents and, with any luck, find the tape that incriminated her.

It seemed almost foolproof, which was why, when Sterling had encouraged her to tell Dante, she had insisted the two of them could do this on their own.

They circled the club, but so far neither of them had been able to find Lucas's group. They'd been there for an hour, and Lexine was getting antsy. Everyone around them was having fun and had no idea the danger they were in with Lucas and his friends out and about. She wanted to shake them and tell them to stop being so naive, but she needed them to be there for cover.

Just when Lexine was beginning to feel like a failure, she sensed them. She grabbed Sterling's arm. "They're here."

He arched his neck up and looked around the throng of vampires. "I know. I can sense them."

She pointed to the bar. "There. They're getting drinks."

This was a good sign. If they had known she was here, they wouldn't have been getting alcohol.

"Do you see Lucas?" Sterling asked.

The only bad part of their plan was, he didn't know what Lucas looked like. She'd realized, when Sterling asked her, she didn't have any photos of him or anything. He'd never let her take pictures of him, and his social media accounts were all minus identifying pictures, too. The closest thing she'd been able to find was an old yearbook photo that was outdated, but at least it had given Sterling an idea.

"No," she said, defeated.

She was sure he'd be there. She scanned the room around Lucas's friends and had almost given up when she saw Lucas walk toward his group. She felt excitement flush through her body. She couldn't wait to take the fucker down.

"There he is! He just fist-bumped Mathis." She pointed out Lucas to Sterling.

He glanced at her and back at Lucas. She couldn't read his look, and all he said was, "Got him."

Due to their distance, she could barely sense the group's blood in her, so there was a strong chance Lucas couldn't sense her. Her blood in him was older and therefore more faded. They had to wait until they felt like it was the right time for her to move closer.

Lexine and Sterling waited until the group had their drinks and were standing at a table, talking. Their defenses were down, and it felt like the right moment.

"I think we should move closer. Are you ready?" she asked Sterling.

"Yep. Let's do this."

They moved slowly and cautiously. They both watched for signs that Lucas sensed her. The group's blood in her veins was getting stronger, and she was happy her plan was working so far.

They were about halfway across the room when she knew Lucas knew she was there. She would have missed it if she had blinked. The guy was good, and it pissed her off.

"He's got me," she told Sterling.

He nodded. "I noticed. Are you ready? I'll be right behind you."

She nodded. With her heart hammering in her chest from excitement, fear, and anticipation, she moved closer to Lucas. She wanted him to think that she didn't know he was there. She got closer to him but not so close that they would spot each other, and she kept herself hidden behind other patrons as much as possible.

When she felt like she had given Lucas enough bait, she headed toward the back of the nightclub. She ran into two males who were in each other's face, looking ready to brawl.

They had a circle of vampires around them with a few chanting, "Fight."

It was a nice distraction for Lexine to get out of the club, except the group was blocking the hallway to the back door.

It took her longer to walk around them than she had anticipated, and she was afraid that Lucas would catch up with her. But, every time she looked back, he wasn't there. She really wished she had been able to get his blood. She hated that he had an advantage over her.

She made her way into the empty alley and hid behind the dumpster, watching the door. She glanced down at her watch several times. *Where is he?*

Just as she was about to give up, the door opened, but it wasn't Lucas who came out. It was Sterling.

Crap.

He was too early. He was supposed to wait for Lucas to

come out first. She stood to go and tell him to hide when she sensed a presence behind her. Even before she felt the knife at her neck and the strong arm around her waist, she knew it was Lucas.

"Put your hands out where I can see them."

"Fuck you," she said. But she did as he'd commanded.

"We already did that." He licked her neck. "But I'd be willing to go at it again."

Lexine shuddered at the thought of sleeping with Lucas again. The only vampire she wanted touching her was Sterling.

"Tell your boyfriend over there to put his hands up."

"I don't know what—"

She felt the knife bite into her neck, and warm blood dripped onto her shoulder.

"Sterling, I'm coming out. Please don't try anything," she said as she unblocked her blood link to him while simultaneously blocking Lucas. If only she'd been able to block her presence and not just her emotions.

Sterling stiffened and opened his blood to her. He was pissed, and it gave her comfort and strength to know he wasn't scared.

Lucas dragged Lexine out in front of Sterling. "So, you thought you could best me, Lexine. Did you really think I was that dumb?"

Sterling was shooting daggers at Lucas. "Let her go, asshole."

"Let me think about it. Hmm…no. If it wasn't for this bitch, we'd be on the next step in our plan. But someone had to grow a conscience."

"I didn't grow one. I always had it. You promised that no

one would get hurt."

"Stupid bitch. You really thought some vandalism was all we were going to do?"

Lexine stiffened. She had been a fool, and she had no one to blame but herself. "How did you find me?"

"Isn't that what you wanted, Lexine? For me to follow you out here? Oh, that's right. You probably thought you were going to get the drop on me. You hadn't planned for me to go out the front door and come around the building."

Lexine gasped slightly. How had he known?

"Did you really think I didn't know you were up to something? Steve had told me right away about what happened at his house. Didn't you find it odd that I hadn't called you for any information in all that time?"

Of course she had. But she had assumed that Lucas was busy with something else.

Lucas laughed mockingly in her ear. "You really are a dumb bitch, you know that? How you even made it as a Guardian is a shock."

If Lucas hadn't had a knife to her throat, she would have hung her head in shame. It had become apparent lately that Lexine was not cut out for this role, but hearing Lucas say it was a blow to the gut.

"Since you double-crossed me, I'm going to have to sacrifice your parents."

"No!" she cried out as Sterling took a step toward her.

"One inch closer, and I'll sacrifice her as well," Lucas told Sterling.

Sterling gritted his teeth, and Lexine tried to tell him she was sorry through their link. It wasn't an exact emotion, but hopefully, he would feel her remorse.

Lucas stuck his mouth in the air and whistled several times in a row.

Lexine felt the rest of the group moving closer, and panic filled her body. Right now, they were two to one. If the rest of her former friends got there, it would be six to two. They were so fucked.

Think, Lexine, think. You might be the worst Guardian in history, but use your training.

Then, it came to her. It seemed so simple that she should have thought of it earlier. She tried to let her happiness at having an idea flow through her blood link to warn Sterling that she was going to try something. His anger and fear turned to alertness, and she knew he'd figured it out.

Lexine grabbed the first finger she found on the arm Lucas had around her waist. She gripped it and bent it backward as she let all her weight go, forcing Lucas to let go of her or go down to the ground.

At the same time, Sterling made a beeline for Lucas and kicked him in the face as he bent over from Lexine's waist. She really wanted to stay and finish him, but they didn't have any time with the rest of the group getting closer.

Lexine hurried and bit into Lucas's arm and sucked as hard and fast as she could. She dropped his limb, not caring that he was bleeding still, as Sterling helped her stand up.

"Let's go."

Lexine nodded and let Sterling grab her hand as they ran for his SUV.

Tonight had undeniably not gone according to plan.

She finally admitted that she was in over her head. "I think it's time I talk to Dante."

Sterling glanced behind himself. "Thank God. Finally."

THIRTY-FIVE

DANTE GLANCED down at the thick manila envelope that lay on his desk. There was no name on it, just the compound's address.

Curious and relieved to have something to keep his mind off Phoenix, he sat down in his chair and opened the envelope. He pulled out the stack of papers. It looked to be a report of some kind on...he shuffled through the paperwork...six different people. Dante didn't recognize any of the names, and the business card that came with the report was for a human private investigator. All vampire businesses were registered with the Guardians. So, Dante didn't know if these were six humans or vampires. Maybe the investigator got the wrong address.

Dante leaned back in his seat and started to read.

An hour later, he heard a commotion in the hallway. Since he had been the only one home, Dante had left his office door open. He now heard Lexine and Sterling whispering as they moved closer to him. He couldn't make out their words, but it was just the vampire he wanted to see.

Sterling knocked on his open door. "Hey, boss."

Dante nodded in greeting. "Sterling."

"Lexine has something she needs to discuss with you."

Dante raised a brow because Lexine was absent from view.

Sterling rolled his eyes and reached over. He pulled Lexine in front of him and pushed her into the office.

"Uh, hello, Dante."

"Lexine."

"I, uh, need to tell you something."

Dante held up the report and envelope. "Does it have to do with the reason you hired a human private investigator to do research on six vampires and why these six vampires are photographed vandalizing both shifter and vampire areas? And does it also have to do with the cut on your neck?"

Lexine's face turned white, and she covered her wound with her hand.

"Why don't you come in and shut the door? I think we have a lot to talk about."

☾

A couple of hours later, Lexine stood in front of all the Guardians—Dante, Lennox, Sterling, Hunter, Morgan, Ram, Tempest, and Declan—and told them her story. Everything, including how Lucas had chained her up, blood-raped her, and how he and the guys had ejaculated all over her. That was the hardest part of all, and she couldn't look at Sterling when she said it. The only thing she hadn't shared was how she'd gotten started hanging with the group.

She couldn't have them knowing she'd done it because she was jealous of Phoenix and Dante.

"So, you knew about this?" Dante asked Sterling.

She'd tried to leave him out of the story, especially when she talked about how she'd turned around and stolen their blood in return. Technically, it was the same thing they had done to her, except she had done it to protect her family. Plus, she and Sterling hadn't taken so much that they could have died from it. But, in the end, Lexine wasn't much better than Lucas and the others.

"Yes," Sterling said without any shame. "But only recently."

With those words, she realized that Sterling had defied Dante, the Council, and the other Guardians. She had made Sterling do something he never would have done without her influence, and her shame deepened.

"Please, don't punish him," Lexine said. "He was only trying to protect me. I asked him not to say anything. I realize now that it was a mistake."

"Ya think?" her brother said.

She could tell he was very angry with her, and he had every right to be.

"I'm not punishing anyone," Dante told her. Lexine felt relief. "The two of you will have to go in front of the Council, and they will decide what happens to you."

Lennox felt a moment of dread. The Council was not going to go easy on them.

"But, first, we need to take down this group. I can't lose you before we eliminate the threat. You and Sterling are too valuable to the mission," Dante said. He walked over to his desk and grabbed a stack of papers and some photos. "Lexine, pass a packet out to everyone, and, Sterling, hang these pictures on the board."

Lexine grabbed the pile of papers while Sterling pulled the whiteboard from the corner of the room.

"What's this?" Lennox asked as Lexine handed the stuff out.

"It's a copy of the report from Lexine's private eye. I want you to look it over now. Sterling is hanging the pictures the investigator took, and I would like you to look at those also. It would have been nice if he had emailed a report, but apparently, Lexine found the only guy who enjoys killing trees."

Lexine winced. She wasn't about to argue, but she'd picked the guy because he left less of a digital trace by doing things the old-fashioned way.

Lexine started poring over her own copy of the report. She was making her way through Michelle's section when Morgan spoke up, "Lexine, where did you say you met these guys?"

"I met them at a bar by the vampire clinic."

Morgan tilted her dark head. "And what's the name of it?"

"Jack's Place."

"What are you thinking, Morgan?" Dante asked.

Her brown eyes glittered. "This is probably far-fetched, but it says Lucas's father and grandfather are both named John, and the nickname for John—"

"Is Jack," Sterling finished.

"Declan?" Dante said.

"Already on it," Declan said as his fingers flew over his laptop keyboard. After a minute, he sat back in his seat. "It looks like Jack's Place is owned by a shell corporation. Hold on." He did some more typing. "Is there anyone with the name Porter?"

They all flipped through their papers.

"Yes," Lexine said. "Lucas's grandmother was Elsbeth Porter before she was married."

More typing. "Yep, it all comes back to Elsbeth Porter."

"Why would they hide their bar?" Hunter said.

"Nothing good," Dante said.

Lexine looked up at everyone with tears in her eyes. "Do you think this is where my parents are?"

"Only one way to find out," Lennox said.

Lexine looked at her watch. "But the sun is going to be up soon. We don't have time."

Dante looked at her. "Well, the thing that your friends don't understand—"

"They're not my friends," she said. She knew she shouldn't have interrupted Dante, but she had to let everyone know those people were not her friends.

"Fine. What your former friends don't understand is that it pays to have an alliance with the shifters. Because they can do things we can't and vice versa."

Lexine hung her head and nodded at her feet. Dante was so right.

"I'm sorry," she told the group. "Thank you for helping me."

"That's why you don't try to do things on your own," Sterling said with some bite. "I'm sure we could have found some of this out earlier. Declan could have found out everything the private investigator did and then some."

"I know. And all I can say is, I was wrong, and I'm sorry."

Dante grabbed his phone from his desk. "I'll call Vance and Damien. We'll have them raid the bar while the vamps are sleeping, and then we'll have him watch Lucas's and the others' homes. At sundown, I want you all to be ready because we're going after them."

They all exited the office, except for Dante, and Lexine waited for her brother. When Lennox saw her, he glared at her and kept walking.

"Lennox, I'm sorry!"

Her brother turned around. "You should be. I can't believe you kept that from me. Mom and Dad? How could you?"

"I didn't want you to get hurt."

"Too late." He swung around and walked away.

Sterling came up beside her.

"I'm a horrible sister."

Sterling put his hand on the back of her neck. "He'll forgive you. Just give him some time."

She looked into his gray eyes. "I sure hope so."

At least she still had Sterling.

THIRTY-SIX

STERLING WOKE to find Lexine staring at the ceiling. It was still several hours before sunset. "Have you slept at all?"

She looked at him. "Not really. I'm incredibly nervous."

He rolled on his back. "Come here."

Lexine moved closer and laid her head on his chest. Sterling pulled her close and breathed in her scent. She smelled like pumpkin pie. How had he never noticed that before? Probably because they'd been more like roommates than anything before.

He was going to miss this.

He had no idea what Lexine had said to Dante the other day in his office, but it seemed like things were over between the cat-shifter and their leader. Sterling knew that Dante wasn't going to date Lexine. Their leader hadn't shown interest in her before Phoenix, and he wasn't likely to show her interest now. But Sterling figured it was only a matter of time before Lexine made a play for Dante again and left him behind.

At least it had been fun while it lasted.

Lexine picked up her head and looked at him. "That was a big sigh. Something on your mind?"

He tucked a piece of hair behind her ear. "Nothing in particular," he lied. "Just that we have a big day ahead of us. I was hoping to hear something about your parents by now."

She put her head back down. "I know. Me, too." She traced the lines of his six-pack. "I'm sorry that I put you in this situation, Sterling. I have no idea what the Council is going to do to you. I should never have made you keep my secret."

Now would be the time to tell her that he loved her and would do almost anything for her, but he kept his mouth shut. Now, he understood why she hadn't wanted to tell anyone about her new group of *friends*. Pity was a bitch, and he didn't want Lexine feeling sorry for him. He might have to seriously think about transferring out of state.

Although he hadn't been able to find his transfer papers since the first night he read them.

Lexine paused where she was touching him, and he realized he'd never responded.

"I forgive you. You didn't make me do anything. I chose to keep your secret. I'll deal with whatever punishment the Council wants to hand out to me."

She looked up again and kissed him. He cupped the back of her head and was getting ready to roll her on her back when there was a pounding at her bedroom door.

"Lexine, open up," Lennox called from the other side.

"Oh my God," she said as she jumped out of bed.

He was about to ask where she wanted him to hide

when she marched toward the door, and he was momentarily distracted.

"Lexine, clothes."

She looked down at her naked body and ran to her closet. She was sliding on her robe when she went and answered her door. She swung it wide, not even bothering to try to hide Sterling.

Sterling quickly sat up as Lexine said, "What's wrong?"

Lennox looked over Lexine's shoulder at Sterling and then to his sister. Sterling, Lexine, Sterling, Lexine. His eyes bounced until they landed on Lexine, and Lennox's mouth turned down in disgust. "That was you the other night when Morgan heard Sterling fucking someone? Barf."

Lexine clapped her hands together. "Lennox, focus. Why did you come knocking?"

Lennox was still focused on Lexine and Sterling. "But you let me go on and on…and it was you the whole time?"

"Lennox," she said sharper this time.

When her brother didn't say anything else, she socked him in the arm.

"Ow," he said, rubbing his arm.

"Why did you come to my door?" she said, frustration in her voice.

"Oh, yeah. The shifters got Mom and Dad out safe. They're on their way here as we speak. And Dante wants to go over tonight's game plan." He looked down at his sister's attire. "So, get dressed." He turned around and shuddered. "Yikes, I can't believe I asked Sterling to share my sister," he said as he walked away.

Lexine closed the door, rushed over to Sterling, and threw herself into his arms. "My parents are okay."

Sterling held her for several minutes. When she pulled away, she had to wipe tears off her face. He was relieved to see that they were happy tears.

"We'd better get ready," she said with a smile.

Sterling grinned at her. "We'd better. I'll meet you down there."

Lexine moved out of the way, so Sterling could get out of bed. He put on last night's clothes and went to his room to shower and dress.

Fifteen minutes later, he was meeting everyone in Dante's office. Lexine had beaten him there and was pacing the room. No sooner had he arrived than two shifters, Saxon and Zane, escorted two figures in black with large brimmed hats and black veils into the room. They removed their hats and veils, and Sterling saw that they were Lexine and Lennox's parents.

The parents hugged their children, and Lexine apologized to them over and over again. Her parents just hugged her again. Thankfully, this part of their mission had ended happily.

Dante spoke with the shifters. Then, he thanked the shifters and told them the vampires would meet them as soon as possible.

"Mr. and Mrs. Harlow, let us give you a room upstairs where you can get cleaned up and rest. Then, later, we can take you to the vampire clinic to get you both checked out," Dante said.

Lexine and Lennox showed them to a room. After they came back, Dante finally told the group what the shifters had said.

"Seems we're either lucky or unlucky."

"What do you mean?" Lennox asked.

"Apparently, all of the vampires are located at one house. We're lucky because they're all in one place, but it'll be hard to take them all at the same time. Something is more likely to go wrong. I'm assuming that is the reason they have stuck together. I don't know what their plans were for Lexine and Sterling the night before, but they have to know someone is coming for them. They'll be ready."

"We're going to be ready, too," Lennox said.

"Now, I need someone to stay back with Mr. and Mrs. Harlow."

"I volunteer Lexine," Lennox said.

Sterling looked at Lexine's face. She didn't like the idea, but she didn't object.

Dante shook his head. "I can't do that. Lexine is the only one who has drunk the blood of all the vampires there. I need her too much."

"I'll stay," Declan volunteered. It wasn't surprising. He was a Guardian for his computer and hacking skills more than his ability to fight.

Dante nodded at the computer genius. "Thank you." Dante turned to the rest of them after glancing at his watch. "Okay, we have about a half hour before we can leave. Let's go over the plan."

The group huddled around and listened to what their leader had to say.

Thirty minutes later, they were inside their SUVs and heading out. The sky was still a little gray and not completely dark yet. They had left as soon as they possibly could.

Dante called someone. "They're still there?" Pause.

"Good. We should be there in ten." He hung up and stepped on the gas.

Once they reached their destination, they all piled out of the vehicles. It was almost completely dark now, and they blended in with their black clothing. The shifters came out of the dark and greeted them. Sterling noticed that Dante was trying not to be obvious that he was looking for Phoenix, but he wasn't succeeding. The female shifter was nowhere to be seen.

"Nobody has come or gone," Damien said.

"Thanks. We owe you," Dante said.

"We'll put it on your tab," the wolf alpha said. "We'll stick around in case you need us," he added.

And the shifters disappeared into the darkness to wait.

Dante turned to them. "Okay, let's do this."

Sterling and Dante circled the house, followed by Lexine, who was trying to keep a distance so that Lucas wouldn't detect her presence. The three of them reconvened in the front with the group.

"Okay," Sterling said. "There is a couple in the back bedroom." He didn't bother with names since none of the other Guardians knew who they were. "Hopefully, they're sleeping. I sensed two more in the next two bedrooms, both female, and one male in the bathroom. We tried to wait for the male in the bathroom to leave, so we could track his movement, but he must have been doing some...big business in there."

"And Lucas is in the kitchen. Of course he's up," Lexine grumbled.

"I had hoped they'd all be sleeping still," Dante said. "But we'll have to make do with what we have. Hunter and

Ram, I want you two to go for the couple in the back bedroom. Morgan, you have the next bedroom, and, Lennox, you have the next. You all can go through the bedroom windows. Tempest, you get the male in the bathroom where he will hopefully stay. There is a patio door not far from there that you'll have to use. Once you're in, head to your left. Sterling, please give them a quick nod if the guy is still in the bathroom when we get up there. And then you're with me. We're going after Lucas through the garage. Everybody ready?"

"What about me?" Lexine asked.

"I want you to stay here. We can't risk Lucas sensing you."

"But—"

Dante lifted an eyebrow.

"I'll wait here."

"Good." Dante turned to the rest of them. "Let's go."

The Guardians approached their targets and spread out around the house. Sterling was cursing himself for not drinking some of Lucas's blood the night before as he rounded the bathroom in the back and headed for the garage. He turned around and gave Tempest a quick nod before continuing on to his destination.

Dante and Sterling approached the rear of the house and headed for the back door to the garage. Dante made a bird call into the night, which signaled everyone to go in. Sterling opened the door to the garage and—

BOOM!

Sterling felt himself flying backward and landing hard on the grass. The next thing he knew was that he had a massive headache, and part of the house was on fire. He must have blacked out for a second, but he wasn't sure. He tried to sit up but hurt everywhere.

There was a lot of commotion around them, but Sterling couldn't hear through the ringing in his ears. It felt like he was wearing earplugs because he couldn't make out what was going on.

Sterling looked over to his side, suddenly remembering that Dante had been beside him when the blast went off. He saw Dante and shouted his name even though Dante probably couldn't hear either. Dante moved his legs, and Sterling breathed a sigh of relief that his leader was alive.

Through the smoke, he saw Lexine emerge and head straight for them. She looked to be shouting something, but he couldn't read her lips. He watched her get closer, but it almost felt like slow motion. He knew how she felt about Dante, so Sterling closed his eyes, not wanting to see her reach their leader's side.

A heavy weight landed on his chest, dislodging what little air he still had in his body. He opened his eyes to see Lexine over him with tears in her eyes. She was talking to him, but he couldn't make out what she was saying.

He caressed her cheek. She'd come to him instead of Dante, and despite the situation, this was one of the happiest moments of his life.

She said something again, and he shook his head.

"I can't hear you!" he shouted while pointing to his ear.

She mouthed, *Police.*

He realized that one of the neighbors, if not all, had probably called the police when they heard the noise from the explosion.

He tried to sit up again, but his head swam, and he was

afraid he was going to pass out. Lexine motioned someone over, saying something, and Ram came into view. He leaned over Sterling and grinned.

We got them, he mouthed. Then, he picked Sterling up in a fireman's hold.

It wasn't the best way to get him out of there, but it was the fastest. While Ram ran for the SUVs, Sterling held on, his head being jarred with every step.

Ram set him down in the back of a vehicle, and someone laid Dante down beside him. Lexine got in after that and put Sterling's head in her lap. He felt the engine turn over, and someone stepped on the gas.

Now that they were out of there, he closed his eyes. He wanted to sleep, but Lexine shook him. He looked up into her hazel-green eyes, and she shook her head.

No sleeping, she mouthed. *Concussion*.

He looked up at her and maybe shouted, maybe whispered, "I love you." It was hard to tell when he couldn't hear himself.

She smiled down at him and mouthed, *I love you, too*.

THIRTY-SEVEN

PHOENIX SAT with Kenzie on her couch, watching a movie. She'd been with the human all day and was still with her even though night had fallen. Vance had called earlier to say that he needed Sawyer for something, so Vance needed Phoenix to stay with Kenzie longer.

When she'd started this assignment, she would have been upset at the overtime. But, now, she thought of Kenzie as a friend and didn't mind hanging out with her. Phoenix never would have thought that the two of them would like each other because they were so different, but Phoenix enjoyed her company and really valued her opinion and advice. She'd even ended up pouring her heart out about Dante to Kenzie. Kenzie thought she was crazy, but Phoenix knew that Kenzie didn't quite understand.

As she shifted her weight, Kenzie groaned in a way that put Phoenix on alert.

"What's wrong?"

Kenzie tried to smile, but she didn't quite succeed. "Nothing."

"Kenzie," Phoenix warned.

The human furrowed her brows. "I think I need to use the bathroom." She threw back the blanket she'd had over her and stood up.

The sight before Phoenix had her heart sinking. "Kenzie, you're bleeding."

Kenzie paled and tried to look at her bottom. When she didn't succeed, she ran to the bathroom. "Oh no," she said from the other side of the door.

Phoenix rushed to the bathroom. "What do you need me to do?" she asked through the wood.

"Please, grab me some clothes."

Phoenix found Kenzie something to wear and helped her get to the car. "Shifter infirmary?"

Kenzie looked at her like she was crazy. "No, we're going to the hospital."

"But your baby is a shifter."

"Half-shifter. And I'm full human. We're going to the hospital."

"Got it," Phoenix said as she took off as fast as she could without breaking the law.

"Have you been able to get ahold of Sawyer?"

Phoenix shook her head. "No, sorry, but I did send him text messages."

Kenzie sighed. "This sucks."

Once they reached the hospital, it was moderately busy, but they managed to get into an ER room right away.

Phoenix stepped out into the hall as the nurse and doctor came in, and she called Sawyer again. Voice mail. "Look, Sawyer, I know you're working, but you need to get down here." She gave him the name of the hospital. "We're in room eighteen. Kenzie is really scared, and she needs you. Hurry."

Phoenix stepped back into Kenzie's room and sat by her friend. It was very difficult because she hated hospitals and anything to do with them. It was easy to ignore how uncomfortable she was when she was helping Kenzie, but now, they were just sitting there and waiting.

Someone came and took Kenzie's blood. Then, radiology came and took her to get an ultrasound. Kenzie looked at Phoenix, and Phoenix prayed she didn't ask the technologist if she could go with. Thankfully, Kenzie didn't say anything.

Then, the tech said, "We'll be back in about twenty minutes."

The second Kenzie was gone from the room, Phoenix headed outside for fresh air. She made note of the time, so she could be there when Kenzie returned. There was an empty bench outside, and Phoenix sat and watched the cars entering the parking lot.

"Come on, Sawyer. Hurry up," she said out loud to the universe.

Time seemed to race by with no arrival of Sawyer, and soon, the twenty minutes were up, so Phoenix headed back inside. Kenzie was already in her room when Phoenix got there.

"Hey, how did it go?"

Kenzie shrugged. "I don't know. They couldn't tell me anything. Did you hear from Sawyer?"

Phoenix hated that she had to tell her no.

Kenzie turned her head away but then looked back at Phoenix. The human's lip trembled, and she said, "That's okay. He'll be here."

Oh, Kenzie.

Phoenix was going to kick Sawyer's ass when she saw him. *Butthole could at least answer his texts.*

The doctor walked into the room, and two seconds later, Sawyer burst through the door.

"Can I help you, sir?" the doctor asked.

"I'm here for my ma—wife."

"Oh, I'm sorry, Ms. Swanson. I thought you were unmarried."

"This is my fiancé," Kenzie corrected Sawyer.

Sawyer frowned. According to shifter law, the two were already mates.

"We just haven't made it to the courthouse yet," she said as she held out her hand to Sawyer.

Sawyer stepped around the doctor and went to Kenzie's side.

"I'm glad to have the both of you together. Ms. Swanson, we got the ultrasound results back, and I'm sorry to tell you that you are miscarrying." The doctor's voice was filled with remorse, and Phoenix could tell he hated delivering this kind of news.

Sawyer fell back in the chair next to Kenzie's bed, as if his legs could no longer hold him up, and Kenzie started crying.

Sawyer pulled his mate into his arms, and Phoenix knew it was time to leave the room.

She pulled the door closed behind her and leaned back

against the wall to take deep breaths. Phoenix felt like she was going to cry as well. It wasn't fair. On top of her failed heat, her friend Kenzie shouldn't have to lose her baby as well.

What if Phoenix hadn't been so jealous? She felt awful now for feeling so envious. Kenzie just wanted a happy life with her mate. Now that Phoenix knew the human better, she knew what a good person she was and that she deserved to have a family. Phoenix never wanted anyone to feel the way she felt.

Phoenix heard soothing noises coming from Kenzie's ER room. Phoenix hadn't managed to latch the door all the way when she pulled it closed, and the sound she heard was Kenzie soothing Sawyer.

"It'll be okay, Sawyer. We'll try again."

"But we already had a baby. I want this baby."

"I know, sweetie. Me, too."

"We didn't even get to meet Peanut."

Phoenix closed her eyes, overwhelmed with sadness upon hearing that they had given their baby a nickname.

"I know," Kenzie agreed with Sawyer.

"Baby?"

"Yeah?"

"I want you to know that I don't blame you at all. I can see your head is going around and around. I really wanted this baby, but I don't want you to feel bad."

"Oh, Sawyer." Kenzie's voice quivered. "I needed to hear you say that."

"Baby, of course I would never blame you. I love you."

"I love you, too."

Phoenix felt like a voyeur, listening in on their conversation, but if she closed the door now, it would be obvious.

But after their *I love you*s, the only sound Phoenix heard was of their almost-silent crying. She waited in the hallway for what felt like hours. She didn't know if she should go or stay. Sawyer was there but was in no shape to be on duty.

After some time, Sawyer walked out of the room and went straight to the restroom. Phoenix was pretty sure he hadn't even noticed her, as he was in such a catatonic state.

After Sawyer left, Phoenix knocked softly and walked in. She had no idea what to say to Kenzie, and she felt incredibly uncomfortable. But this wasn't about her. This was about her friend.

"Hey, Kenzie. I'm so sorry."

Kenzie wiped her cheeks and sat up. "Come here."

Phoenix stepped closer to Kenzie until the human grabbed her hand and forced her to sit on the bed with her. "Thank you for bringing me here and for tracking down Sawyer."

"Of course. Are you going to be okay?"

"I'm not going to die or anything. The doctor said I'll pass…I'll pass the baby and everything, so at least I won't have to have surgery. He told me to go see my doctor, and we can probably try again in a few months."

"Are you even going to?" Phoenix asked.

"Definitely. Why wouldn't I?"

"Because of how much pain you're in. Because of how much pain Sawyer is in."

"Oh, Phoenix," Kenzie said. She still held Phoenix's hand, and she squeezed. "Sure, it might be easier to hide away and never try again. But I would rather have a miscarriage and the pain that comes with it if it means I might get to have a baby someday rather than never getting pregnant at all and avoiding the heartache. Life is full of ups and downs, good things and bad things. That's just the way it works. If I have to take the bad things to get the good things, then bring on the crap. Because being with Sawyer is worth it. Eventually having a baby, even if it means adopting, is worth it. Having friends is worth it. Living isn't simply not dying, Phoenix." Kenzie reached forward, and this time, she wiped Phoenix's cheeks. "Honey, why are you crying?"

"Because I'm not as strong as you. And I want to be."

Kenzie smiled. "Sure you are. You're stronger. Do you care about Dante?"

"Yes," she answered without hesitation.

"So, if something happened to Dante tomorrow or next week or next month, wouldn't you be happy with him for a day, a week, a month rather than live this lonely existence? Because, sure, you can try to protect your heart, but you already care about him, Phoenix. And, if you don't go after him, you've lost him anyway."

Phoenix pulled Kenzie into a hug. "You are an amazing person. I should be comforting you, not the other way around. Sawyer is an absolute fool for taking so long to see that."

Kenzie hugged her back. "I tell him that all the time."

Phoenix released Kenzie and sat back to see Sawyer standing in the doorway, looking shell-shocked.

"Sawyer, what's wrong?" Kenzie asked, alarmed.

"I don't think I've ever seen Phoenix hug anyone."

"Ha-ha," Phoenix said.

Sawyer stepped into the room. "Thank you, Phoenix, for taking care of Kenzie today."

"No problem. She's my friend."

Sawyer raised his brow. "Still, I thought you'd be out of here the minute you heard about Dante."

Phoenix frowned. "Dante? What about him?"

Sawyer blew out a breath and rubbed the back of his neck. "Uh-oh."

Her whole body went on alert. "Uh-oh what?" The first thought that came to mind was that he'd already replaced her. Phoenix looked at Kenzie, who shook her head and shrugged.

"The vamps ran into some trouble. They figured out who was behind all the trouble we'd been having."

Phoenix jumped to her feet. "They did? Are they going after them? How did they find out?"

"It's a long story, but that's where I've been all day until I got here. The vampires behind this mess are already in the Guardians' custody. But, Phoenix, Dante was hurt today."

Phoenix felt like her world was tilting, and she realized that Sawyer had rushed to her, so she didn't fall over. "Is he…" She swallowed. "Is he…"

"He's alive, but he's at the vampire clinic. There was an explosion, and he was thrown pretty far."

Her head was starting to clear, and she pushed Sawyer out of the way. "I have to go."

She finally understood exactly what Kenzie had been saying. She had wasted this whole week when she could have been with him. And, now, he might die without knowing how she felt about him.

"I can drive you," Sawyer said.

"No, you stay with your mate. And, for God's sake, take her to the courthouse and marry her already," Phoenix said as she walked out of the room.

"You heard her," Sawyer said, his voice trailing as she walked farther away. "Now, you have to marry me."

Once out of the building, Phoenix ran for her car and sped out of the parking lot. She had to get to Dante.

THIRTY-EIGHT

LEXINE WAS SNEAKING food in for Sterling when she found Phoenix at the front desk.

"Please, I need to see him."

"I'm sorry, miss," the receptionist who didn't sound the least bit sorry said, "but you don't have any right to go back there. And Mr. Leonidas is sleeping. I will not wake him for this."

Lexine walked over to the two of them. "Hey, Phoenix."

The cat-shifter turned to Lexine. "Uh...hey, Lexine."

"Listen"—Lexine looked at the receptionist—"this is Dante's future mate, so if I were you, I would not want to piss off the leader of the Guardians. You feel me?"

The receptionist nodded. "Yes, ma'am."

"Come on, Phoenix. I'll take you to Dante," she said. "And don't *ma'am* me," she told the receptionist. "I'm not that old."

Phoenix followed her down the hall.

When they got to the door to the room that Dante and

Sterling were sharing, Lexine turned around. "Look, I just wanted to tell you that I'm sorry. I know I haven't been nice to you in the past."

Phoenix looked like she didn't know what to say. "Thank you."

"I was jealous before. I always thought I had a crush on Dante, so when you came along, I didn't like it. But, now, I see that I didn't really like him like that. I liked the idea of him. Anyway, you and Dante are meant to be together. And I hope you came here to set things straight with him."

"I did."

Lexine smiled. "Good. Otherwise, I'd have to kill you."

Phoenix laughed, not the least bit intimidated. "You could try."

Lexine pushed open the door and walked past a sleeping Dante to Sterling's bed.

His gray eyes opened when she got to his bedside. "Hey."

"Hey," she said. She held up her backpack. "I brought you food."

"I know. I can smell it."

She set her backpack down and pulled out the burger and fries for Sterling.

"God, you are awesome," Sterling said. "Now, if you could just fit me in your backpack and sneak me out of here, that would be great."

Lexine sat next to Sterling and lay back on the raised head of the bed. "You'll get out of here soon."

"Not soon enough," he said, already taking a bite of his food.

"You're lucky the booby-trap bomb that Lucas had set was only enough to blow off the door and send you and Dante through the air. It could have been a lot worse."

"I know," he agreed.

There was a noise over by Dante's bed. Sterling looked up to see Phoenix sitting by Dante's bedside now that Lexine wasn't blocking his view anymore.

"When did she get here?"

"Just now."

"And you're okay with this?"

"Of course. Why wouldn't I be?"

Sterling looked at her like she'd told a bad joke or something. "Because you've been in love with him forever."

She closed her eyes and relaxed. "Nah. I was just telling Phoenix that I was in love with the idea of him, not Dante himself. I wanted a strong alpha male who would boss me around in bed, but it turns out, I've already found that." Lexine settled in, ready to take a short nap while Sterling ate, when another thought crossed her mind. She opened her eyes and sat up. "Wait a second. How did you know I liked Dante?"

"Babe, everyone in the house knew." He tilted his head to the side. "Well, almost everyone. Dante never knew. At least, I don't think he did."

"Ugh, how embarrassing."

Sterling lifted his brow.

"You're right. After everything we've gone through recently, that's not very embarrassing." She laid her head back again while Sterling polished off his burger.

"So, if you realized you no longer loved or liked Dante,

what did you say to him that night in his office after he came back from seeing Phoenix?" Sterling looked worried.

"Did you think I went and propositioned him or something?"

"No. Yes." He shrugged. "I don't know."

Lexine laughed. "I went and told him about you and me. I know there are no rules on fraternizing, but I wanted to be honest with him. After everything I put the Guardians through, I felt like it was best to start being honest."

Sterling paused with a fry halfway to his mouth. "You told him about the two of us?"

"Yeah," she said in her best duh voice. "You didn't really think I was going to let you move to California, did you?"

Sterling leaned over and kissed her. "God, I love you."

Lexine smiled against his lips. "I love you, too."

Sterling sat back and popped a fry in his mouth. "Good, because, when we get home, I'm going to make you prove it."

☾

Dante woke with a crushing weight on his chest and what sounded like a motor running. The room was pitch-black, except for his monitor in the corner. But even the light from that hurt his eyes. He still had a massive headache from the bomb that stupid fucker Lucas had set. Dante couldn't wait for the Council to throw the book at him.

The physical ache didn't help with his mental ache though. He still missed Phoenix. One would think getting thrown twenty feet in the air would help one forget about missing the individual they couldn't have, but instead, he missed her so much that it felt like she were in his room.

Man, he wanted to go home. But first things first. Dante grabbed his call button and pressed. His hand still hurt where it had gotten burned, and he hoped that he would heal from this whole ordeal soon.

A nurse walked into his room, and he had to shut his eyes from the sliver of light from the hallway.

"What can I get you, Dante?"

"I think I need to see the doctor again."

He felt more than saw the nurse get tense. "What symptoms are you having?"

"I'm having trouble breathing. I feel like something is crushing my chest. I feel hot, and the ringing in my ears has changed to what sounds like a car running."

The nurse's body sagged, and it sounded like she stifled a laugh. "I'm sorry."

"About what?"

"I shouldn't laugh. Dante, you're fine. I mean, except for your concussion and burns. You just have a full-grown cat-shifter purring and lying on top of you."

"What?" Dante said as he looked down. He could barely make out the outline of Phoenix in the dark, and mostly because he knew she was there. He put his hands out and felt her hair and then the rest of her body.

The nurse smiled sweetly, turned, and walked out the door.

Phoenix moved as he continued to touch her, and the purring stopped. "Dante," she said, her voice groggy.

"What are you doing here?"

"I came to see you."

"Thank you, Captain Obvious. But why did you come to see me?"

"Because I realized that I almost lost you today."

"It wasn't that bad. Lucas set a small bomb to blow off his garage door, but that was the extent of the damage. Only Sterling and I were hurt."

"But it could have been worse. And I figured out that I couldn't go another second without telling you that I love you."

Dante's heart skipped a beat. Not literally. He heard the rhythmic pulses of his heart monitor continue on, but it felt like his heart had skipped a beat. "You do?"

"Yes. I want to be with you, and I hope you still want to be with me, too."

"Of course I do. But what about your heat?"

"I'm still disappointed in my body, but we can try again. And we can have a lot of fun preparing in between."

Dante pulled Phoenix up to his mouth and kissed her. "God, I can't believe you're here."

"Me either, but I am so glad I am."

"Phoenix?"

"What?"

"Will you tell me what happened to you?"

He felt her body go on alert, and his hopes fell. He didn't want to know what had happened to his cat-shifter because he was curious; he wanted her to trust him enough to tell him.

Her body sank back into his, and she said, "Sorry, I just had to make sure Sterling and Lexine were sleeping first."

Is she actually going to tell me?

She took a deep breath. "I started developing early. Early by human standards and really early for a shifter. My dad died when I was young, and my uncle moved in. My mom got free help, and my uncle got a place to stay for cheap. He lived with us for as long as I can remember. He wasn't actually my uncle. He was my mom's cousin, so that would technically make him my cousin, but he and my mom were close like brother and sister, so uncle seemed easier. Well, my uncle never married. When I started developing, he took notice in me."

Dante had almost told her to stop when she first muttered *uncle*. Now, he had to literally bite on his tongue, so he wouldn't say anything. He knew it was good for Phoenix to talk to him about this.

"You're probably going to think I'm crazy because he never raped me or anything. I think he knew that was a bad thing. But feeling my breasts and making me take my shirt off, so he could look at me while he beat off was apparently okay with him."

Dante closed his eyes. "Oh, Phoenix."

"Yeah, this went on for a while. When I finally got up enough nerve to tell my mother, she blew me off. When I told her how he looked at me, she told me I was misinterpreting things. Then, when I said he touched me, she flat-out refused to believe me. I know he was like a sibling to her, but I was her daughter. What did I have to gain by telling her that?"

"Your mom's a bitch," Dante said. "Sorry. Please continue."

"You're right; she is a bitch," Phoenix agreed. He could

hear the smile in her voice for that second. "That's why, the day I turned eighteen, I moved out. I had already begun training myself to fight off my uncle, so I went and knocked on my alpha's door and insisted he hire me, which he did. I think he sensed that I needed to be a sentinel more than he needed me to be one."

"So, that's why you wear baggy clothes and hide your body."

"Yeah, because it wasn't just my uncle; he was just the worst. Guys at school grabbed my breasts all the time, as if having a large chest was an invitation to touch someone inappropriately. I couldn't help the way I had grown. But, even after I grew stronger and tougher—"

"And practiced your resting bitch face."

"Hey! But, yes, after all that, I never changed the way I dressed. I felt more comfortable with hiding my body."

Dante rubbed her back. "Thank you for telling me. But two things."

"What's that?"

"One, I don't think you're crazy. What happened to you was a crime, and that bastard should be locked away. Yes, it could have been worse, but that does not negate your trauma. He never should have treated you like that. And, when you told your mother, she should have at the very least kicked him out."

Phoenix kissed him. "And what's number two?"

"Where is the asshole? I want to watch the life leave his eyes as I squeeze his neck."

"Sorry, Dante. He's already dead. Car accident five years ago."

"Damn," he said, disappointed that he wouldn't get to

confront the guy. "I'm sorry for what happened to you, Red."

"Me, too. But at least I have you, right?"

Dante pulled her close. "At least you have me. I'm not going anywhere, Red."

THIRTY-NINE

HUNTER WATCHED Lexine and Sterling walk to the front of the room to face the Vampire Council. It was their monthly meeting, and now, five men and three women would control Lexine's and Sterling's fates. It was time for them to discover their punishment.

Lucas and his friends had already received their punishments. Life in prison. Not only had they played a role in the vandalism, but there was also arson, blood-raping Lexine and sexually assaulting her, and attempted murder of two Guardians. Lucas had explained that he never meant for anyone to get hurt in the blast. He had set a small enough blast, only planning to stun Lexine and Sterling, figuring they would come after him after the failed incident behind the nightclub. The Council hadn't cared and decided to throw the book at him and his accomplices.

Lucas and his group were going to a private prison that housed only vampires and was off the grid to humans.

"Lexine Harlow and Sterling Wardell, we've been filled in on what happened," Councilman Hutton said. He then listed their transgressions. Lexine's was much longer than Sterling's. "How do you plead?"

"Guilty," Lexine said.

"Guilty," Sterling said.

The council members didn't look surprised because Dante had been talking to them for the last two weeks.

"Sterling," the councilman said, "you are now on probation for three months for your failure to inform your leader, the king and queen"—he pointed to where the king and queen sat off to the side—"or us about your knowledge of who was behind the attacks and Lexine's involvement with them."

Sterling bowed and nodded. "I understand and accept my penalty."

"Lexine," the councilman said, "you are hereby stripped of your role and title as Guardian. We can no longer trust you to take the interest of our people above your own. You will have to immediately turn over all your weapons and anything else tied to the Guardians. Do you understand this?"

"Yes, sir." Lexine bowed her head.

"Do either of you have questions?" Councilwoman Vanderbilt asked.

"No, ma'am," they both said.

"Then, you may be seated."

Hunter was amazed that Lexine wasn't fighting this. Yes, she was guilty, but Hunter couldn't imagine not being a Guardian. It was such a big part of who he was. He couldn't imagine doing anything else with his life.

"Guardians," the councilwoman said, "let this be a

reminder that who you fraternize with and what you do on your off time can affect your position."

Hunter didn't know if he was imagining it, but it seemed like the councilwoman was looking right at him. Had she somehow found out he was involved with another male? Sweat began to form on his forehead. Would they call him out in front of everyone? Would they ask him to come to the front of the room and tell him he was suspended, too? Or worse, fired?

"I would like you all to be careful about who you let into your lives. You are Guardians first and foremost. You are being watched all the time, and nothing you do goes unnoticed."

Sweat now covered Hunter's body. They had to be talking about him.

"Do you understand this?"

"Yes," he heard the other Guardians respond around him.

"Hunter?"

He looked up at Councilwoman Vanderbilt and tried not to cower. "Ma'am?"

"Do you understand what I am saying?"

He swallowed. "Yes."

"Good. Guardians are dismissed."

Hunter watched the Guardians, along with Sterling and Lexine, get up and file out of the room, and then he came up on their tail. Once they were outside, the group of them stopped.

"Lexine, are you okay?" Morgan asked.

"Yes. I figured this would happen. I was prepared. Besides, after these past few months, I've begun to realize this isn't the job for me. I think I did it because my brother did. But he's a far better Guardian than I am."

"We're going to miss you," Tempest said.

"Well, the good news is, I'm not moving out."

"You're not?" Lennox asked.

"Nope. I already talked to Dante, and he gave me permission to live with Sterling. I thought I'd go back to school or something. I'm keeping my options open."

There was a group of cheers all around, except for Lennox, who looked at Sterling. "I still don't know if I like it."

"You just have your panties in a twist because you found out the screamer was your sister," Morgan said.

Lennox gagged, and everyone laughed.

"Let's go home," Dante said.

"I have to make one stop," Hunter told the group. "Then, I'll meet you guys back at the compound."

Everyone told him good-bye. He got in his car and made his way over to the Minneapolis side of the river. He drove to the wolf-shifters' mansion and went to the door.

When he knocked, Damien answered. "Hunter, what can I do for you?"

"Is Quentin around? I need to speak with him."

"Sure. You want to come in?" he asked as he held the door open further.

"No, thanks. Just have him meet me outside."

"Okay. Will do."

Damien shut the door, and Hunter was left alone to wait.

Some would maybe think he was crazy for what he was about to do with all the interspecies relationships going on, but it just wasn't the same as a homosexual relationship. After all, interracial marriages had become legal in the United States in 1967 while same-sex marriages just became legal in 2015, almost fifty years later. And he was pretty sure the Council still wasn't happy with Naya and Vaughn's relationship. Ultimately, they were the ones with the control, and he couldn't risk their disapproval.

Until recently, he had always thought he was asexual, so being a Guardian was all he'd ever had and known. Finding Quentin had been a surprise and not something he had ever considered for his future. While he was very into the wolf, Hunter had only known him a month and not very well. He couldn't risk throwing his whole career away for a relationship that might not last. Because then he would really be alone. Hunter didn't like what he was about to do, but he knew he was making the right decision.

A few minutes later, the door opened again, and Quentin stepped outside. "Hey, what are you doing here?" He moved to step closer to Hunter but stopped when he saw the vampire's face.

"I need to talk to you."

Quentin sighed in defeat. "You can talk, but I can already see that tomorrow's finally arrived."

"Tomorrow?"

"Remember how I told you about the honeymoon phase? How you think you have everything all figured out, but tomorrow, you might wake up and feel differently?"

"Yes."

Quentin crossed his arms over his chest. "Well, I can see that tomorrow has arrived. Reality has finally reared its ugly head, and you've decided you're not ready."

"You don't even know what I'm going to say."

"Okay then. Prove me wrong. What do you want to talk about, Hunter?"

Hunter didn't say anything.

"Yeah, man, that's what I thought. I do have a question for you though."

"What?"

"You recently had a female in heat at your place, right?"

"Yes."

"How'd that work out for you?" Quentin shook his head. "You didn't feel a single thing, did ya?"

Quentin was right. When Lennox had asked him how Phoenix's heat affected him, he'd known that he wasn't like the other guys in the house. Hunter didn't say anything again.

Quentin dropped his arms. "Is there any changing your mind?"

Yes. "No."

"Then, we're done here."

"I'm sorry, Quentin." Hunter had to get it out before the shifter went back inside.

"I'm sorry, too."

"You don't understand. Sterling and Lexine were punished tonight. The Council talked about our social lives and how it could affect our positions. They looked right at me, and I swear, they were talking about you and me. Please, you have to understand. I can't lose being a Guardian."

Quentin's shoulders sagged, and he stepped closer to Hunter. So close, their chests almost touched. Quentin reached up and cupped Hunter's cheek. "Oh, Hunter, I'm not sorry for me. I'm sorry for you. I'm sad that you're going to live every day suppressing yourself and telling a lie. Have you even talked to Dante about it?"

Hunter shook his head. "What if he tells the Council?"

Quentin dropped his arm and leaned over to give Hunter one last kiss. "Good-bye, Hunter," the shifter said. Quentin turned around and headed back to the house. "I'll see you around. I hope everything works out for you." He opened the door and went inside.

"Good-bye, Quentin."

FORTY

PHOENIX WOKE to the feeling of being truly loved. The emotion flowed around her, in her, through her. She rolled onto her back to see her mate watching her. And the love she felt wasn't just any love; it was coming from Dante himself.

Now that they were together, he'd opened the blood link he shared with her at times when he wanted her to know exactly how he was feeling. She'd been both awed and miffed when she found out about the link. No one had told her about it, so all these months, Dante had been able to feel what she felt. Although with her natural habit of hiding her emotions from even herself, Dante had told her she did a pretty good job of naturally blocking her feelings.

But, now, he was helping her do it on a conscious level, and she was working on letting him in more. It was hard sometimes. She was still afraid of being hurt, but she was trying more and more every day.

"Good evening," she said.

Dante leaned over and kissed her. "Do you have any

plans tonight?"

Phoenix did some mental calculating on what day it was. She had mostly adjusted her schedule to sleeping during the day and being awake at night like Dante, but sometimes, Vance would still ask her to do things during light hours. And, now that the threat that had hung over the shifter and vampire communities was eliminated, things had gone back to being less hectic and on a more even level.

"I have to check my messages, but I don't think Vance has anything important for me."

"Well, we kind of have something for you to do today."

"We? As in, you and my alpha?"

"Yep." Dante glanced behind him at his alarm clock. "You have an hour."

Phoenix sat up in bed, letting the covers fall to her lap. Now that she had told Dante everything about her past, she found it easier to be naked around him. Every night, he would help her become more comfortable with her body. Her incredible vampire was even teaching her to enjoy her breasts.

"Where are we going?" she asked, getting excited. She couldn't imagine what Dante and Vance would plan together.

Dante threw back the bedding and stood. He stretched as his morning, or night, erection stood out from his body. She was still amazed that he could fit that thing inside her, but she was definitely no longer afraid of it and loved when he made love to her. She thought back to the first time she'd seen it covered by his boxers months ago and how she'd almost been afraid of it even though Dante was sleeping. Things had certainly changed.

"We are going to the shifter infirmary. Vance made an appointment for you," her mate said.

And all her excitement turned to annoyance.

"I'm not going."

"Yes, you are."

"And if I don't?"

"Then, I will hog-tie you and throw you in the back of my SUV."

She scowled. "But I don't wanna," she whined. Actually whined.

Dante, with the help of Kenzie and her pedicures and clothes shopping, was turning her into a girlie girl.

Dante sat on the bed and took her hand. "Phoenix, don't you think you've avoided the heat thing long enough? It's time you go see your doctor and find out if something's wrong."

But she didn't want to find out if anything was wrong. She might have made progress in opening up her heart and mind to being with Dante, but she was still herself. If she didn't know anything was wrong, then nothing was wrong.

"Plus, Red, in light of your other symptoms, you know it's a good idea."

She hung her head in defeat. "I know."

"Speaking of that, do you need to feed?"

She eyed her mate's neck where she'd marked him the night of her heat. Although she could already practically taste his blood in her mouth, she was good for now. "No."

"I'm going to go shower then." Dante got up from the bed and headed for the bathroom.

Phoenix lay back on the bed. She knew her mate was right. In the month and a half since her failed heat, she had been having unusual cravings. Like for Dante's blood. So much so that he hadn't fed from her for the last two months because he was worried something was wrong with her. He had gone to a feeding facility, and Phoenix had stayed with him the whole time. She had tried to get Dante to feed from her, but he was too worried.

She had also begun to smell like Dante so much that vampires and shifters would think it was him until they saw her. She didn't know if it was because she had been consuming so much of his blood or because they had mated or what. But, if she didn't know it was impossible, she would think that she was turning into a vampire.

Thankfully, she could still go out in the sunlight without any problems, and she could still shift although her body seemed slower to respond, which was also worrisome.

Dante came out of the bathroom in a cloud of steam with a towel wrapped around his waist. "Red? You okay?"

She met his beautiful brown eyes. "Did you know Leonidas means lion?"

He smiled. "I did. Coincidence? I think not."

She smiled back. "What do you think of Phoenix Leonidas?"

His smile turned into a grin. "Are you saying, you want to change your last name? I'm shocked. I've always seen you as a feminist."

"Oh, I am. But the point of being a feminist is that you have choices. And I choose to take your last name. As long as it's okay with you?"

Dante jumped onto the bed, landing on his stomach beside her. "Of course." He leaned over and kissed her. "I would love for you to take my last name."

"That means, we'll have to get married the human way."

He shrugged. "I know."

"Good. Let's go to the courthouse today."

Dante dropped his head down and laughed. When he looked up at her, he said, "Nice try. You're still going to the doctor."

She glowered at him.

"But maybe, tomorrow, we can go to the courthouse."

"Fine," she said, throwing back the covers. She marched to the bathroom, making sure Dante was aware of her aggravation.

☾

About two hours later, Phoenix sat in the exam room at the shifter infirmary, kicking her legs against the exam table out of boredom. She'd already seen the doctor and the nurse, had her blood drawn, and been poked and prodded, and she was ready to go home.

There was a knock at the door, and a third vampire, different from the last nurse and doctor, stepped in. She handed Phoenix a piece of paper. "Here is your list of appointment times. We find it easier to just make them for our patients. We made them all in the evening. But you are more than welcome to change them at any time."

"I'm sorry," Phoenix said, her boredom turning to anxiety. "What is this about?"

The female pulled her clipboard away from her chest and frowned. "Are you not Phoenix Kaplan?"

"I am."

The female looked relieved. "Oh, good." She went back to the door and opened it.

"Wait," Phoenix said. "I don't know what these are for."

The female shrugged. "I'm sorry, miss. I just do what I'm told." She stepped out of the room and closed the door behind her.

Phoenix looked down at the sheet of paper and saw what had to be at least thirty appointments listed. She looked up at Dante, who was sitting across from her, waving the paper around. "See? This is why I didn't want to come."

"Let's not panic until we have to," he said calmly.

It irked her that he wasn't freaking out like she was.

She looked at the list again. "There are several appointments for when I should be in heat again." She looked up at her mate with what had to be a horrified expression on her face. "You don't think they'll want to monitor us during that time, do you? I am not having sex in front of others. I don't care if they are medical professionals."

"Damn, there goes my porn career."

"Ha-ha. You're not funny."

Dante chuckled. "Phoenix, can we just wait for the doctor before we assume the worst?"

There was another knock at the door, and the nurse from earlier walked in. She handed Phoenix another piece of paper. "Here is your prescription. Did you already get your packet?"

Phoenix gritted her teeth. "No, I have no idea what the hell is going on." She held up one hand. "I have appointments for who knows what." Then, she held up her other hand. "And, now, I have a prescription that I don't know anything about."

R.L. KENDERSON

The nurse looked confused. That made two of them. "Dr. Houseman hasn't come back and talked to you?"

"No."

"Oh, dear," the nurse said. She spun around on her heel and headed for the door.

"Oh, dear what?" Phoenix called out.

But the female was already gone.

Phoenix turned her eyes to Dante to show him how frustrated she was, but now, there was worry in his eyes, and she was suddenly scared.

If Dante, her rock, was worried, then that meant she should be worried.

A third knock sounded at the door, and the doctor walked in like her feet were on fire. "I am so sorry, Phoenix. There was a slight emergency with another patient out front. My nurse and medical assistant didn't realize that I was with that patient and that I hadn't talked to you yet."

Phoenix swallowed and stiffened her spine. "Am I sick?"

Dr. Houseman looked alarmed. "Heavens no." She handed Phoenix a thick folder. "This should explain everything."

Dante stood up and came to her side. They both looked down at the words on the outside. Her eyes locked on to one word.

"Pregnant?" she whispered. She lifted her head and looked at the doctor, who was now blurry. Phoenix wiped the tears from her eyes. "How? I don't understand. I was barely in heat."

Dante put his arm around her as the doctor said, "My best guess is, you got pregnant that first night. And, since that's the goal of mating heat, it was over after that."

320

"But I bled."

"Yes, but you said only lightly, correct?"

"Yes." Phoenix had assumed that, since her heat had been short, her bleeding had been light, too.

"And you haven't had any other bleeding since then?"

Phoenix shook her head.

"There you go then. You have nothing to worry about."

"I still don't understand," Phoenix said, still in shock.

"Well, we still don't know a whole lot about shifter-vampire conception, but as you know, there has been another couple who conceived rather easily. We might be seeing a trend. We won't know until more mating and pregnancies, or lack of pregnancies, happen. It's obviously not something we can make a case study out of, so we just have to go with the info we have right now."

"Is this why she's been craving my blood?" Dante asked.

"Again, we—the vampire doctors and those of us here at the infirmary—are going by assumptions. But it would seem that the vampire half of the baby needs your blood. So, my suggestion is to just give in to the cravings. Your body will tell you what it needs. Just don't ignore it," she said to Phoenix. Then, she turned to Dante. "But I would hold off on feeding from her until she gives birth, for safety's sake."

"Done," Dante said.

Phoenix wasn't happy about watching Dante feed from someone else for several months, but if it meant they got to be parents, it would be worth it.

"Any other questions?"

Phoenix shook her head.

"All right. Feel free to call anytime. Otherwise, we'll see you back here in a few weeks."

Dante led Phoenix out to the SUV while she felt like she was still in a daze. She looked over at her mate, who was practically strutting to the car.

"You're pretty proud of yourself, aren't you?"

Dante grinned. "Fuck yeah."

Phoenix rolled her eyes.

"I'm sorry, Red. It's a guy thing. I can't help feeling like a stud. I wish I could explain it to you." He put his arm around her and kissed her head. "Do you still love me despite my caveman mentality?"

"I suppose."

He stopped halfway to the vehicle, lifted her chin, and kissed her long and hard. "You'd better because I love you." He started walking again, taking Phoenix with him. "I can't wait to tell everyone."

"Me either." *Except...*

This time, Phoenix paused.

"What's wrong?" Dante asked, concerned.

"How am I going to tell Kenzie and Sawyer?"

Despite Kenzie's strong attitude at the hospital, she definitely had good days and bad days. She was trying to continue with life, but she would never forget about the baby she'd lost. Phoenix didn't want to add to her friend's pain.

"That's a tough one. But I'm sure Kenzie will be happy for you, no matter what."

"I know, but I still feel bad."

Dante kissed her again. "You're a good person, you know that?"

"What? Like you ever had any doubts."

"You're right. No doubts," he said with a glint in his eye.

"Come on, stud. Let's go home."

EPILOGUE

SEVERAL MONTHS LATER

DANTE FLIPPED THROUGH HIS PAPERWORK, going over applicants. Months later, they still hadn't found a good replacement for Lexine. Thankfully, things had been pretty calm lately, so they weren't short. And having Sterling off suspension also helped, but Dante still wanted this whole recruiting process to be over with.

But, if that was all he had to complain about, life was pretty good.

Just then, Hunter walked by the open office door.

Well, finding a new Guardian and Hunter's sullen mood were his only complaints. The normally content Hunter had turned into someone no one wanted to be around lately. Dante had tried to talk to him, but the Guardian refused. He just hoped they weren't headed toward another Lexine situation, though he hadn't been getting that vibe from Hunter.

Dante put his head down and read over a few more

applications when he smelled her. He looked up to see his beautiful, vibrant, and quite pregnant mate enter his office. She shut the door behind her and leaned against it with a mischievous smile on her face.

"Red, I need to get through these applications," he told her.

He could tell his words went in one ear and out the other as she stalked toward him.

"Phoenix," he warned, but he couldn't quite get the stern tone into his voice.

She continued toward him, her eyes completely feline, and he knew what she had in store for him. He should kick her out, but his dick was already hard and telling his brain to shut the fuck up.

Dante loved the confident sexual look in her eyes, and he was so proud to be the one who had helped her achieve it. Although the real credit went to Phoenix. She'd decided she wanted to change, and she had done it.

She reached his office chair, put her hands on the armrests, and pushed his seat back. She leaned over and kissed him. She pulled back and smiled at him again. Using the armrests, she lowered her body until she was kneeling before him.

She slowly lowered his zipper and pulled him out of his pants. She took him in her hand and licked him from base to tip before taking him in her mouth. Dante's eyes rolled back in his head.

Yes, his mate had come a long way. She had gone from being sexually repressed to giving the best blow jobs.

She finished him off and then stood up to get in his lap. Dante had to help her up now because her belly got in the way often. He tucked himself back inside his pants, and Phoenix curled up against him.

He rubbed her expanding belly. "Any contractions so far tonight?"

"Nope."

Dante sighed with relief. "Good."

Phoenix had begun getting contractions about a month ago. Because of this, they weren't allowed to have sex, and she was definitely not allowed any orgasms because that was what had started the contractions in the first place. He missed being inside her, but he couldn't deny that he loved how much oral sex he'd been receiving. He would worry she did it just to make him happy, except he could tell how much she liked it from their blood link. He wasn't supposed to feed from her, but Phoenix insisted that he take enough for him to stay connected to her. How could he not love this female?

"Are you sore anywhere?" he asked her.

"My back a little."

"Lean forward."

Since he couldn't return the favor, he'd been trying to give her as many back rubs and foot rubs as she wanted. He dug his fingers into her lower back, where he knew she was usually the most sore, as she rested her arms and head on his desk.

"So, no luck with finding a new Guardian?" she asked.

"No." Sigh. "Maybe I should just hire you."

She sat up so fast that she almost hit him in the nose. "Dante, you're a genius."

"Not going to argue, but why?"

She turned around on his lap. "To further our alliance

with each other—shifter and vampire—why don't we have something like a liaison program? We could have shifters, both cat and wolf, be Guardians, and you could send one Guardian to be a cat-shifter sentinel and one to be a wolf-shifter sentinel." She frowned. "Of course, you'd still have to replace Lexine, but it's still a good idea. I already live here, and it would be easier to work here than go back and forth between the bunkhouse and here."

"Wow, Red, that's a really good idea."

She smirked. "I know."

Dante laughed. "I'll talk to Vance and Damien about it and then the Guardians. I feel like it's something we all have to agree with." Dante kissed her. "You're the real genius."

She smiled and turned back around. "Well then, this genius needs you to continue with that back rub."

Dante laughed and began kneading his fingers over her again. After a few minutes, it became pretty apparent that she wasn't going to stay awake much longer.

"Dante?" Phoenix said, her voice low and sleepy.

"Yeah?"

"I really do love you, you know."

He smiled. "I know. I love you, too, Red."

FORBIDDEN CLAIM SAMPLE

Isabelle Rand kissed her boyfriend, Bram, on the cheek and exited his vehicle. As she walked to the front of the school, she took a deep breath. When she reached the doors, she turned around and waved at Bram, knowing he wouldn't leave until he saw her walk into the building.

She made no move to look and see if he drove away as she walked down the hall to her classroom. But, instead of going to the end of the corridor, she took a right into the school's office.

"He's gone," her coworker, Jessica, said.

Isabelle breathed a sigh of relief, but it didn't last long. She was only a fourth of the way through her plan.

Two more teachers, Danni and Alice, with their arms full, came from the back office area along with their principal, Noah.

Danni and Alice dropped the huge, mismatched luggage at Isabelle's feet.

"Here are most of your clothes," Danni told her.

"And here are the rest of your clothes and toiletries,"

Alice said.

Jessica came over from where she'd been watching the window and took Isabelle's hand, placing a set of car keys in it. "Here's your new car. It's nothing great, but it's bought and paid for."

"Give me the keys," Noah said. "I'll pull the car around."

Isabelle handed them over.

Noah looked at Jessica.

"It's a black Kia," she told him.

Isabelle swallowed hard as she tried not to cry. "I don't know what I'd do without you guys."

Jessica hugged Isabelle first. "This is what friends do for each other."

"Help them go on the run like a criminal in the night?" Isabelle joked as the first tear fell.

Alice embraced Isabelle next. When she pulled away, she squeezed Isabelle's arms. "No, we're helping you escape an abusive boyfriend who doesn't deserve to call you his."

Isabelle smiled as best she could.

Danni enveloped Isabelle last.

"I'm scared," Isabelle said in her friend's ear.

Danni drew away and looked into Isabelle's eyes. "I know. I would be scared, too. But we've been planning this for a month. Minneapolis is less than two hours away. You will make it before he even knows you're gone."

"Honey, are you sure you don't want to go to a shelter? Are you sure your friends in Minneapolis can keep you safe?" Alice, twenty years Isabelle's senior, asked.

There was no way Isabelle could tell these wonderful humans that she was going to the safest place in the world for her. Not only was Damien her friend, but he was also the alpha of the Minnesota Wolf Pack. And her other friends whom she was seeking solace from were the wolf-shifter sentinels. Once she told Damien about Bram, he would do everything to help her. And Bram wouldn't dare take on the alpha of their pack. Not if he wanted to live to tell about it.

"I'm absolutely sure. I just need to get there."

"Okay, honey. We trust your decision."

"We'd better go. I'm sure Noah has pulled the car to the side door by now."

Isabelle took one of the handles to wheel the bag outside, and Danni took the other.

Once they walked outside, Noah popped open the trunk and then got out of Isabelle's new car. The bags were loaded into the trunk, and then Noah hugged Isabelle.

When he stepped away, he held out his hand. "Phone."

"What?"

With his other hand, he reached into his back pocket. "Your phone."

"Oh. Yeah. I almost forgot."

The four of them had discussed the unlikelihood of Bram tracking her phone since he wasn't on her plan, but they didn't think it was a risk she should take. Plus, she didn't want to deal with the numerous phone calls he was bound to make once he realized she was gone.

She opened her purse and took out her phone. With a silent good-bye, she handed it over, and Noah gave her a new prepaid phone.

"I programmed all our numbers into it, just in case you need anything. And please let us know when you make it there safely."

"I will." She looked around at her friends. "I don't know how I'll ever repay you."

"I do," Alice said. "You can repay us by getting yourself to safety and staying there."

Isabelle smiled. "I will. I promise."

"You'd better."

Isabelle walked around to the driver's side of her new car but stopped before getting in. She'd almost forgotten. "Please be careful. Bram is not a good guy, and he's not what he seems. He's very strong and very dangerous."

She wished she could come out and warn them that Bram was a wolf-shifter, stronger than all of them combined, and capable of turning into a wild animal that could rip them to shreds. But she couldn't. They were her friends, but she couldn't give away her species.

"Honey, please don't concern yourself with us. It's a teacher in-service today, so no students to worry about, and we'll just tell everyone else you called in sick. We know nothing."

Noah waved the phone. "As soon as you leave, I'm going to call my office with your phone. It'll show up on your statement that you called in. Like Alice said, don't worry about us."

Isabelle closed her eyes. "You know that's never going to happen. But I will try to worry less. As long as you promise to be careful."

"We promise," Alice said for all of them.

And, with one last good-bye, Isabelle took off for Minneapolis…and for freedom.

Order Now!

ABOUT THE AUTHOR

R.L. Kenderson is two best friends writing under one name.

Renae has always loved reading, and in third grade, she wrote her first poem where she learned she might have a knack for this writing thing. Lara remembers sneaking her grandmother's Harlequin novels when she was probably too young to be reading them, and since then, she knew she wanted to write her own.

When they met in college, they bonded over their love of reading and the TV show *Charmed*. What really spiced up their friendship was when Lara introduced Renae to romance novels. When they discovered their first vampire romance, they knew there would always be a special place in their hearts for paranormal romance. After being unable to find certain storylines and characteristics they wanted to read about in the hundreds of books they consumed, they decided to write their own.

One lives in the Minneapolis-St. Paul area and the other in the Kansas City area where they're a sonographer/stay-at-home mom/wife and pharmacist/mother by day, and together they're a sexy author by night. They communicate through phone, email, and whole lot of messaging.

You can find them at http://www.rlkenderson.com, Facebook, Instagram, TikTok, Twitter, and Goodreads. Join their reader group! Or you can email them at rlkenderson@rlkenderson.com, or sign up for their newsletter. They always love hearing from their readers.

www.ingramcontent.com/pod-product-compliance
Lightning Source LLC
Chambersburg PA
CBHW062020170626
46813CB00001B/240